A
Harlequin
Romance

OTHER
Harlequin Romances
by ESSIE SUMMERS

Many of these titles are available at your local bookseller,
or through the Harlequin Reader Service.

For a free catalogue listing all available Harlequin Romances,
send your name and address to:

HARLEQUIN READER SERVICE,
M.P.O. Box 707, Niagara Falls, N.Y. 14302
Canadian address: Stratford, Ontario, Canada.

or use order coupon at back of book.

THE
FORBIDDEN VALLEY

by

ESSIE SUMMERS

HARLEQUIN BOOKS

TORONTO
WINNIPEG

Original hard cover edition published in 1973
by Mills & Boon Limited.

© Essie Summers 1973

SBN 373-01731-6

Harlequin edition published November 1973

Printed in Canada

To my dear cousins, Helen Davidson and William Summers, of Newcastle-upon-Tyne, with love. This book links the hero with his pioneering ancestors, and the dedication is in thanks to the two people who, from their own treasured memories, brought alive for me, a New Zealander, the grandparents I was never privileged to know.

CHAPTER ONE

CHARLOTTE DE LACEY SMITH looked down a wide sweep of coastline at the end of a flight that had taken her from England to Auckland and was now dropping down to Wellington. It was somehow comforting, after all those leagues of untenanted ocean so recently covered, to see land encircling bays, a network of hedged fields, clusters of houses, trees and rivers, and to know that journey's end came when her parents would greet her . . . or, more correctly, her mother and stepfather.

They'd wanted to meet her at Auckland, but Charlotte had decreed otherwise. 'When I meet you, my darlings,' she had written, 'I want us to be within reach of home, not still in transit, so we can relax and talk to our hearts' content. We've more than a year of conversation to catch up on.'

The usual instructions for landing came over the intercom; Charlotte saw green hills upthrusting, a deeply indented harbour with an island in the middle of it and blue waters thick with shipping, a glimpse of high-rise buildings, and houses with multi-coloured roofs and bright gardens crowding the hillsides, then the plane dipped down and levelled out to skim between two ridges on a long runway that looked as if it finished up in the sea itself.

The plane touched down, taxied to the terminal building and Charlotte knew the sensation, familiar to all air-travellers, of relief at the thought of *terra firma* reached safely. Though it was a wonderful way to travel, with a minimum of effort and a maximum of comfort, dozing in one's seat, or watching the sunset flame and fade above spun floss clouds, stars prick out in an atmosphere so clear you felt as if the world had grown young again, and then, as the night hours passed, to see the living wonder of the sun come up, striking gold and rose and violet rays from the rim of the earth.

How strange to leave England in autumn and arrive in New Zealand in spring . . . the sunshine outside looked hot and golden, but no doubt here too, spring winds could be treacherous. Charlotte took her white fleecy coat down and slipped it on, picked up her overnight bag and began to edge out.

Here a new life awaited her, if she decided to settle. Mother and Dad loved it, so it seemed quite likely she would too. Nice for Dad that when this chance of promotion had come at the New Zealand branch of his firm, his son and daughter had already emigrated here.

What a blessing all the Customs formalities had been gone through in Auckland ... no impatient waiting to see her family ... suddenly Charlotte glimpsed them through glass and went running swiftly along the tarmac, skirting the file of orderly passengers, her bright auburn hair, shoulder-length, streaming out behind her.

She was first through the door and was engulfed by two pairs of arms. Three pairs of eyes were suspiciously bright. Charlotte's mother hastily mopped hers. 'Oh, dear, I wish I wasn't so emotional at times like this ... but what a long year it's been!'

Charlotte hugged her. 'I'd hate it if you took it too calmly, pet. Besides, look at Dad. All that nose-blowing is simply camouflage ... he's having trouble with his tear-ducts too. Bless him ... Dad, I could dance for joy ... I'm here at last!'

'We ordered this sort of day for you, Sharlie,' said Hugh Ward happily when they'd collected her luggage and had set off in the Holden station wagon, for Khandallah, a suburb five miles out. As they threaded through narrow streets where quaint pioneer buildings were jostled and dwarfed by modern skyscrapers and all the clamour of a busy port seemed about them, Charlotte could well believe this was the capital city, but presently they were threading through the Ngaio Gorge, where the hillsides were covered with lush evergreen bush, and houses were tucked into hollows or perched on man-made plateaus, or clung desperately, it seemed, to the steep sides. An electric railway went down one side of the cutting to transport suburban dwellers to the city, but the road kept climbing, climbing.

They came into Khandallah where all the streets had Indian names and up the steepest hillside of all, twisting round an access road that wound right up into the bush on the west side, where houses dwelt in green seclusion and they ran out on to a levelled-out plateau where a white timbered house with gables and a green-tiled roof sat in a garden sweet with daffodils and blossoming cherry trees, so like England Charlotte couldn't believe it. But all around them and above them, the bush luxur-

8

iated, an example of nature abhorring a vacuum and clothing every inch with virile growth. Loveliest of all, it was starred symmetrically with the pale-green of giant tree ferns. Hugh Ward told her they called them *pungas*, but the pronunciation was deceiving, as the spelling was *pongas*.

As they got out of the car Charlotte gazed round her in sheer delight . . . hill upon hill upon hill with, across the harbour and behind them, range upon range, purplish and beckoning, standing out in sharp silhouette in this clear, bracing air. The harbour waters glinted so brightly one needed sunglasses and the air here was full of a strange zizzing sound, a hot, contented murmuring or singing.

Charlotte put her head on one side to try to listen and identify. Rhoda Ward laughed. 'They're cicadas . . . sort of flying crickets or locusts . . . at least to me they look like that. It would probably make a naturalist squirm to hear my description! They're sun-worshippers, so are more numerous in the North Island, though there are plenty round Kaikoura where John and Diana are. They have a soporific effect on me, though. In the afternoons here, if I sit down with a book, they lullaby me to sleep.'

At that moment the sound was cut off as by a signal. Rhoda laughed. 'See . . . that cloud has just passed over the sun.' Sure enough a billowing mass was hastening beyond a hilltop and had cut off the sun which, at this hour of noon, was high in the sky. It passed, the cicadas resumed their chirring, and they went inside, all talking at once.

'We've only three rooms upstairs,' said Hugh, 'but we've given you the one that faces south . . . it's the smallest but has the best view of all. You can see the mountains of the South Island from there. Come on, Sharlie, I'm dying to show you.' He seized her largest case and tore for the stairs, with boyish enthusiasm.

Sharlie turned to hug her mother before taking off after him. 'He'll never grow up, will he? He's gorgeous! Come on.'

The casements under the eaves were flung wide by the time they got there. Hugh said, 'Whoever built this house – it's about ten years old – must have designed it to frame that view. Isn't it perfect?'

It was. They looked straight out between the hills and presumably over the waters of Cook Strait that they could not see, to the upper half of a mountain that could have been the setting for a castle-in-the-air picture, capped with snow, glittering silver against the azure sky.

It was many miles down the East Coast of the South Island, Hugh explained, and was the highest peak of the Kaikoura Mountains, Tapuaenuku, which meant *The Footprints of the Rainbow God*.

Charlotte tried the word out, rolling its musical vowels over her tongue in imitation of her stepfather's pronunciation.

'How far away is the South Island from the North Island, Dad?'

He considered that. 'I can't tell you in miles – or in leagues of ocean, but to cross from Wellington to Picton takes over three hours by steamer, so it's about the same as from Dover to Ostend, I guess. A glorious trip, because so soon you're threading through the waters of the Sounds, with innumerable bays on each side, and of course that makes the journey seem shorter. But if you go from here to Christchurch – the main city of the South Island, half-way down the East Coast – it's an all-night trip with sleeping cabins.'

Charlotte looked at Tapuaenuku again. 'The Tapu part of it is rather like the name of the place where Phyllis lives, isn't it?'

Hugh nodded. 'Yes, *tapu* occurs often in place-names, because so often a place was made *tapu* by some tragedy. It means a sacred place, undefiled, forbidden. So Tapuwharua must be *The Forbidden Valley*.'

'Well, it certainly won't be forbidden to me,' said Charlotte, all unknowing. 'Phyl wants me to go down there as soon as possible.'

She wouldn't say yet, in this hour of glad reunion, that Phyllis seemed to be desperately needing someone of her own.

Rhoda nodded. 'Nothing forbidding about that valley, anyway. You'll get a marvellous welcome there. Phyl deserves every bit of her happiness. We spent two wonderful weeks with them shortly after we arrived. Owen is the sort of stepfather to Phyllis's children that Hugh was to you and John. And his parents seemed delighted to have some ready-made grandchildren. They're retired from the farm, into the township of Oxford itself – Tapuwharua is in the Oxford district – but at present they've gone off to Canada to see their married daughter who lives there.'

Charlotte decided that in that case it couldn't be mother-in-law trouble that was worrying Phyl so dreadfully. She had written Charlotte just before she left England: 'Lacey,' (she had always called her cousin that) 'it's just wonderful to know you're coming out here – someone of my very own. And just when I most need you. I won't tell you about it. I can't face writing it. Put down in black-and-white might make it seem real. It's the sort of thing you only imagine happens to other people. If you hadn't been coming so soon, I'd have written it all out, of course. But face-to-face it will be easier. I just don't know what to do. You may be able to help me to a decision. I can't say anything to Owen just now – it would be cruel. He's in the thick of lambing, so I'm going to play it along.

'Oh, I'd better not start or I'll tell you all. But believe me, Lacey, I need you desperately just now. I've got a breathing space before I must make up my mind. It's too hideous. I'd have liked to have flown up to have seen Aunt Rhoda, but thought Owen might suggest he came. And I can't – yet – face telling him, though I'll have to. Anyway, I don't want to leave him at lambing-time, though we have two good men. Oh dear, I keep hinting, I can't seem to stop, but I must and I will. It would take reams to explain it to you, and I must catch this mail to ask you to make your way to Amberleigh as soon as possible. I've a feeling that only you can sort out my chaotic feelings. We've always been such kindred spirits. I'm too close to my problem at the moment. Say nothing to anyone. Just come. It's like a miracle to know you're coming to this far-flung corner of the globe. Much love, in haste, Phyl.'

Well, if there was anything Charlotte could do to ease any problem of Phyl's, she would. It had been Phyllis's mother who had cared for Charlotte and John, her brother, when their father had died, and their mother, worn out by a year of heroic nursing, had had a breakdown.

Aunt Susan and Phyllis had been their only comfort and security in an unstable world just then. Phyl had been considerably older than Charlotte, but the gap in their ages had mattered little then or now. Aunt Susan, later, had nursed their mother back to full health after long hospitalization. Then had come the rewarding, compensating years, when their mother had married Hugh Ward.

Charlotte would go down to the Amberleigh estate in that valley with the long name, in North Canterbury, as soon as possible. She had written Phyl on the plane and had posted it airmail in Auckland, saying she'd give her parents a few days, then say she was dying to see John and Diana in the South Island, and would stay only one night with them and continue on to Phyl.

It was after lunch before she managed to bring the subject up and was amazed to see her parents exchange a quick look of — could it be relief? She gazed from one to the other swiftly. 'Come on, you two, give . . . you're up to something. What is it?'

She had a feeling they might be matchmaking! And Ivan, Hugh's son, was a partner on John's farm. Just because Charlotte's brother John had married Hugh's daughter Diana, they mustn't expect her to fall for Ivan, dearly as she loved him in a sisterly sort of way.

Hugh spread his hands out. 'It would suit us very well if you did take off to spend time on both farms, because something's cropped up out of the blue. I've been asked to go to the branch in Fiji for two months or so, because the manager in Suva has to bring his wife to Auckland for a very tricky heart operation. Any other time we'd have welcomed the experience, but to have it come just as you arrived was a bit thick. We wondered if you'd like to go south for a bit to the others, then join us in Fiji when we find a larger flat. We don't like the idea of you staying here alone — all this bush so close makes it rather lonely. If you go south to John and Diana, you could have our car. You can take it on one of the drive-on-drive-off steamers, disembark at Picton, and go down to Kaïkoura to the others, then after a week or two go to Tapuwharua, then follow us to Fiji.'

I was a happy solution. Charlotte doubted she'd make it to Fiji, as Phyl might want her to stay on for a bit, unless whatever trouble it was resolved itself quickly. She decided not to mention it to her parents. They had both of them known grievous loss in their lives and now, in the autumn years, were finding tranquillity and freedom from care, and even adventure, seeing new places and meeting new people. It couldn't have been easy, fitting their families into one harmonious relationship, but they had achieved it admirably. She thought they deserved this time in a South Pacific playground to themselves.

For two it could be an idyll.

Things happened more quickly than they'd imagined, because the need for the heart surgery became more urgent, and in forty-eight hours' time, Charlotte found herself on the *Aranui*, easing into the incredible beauty of the Marlborough Sounds on a late September day that had in it the balmy promise of summer-to-come.

She looked about her with enchanted eyes. How she would love to spend a holiday here in one of these myriad bays that further indented the vast fretwork of the Sounds. This beauty eased a little the pain of tearing herself away from England. It was the rest of the family who'd wanted to emigrate, not Charlotte. How wonderful it was going to be to see John and Diana and Ivan again. John had emigrated years ago, returning briefly to marry Diana, his stepsister, when she had grown up. He had adored her, even as a child. Ivan had gone out a few months later. How wonderful to be a foursome again.

The only thing that had worried Charlotte was that there had been no word from Phyl awaiting her in Wellington. Her mother had commented on it, even in the rush of packing. 'I'd have thought Phyl, like the others, might have sent you a wire of welcome. Or a greeting card with "Happy Landing" on it. How about putting a long-distance call through to her?'

Charlotte had shaken her head. Who knew? Phyl might break down on the phone. 'I'll ring her from John's place. Be cheaper and we can talk longer and I'll be able to give her a definite date to say when I'm going down to visit her. I expect they're still terrifically busy after the lambing. After all, I know what a hectic life farming is!'

The call came for drivers to go below to their cars and she negotiated the ramps and what-have-you to the wharf, a tiny little port that reminded Charlotte of Oban and a certain holiday she'd spent in Scotland. New Zealand was like that, she was finding with great similarities and yet intriguing differences. The road south was glorious, skirting the East Coast, running through tussocky mountain passes and then skirting huge bluffs where once, she was told, when she stopped at a lookout point and went on to a rocky headland, there had been no way round. The mountains simply dropped into the sea, with chopped-off cliffs. But now rail and road tunnels had pierced the barriers of rock, and access was easy, mocking the heights.

The Pacific surged up to the shore in curling surf, fishing-

13

boats showed here and there, gulls screamed and wheeled, their wings flashing silver against the sun and cobalt sky. Where the narrow coastal strip widened into rolling country, the hillsides were dotted with the dazzling white fleeces of ewes and lambs, daffodils blew in a golden wave outside some homesteads and small orchards were a glory of pink and white bloom, like coconut ice. Charlotte sang as she drove.

She stopped in Kaikoura and had some of the *koura* which she called lobster and they called crayfish. Freshly caught crays were out of this world, she decided. Charlotte had hers in a salad, flaked and tossed in some tangy dressing. A few miles on, past Goose Bay, she turned inland at Oaro and began to climb the Hundalee, a winding road, beautifully scenic, through forest and bush, and named, John had once written Charlotte, after Hundalee Tower at Jedburgh in Scotland.

Soon, on the other side, she would see a signpost to Huntress Hill – John had named his farm that before ever he married Diana, quoting Ben Jonson's *Hymn to Diana*: 'Queen and Huntress . . .'

They'd said when she saw the sign she must clatter in over the cattle-grid – though she'd find they called them cattle-stops here – to a rough hillside track. Not to worry, it led to their farm all right, but it was out of sight, a mile and more into the hills.

What a welcome! As she turned the shoulder of the last hill and saw the homestead nestling into the side of it, it was as if an alarm clock had rung. Dogs barked, calves bawled, sheep and lambs baaed, and three figures came rushing out of the house and reached the car as she drew up in the U-turn of the drive below a terrace ribboned with the blue of grape-hyacinth borders and bay with ranunculus and anemones.

John was in the lead of the figures streaming out and down. 'Sharlie! How magnificent that you're here at last. Family all together again.'

Diana pushed him aside. 'Oh, it's too marvellous! I've been just consumed with excitement these last few weeks. I thought the time would never go.'

In turn she was pushed aside, and Ivan danced Charlotte up and down, then kissed her resoundingly. 'Stepbrother's privilege. Come on in . . . Di wouldn't let us start in on what she's baked to welcome you and I'm starving. Let's eat before young Robert wakes up or you girls will ooh and aah over his charms

14

so long, we'll be ravenous!'

Oh, it was heart-warming to be one of the gang again. Charlotte had felt she couldn't desert her post as a nanny the year her parents had left for New Zealand. A new boy had been on the way there and her employer, more of a friend really, would have fretted had the other children been left to the care of someone strange. Charlotte had waited till the new baby was three months old, then made her plans.

The afternoon tea was over, the adorable nine-months-old Robert had been lifted and the baby-worship done, when John and Ivan decided to go down to the roadway to collect the mail from the box down there. Charlotte said, 'I do so hope there'll be a letter for me from Phyl. She didn't even send a greetings telegram. But Dad put in the re-direction order to the Post Office, so if anything went to Khandallah, it would be forwarded from there – he made it as from yesterday, would it be too early to expect anything?' She added, 'Anyway, if there isn't, I'll ring her tonight. I'm going to stay with her later on.' (Not too much later, but she wouldn't mention leaving here yet.)

They all three seemed to stiffen. She looked at them, an interrogatory crease between her tawny brows, a questioning look in her hazel eyes. Diana said slowly, 'We're just wondering ... wondering what on earth's going on down there. You see—'

Charlotte said anxiously, 'Has she been in touch with you? Has she told you something about—'

Di broke in. 'No, she's not rung for ages, or been up to see us, but we hadn't realized how long because we've been so busy during and after lambing, and knew they would be too. But it's so odd. In yesterday morning's *Press* we saw an advert – for a housekeeper at Amberleigh Homestead, Tapuwharua. It said "must be used to children". So I—'

'So you think Phyl's ill?'

'We don't know what to think. Fact is, we didn't see this ad till today. Just before lunch, I went to wrap some garbage in yesterday's paper and it caught my eye – the name. I tore it out. We decided not to ring the homestead till you arrived, because if Phyl was ill, we knew you'd be the very person – a trained nanny, and a relation. We thought you'd perhaps know something. That if Phyl *was* ill, Owen would have rung your mother – unless, of course, he knew she was going to Fiji. Though in that case he'd have rung here. Still, our phone was out of order

15

for a couple of days. But we did think, if they needed someone, knowing you were arriving and would be looking for a job, they'd have offered it to you. But there was another thing. We can't make it—'

John broke in. 'We can't make it out because the advert wasn't in Owen's name. It's in his brother's. We thought this brother was still overseas. He's been away since before Phyl married Owen. Last time we saw them, Owen said his brother might be back soon. Owen had the chance of buying in some adjacent property – it was all one big estate once but had gone out of the family's hands a generation or so ago. So the brother would take over the other property. Look, see for yourself.'

Charlotte peered at the advert. 'Position offered housekeeper. Must be used to and fond of children (school-age) and must not mind isolation, though transport or use of a car will be provided. Excellent wages offered suitable applicant. Sole charge of house. Apply Edmund Leigh, Amberleigh Homestead, Tapuwharua, near Oxford, North Canterbury.'

Charlotte blinked at it, trying to fathom what it could mean. Then her brow cleared. 'I've got it! They'll be his children, not Phyl's. He'll want someone to look after them in the house on the other property they've just acquired. Perhaps he's a widower, or his wife is sick or something. And maybe he's staying at Amberleigh till they get the other place furnished.'

John shook his head decidedly. 'No go. Though it was very bright. Edmund is a bachelor. If Phyl is ill, then you'd expect Owen to do the advertising. We'll have to ring them.'

Charlotte said slowly, 'Look, I don't want to break a confidence, but I think I'd better tell you that Phyl wanted me to go to her as soon as I decently could. She was very worried about something. In fact, for Phyl, who's always so calm, I thought she sounded frantic. She had no time to tell me. Wanted me to get the letter before I left England, so I could make arrangements to visit her as soon as possible. I said nothing to Mother and Dad. Of course, when they were just off to Fiji they couldn't have done anything. But in view of this I've got to tell you.'

Ivan said, 'Well, best thing is to ring tonight. They could be out now – in the paddocks. Then you can get hold of this Edmund and if the kids are in bed, he'll be able to speak freely. Could it possibly be that both Owen and Phyl are in bed ill? Didn't Phyl give any hint at all? Say she wasn't well or—'

'Not a thing like that. I'm sure it was more emotional than physical. It worried me, because she doesn't panic easily, or imagine things. Said she'd rather tell me face-to-face. She did say it was too hideous, and that she needed help in making a decision. Phyl's so alone now that her mother's gone too. But she's always been so self-sufficient. We all know that the kindest thing we could ever say about Ranulf was that he was a weak reed to lean upon.

'When he was drowned I felt rather remorseful because all I could think of was that I knew, in my inner self, that Phyl and the children would have a much better life without him. Always up to his ears in debt, getting into trouble, disillusioning his wife at every turn. No, this is beyond me. I can't even guess at what lies beyond that advert. However, best thing will be to ring tonight. It may have some simple explanation. But the best thing of all for us would be if Phyl herself answered the phone.'

Diana said hopefully, 'Anyway, whatever was bothering her may have been solved by now. Things often work out that way, given time. And Owen's one in a million. Have a talk to her and if she'd like to come here for a few days she'd be most welcome, though she may prefer to explain it to only one person at first — you, Sharlie. Play it by ear, and we'll fit in with whatever you feel you should do. Right, boys, if you go down for the mail, there just may be a letter from Phyl.'

They came back with a letter from Amberleigh all right, but they had worried expressions. 'It's not from Phyl. It's from this Edmund Leigh . . . look, the address is on the back.' They all gazed at the writing, thick, black, positive. Somehow it sent a chill through Charlotte, which was absurd, she told herself.

'But that's not the oddest thing of all,' said Ivan, still holding the letter. 'This is! It's undoubtedly meant for you, Sharlie, because it's been forwarded from Wellington, but look!'

It was addressed to 'Miss Lacey Ward'.

They gazed at it blankly. 'So he knows Phyl calls me Lacey, but how in the world does he — oh, I suppose it's just a mix-up. Phyl must've said my mother's name was Mrs. Ward, but not that I had a stepfather. But I think this is ominous. I think Phyl and Owen *must* be ill. Well, only one way to find out.' She ripped it open. They crowded round her.

They read it all at once, trying to race down the page to make sense of it, to take it in . . . to credit it.

'Dear Miss Ward,

'I'm afraid that as your cousin is not here and none of us knows where she is, I could do nothing but open your letter to her. I think, from what you have written, you must have had a fair idea that she was playing round with someone. You say you're sorry she's not happy at the moment – I presume from this my brother's happiness doesn't count! And you state you'll come to stay with her as soon as you arrive in New Zealand. I must ask you not to do that. It would be only one more complication in a horrible situation. Her running-away has been cruelly timed. I've just arrived back myself from overseas. I've heard nothing but good of my brother's wife from my parents and for sure I didn't expect to be pitchforked into anything as unsavoury as this on arrival. She left an extremely callous note for my brother – sent the children off for the day – and put him into such a state of mind when he read it that he hared after her, no doubt at excess speed and perhaps trying to stop her, and has almost killed himself. There's a chance – no more – that he may recover, but he's deeply unconscious in a Christchurch hospital.

'Under these circumstances I'm sure you will understand I can't cope with a visitor. A neighbour is looking after the children till I can get a housekeeper. I'm told my brother regards the children as he would have his own, so I can do nothing about them till he either recovers consciousness, or succumbs. I can't even send for my parents because at the moment they're on a ship, with my sister and her husband, en route for Alaska, and I am most reluctant to send them news by radio-telegram till I see how it goes with Owen.

Yours truly,
Edmund Leigh.'

They were all appalled. They stood and looked at each other aghast.

Then, 'I just don't believe it,' said Charlotte flatly.

'Neither do I,' said her brother. 'Phyl is a wonderful person. Besides, she adored Owen. And she would never, under any circumstances, desert her children. In fact, I can't even begin to believe her casting as much as a look at any man not her husband.'

18

Diana said slowly and unhappily, 'I don't know if you can ever say that about anyone. I've had no personal experience – or even among my friends – of such a thing, but some folk do suddenly go haywire over someone else. The sort of people you'd expect it least to happen to. Oh, don't look at me like that, it makes me feel so disloyal. I only mean Phyl might be *capable* of a grand and consuming passion for someone, but I, too, am sure she'd never go back on her marriage vows or desert her children. I mean, despite all Ranulf's infidelity, because he was truly a sailor with a wife in every port, she never wavered herself. So even if she did fancy someone, she'd never run away with anyone.'

Charlotte squeezed her hand. 'Yes, we'd all feel like that about Phyl. Even Aunt Susan, who was very orthodox, thought Phyl ought to leave Ranulf. But when he got that job with the Eastern shipping company, even though she hated leaving her mother and England and all she knew and loved, she went out to Australia so he could have a home in some port nearer than any English one. It was to try to preserve her marriage, to keep Ran on the straight and narrow. And she worked, oh, how she worked. Because money went through his fingers like quick-silver.'

They gazed hopelessly at the uncompromising black-and-white of Edmund Leigh's letter. He had stated that Phyl had left a note saying she was running away with someone. It wasn't the sort of thing you could argue about. And Owen had almost killed himself chasing the pair of them. John said helplessly, 'We know so little. I wonder where they were making for. Might have been to Harewood Airport near Christchurch if he's landed up in hospital there. They could have been flying off to the North Island.'

Charlotte said bleakly to her brother: 'John, you're accepting this, aren't you? That Phyl *has* been unfaithful, *has* run off with another man?'

John look wretched. 'Sis, it's hard to get away from that, isn't it?' He gestured towards the hateful letter.

Diana wiped tears away. Charlotte said savagely, 'I *won't* believe it. I *won't*! It would have to be proved to me beyond shadow of doubt.'

The men said nothing. Their silence began to set up the first doubt in Charlotte's mind.

'Oh, hell and damnation!' said John. 'Just when we were

looking forward to having a whale of a time with you, showing you round the farm and the countryside . . . all the glorious summer ahead . . . the bathing on the coast, climbing these hills and mountains.'

Charlotte hugged him. 'The timing has been horrible, but—' and they were struck silent again, because that was exactly what that irate, justly irate, Edmund Leigh had said.

Finally John said, 'How about coming round the estate with us? We can't do any good mulling round the problem, here inside, and we need to go round the sheep, anyway. Bring Robert, Di, and we'll take the Land Rover. Perhaps tonight I should ring this chap Leigh and find out a few more details.'

Diana said miserably, 'I've a horrible feeling that from the very terseness of his letter there isn't much more to find out. There's a terrible sound of finality about it. You're Phyl's cousin and he's probably so angry, John, he won't want a thing to do with any of us. We could do more harm than good. I hope he's not the sort to take out his temper on the children. Even the best of us can do that at times, when on edge, and in a situation like this, anything could happen.'

Charlotte hadn't seen the children for over four years. Mark had been a babe younger than Robert then, when Phyl had gone out to Australia, and Barbie had been an elf of a child, a little brown pixie like Phyl, and only two and a half – darling mites. A desire to protect them surged over her. When she and John had been alone, with one parent dead, and one in hospital desperately ill, Phyl and her mother had taken them in, loved them, cared for them. Now Phyl's children were even more desolately alone, more vulnerable, facing up to the fact that their mother had deserted them. What would that man have told them? How would he have broken it to them?

Oh, if only she'd arrived a few days sooner, if she could have seen Phyl! If only she had rung her from Wellington. Might Phyl have acted differently then, less precipitately? Charlotte perceived that she too was beginning to accept this horrible thing, and a wave of revulsion against herself swept her. She mustn't. Phyl wouldn't. Oh, if only she could be there, instead of some strange housekeeper who might be lured to Amberleigh with the promise of high wages . . . who might pretend to like children, and who might be callous and indifferent to them.

It was then that the idea was born. It hit her right between the eyes – she almost reeled from the impact. But she wouldn't

20

come out with it right now. She'd wait till they'd adjusted themselves to the news, till they'd had their evening meal, and talk it over with them then.

When she'd written that letter on the plane she'd naturally signed it 'Lacey' seeing Phyl had called her that, always, and on the back of the envelope, in haste, she had scribbled: 'C/O Mr. H. Ward' and the Kandallah address. So the name Charlotte Smith wasn't going to mean a thing to one Edmund Leigh!

Housekeepers were hard to get, and someone who was a trained English nanny would surely be acceptable, even if she might have to convince him she was a fair-to-average cook and didn't mind housework. Anyway, it was worth a try. Oh, if only no one else had applied yet and been accepted! Yes, she'd wait till after dinner so they did not think she was acting on swift impulse.

Even so, it was hard to persuade them to let her apply, but finally, John, seeing her real distress, gave in. 'I suppose, at the most, it would only make an unpleasant scene if he found out who she was, and by that time Sharlie would have found out the ins and outs of it. Someone from the family, even though the Leighs wouldn't know it, would be looking after the children and we'd know, step by step, day by day, what was happening. How Owen Leigh is, for example; whether or not his parents will return once they get to Alaska and can be reached by Edmund Leigh. We've met the parents, and the children would be all right with them if only they were here. Actually, I should imagine, everything will depend on whether or not Owen Leigh regains consciousness or—'

'Or dies,' said Charlotte heavily. 'And if so, how his mother would react towards the children whose mother had brought about that accident. Well, let's agree not to let Mum and Dad know yet. They'll be writing here at first. I said I'd let them know when I decided to go to Phyl's. If need be we can just let them think we've run down by car to see her for a day, and that I'm staying on with you.'

Charlotte rang at eight. She felt her heart thud when a voice said, 'Edmund Leigh, Amberleigh, speaking.'

She said quickly, 'My name is Miss Charlotte Smith. I wanted to apply for the post of housekeeper if it's still open. Have you got anybody yet?'

His voice sounded grim and tired. 'Haven't had as much as

an inquiry. I'd better mention that when I said isolated in the ad, I *meant* isolated. You sound English, and to you isolated may mean a village in the country with one village just about running into the other. We're back in a valley beyond Ashley Gorge, cut deeply into the hills. Floods and snow can cut us off – though very infrequently and at least the worst weather is behind us, but I thought it only fair to mention that our nearest neighbour is miles off, no theatre nearer than Oxford, and nothing but a store, a garage and a church in the valley. Better to say this even if it puts you off than have you come and stay no longer than a few days.'

Charlotte said crisply, 'That wouldn't worry me at all. I'm a trained nanny and quite a fair cook – though just of plain meals – and I spent the last three years on a remote Welsh farm in the mountains. I know what it is to be cut off by snow and I was so happy there I didn't want to leave the place.'

'Why come out here, then?'

She had to be guarded in her reply. 'I have a brother in New Zealand. He didn't like me being so far away and on my own as far as close family was concerned.'

She dared not elaborate. If she invented too much she might get tripped up, and she'd no idea how much he knew about Phyl's cousin. He asked where she was ringing from. She said, cagily, from Kaikoura, that she was on a sightseeing trip round the South Island but had thought, on seeing his advertisement, that it might suit her very well. She didn't care for city positions. She added that she had excellent references and would bring them with her if he granted her an interview.

He agreed to this and was about to tell her how to get to Amberleigh when she broke in, because she needed to know something more of the situation, as any woman might, yet she must not reveal any pre-knowledge of it. So she said, 'How old are your children, Mr. Leigh?'

His voice rasped. 'They aren't my children. They're my brother's stepchildren. The boy is just five, has just started school, and the girl is almost seven. I'll have to explain the situation to you – hope it won't put you off. I've just arrived home from some time in Canada. My parents, recently retired from this farm, are over there now, visiting my only sister, who lives there, so I've no one to take these children. While I was away, my brother married a young widow with two children. He even adopted them legally, giving them his name. On the

22

surface, things seemed ideal. What went on below the surface I've no idea. Briefly, I arrived home to a hell of a mess. My sister-in-law has run away with someone, deserting her children, and my brother, presumably haring after his wife at speed, crashed his car and is on the seriously ill list in a hospital in Christchurch. It's a busy time of year. I haven't even got a married couple on the farm, so I must have someone. There's only one thing. You sound too young. I'd have preferred a middle-aged woman.'

Charlotte made a lightning decision and advanced her age by five years. 'I'm thirty,' she said crisply. 'Over thirty. To a teenager that's old. To the middle-aged it's young. You can take your pick which way you regard me. How does it sound to you, Mr. Leigh?' She made her voice sound waspish on purpose.

He said stolidly, 'Younger than I'd have wished, but, as I said before, I've had no other applicants. Beggars can't be choosers.'

'Any particular reason for not wanting someone young . . . or youngish?'

'Yes, I'm a bachelor.'

It was out before Charlotte could help herself. 'Mr. Leigh, if you're nervous in case I should develop ideas about you . . . if you think I'm an English female on the prowl, looking for a wealthy farmer, you needn't worry.'

Now real feeling crisped his tone. 'Why needn't I? I've seen a fair bit of this sort of thing happen in bachelor households. That's why most of us prefer baching even if we detest cooking. But I have to have someone to look after the children.'

'I'll tell you why you needn't. I find I don't care much for the New Zealand male. And in any case I'm not the husband-hunting type. Neither am I Women's Lib. I simply enjoy my work and my freedom.'

'Fair enough. We should do well together. I wouldn't be quite so sweeping, but as my brother's English wife has slightly jaundiced my attitude towards English women, the situation between us can be one of armed neutrality.'

'That would suit me very well indeed. We've got off to a good, frank start, haven't we?'

Over the telephone she met three pairs of startled eyes and wanted to giggle. First bit of humour she'd found in this set-up!

He went on, 'I'll tell you how to get here. You said you had a car? It's a steep road. How's your driving? You may be used to English roads and so far have been on only our main roads. Our side-roads are quite different, and this one leading back into the valley, and ending there, is anything but tar-sealed.'

She reminded him of that Welsh mountain farm.

'Oh yes, good show. I'll expect you tomorrow afternoon, then. I'll just give this to you slowly, from where you turn off the main road. Got a pencil ready . . . okay. . .'

When he had finished he said, 'If I'm not at the house bang the gong by the back door and I'll hear you. I'll try to be in, or near, but on a property like ours, you never know. I'll be in at the hospital tomorrow morning to see my brother and if he's holding his own, I'll be here. If he should – should worsen, I'll leave a message pinned to the back door, and you can come on down to the hospital to see me. You'd better take a good look at our valley and see if you can stand living there. That's about as definite an arrangement as I can make. Thanks for ringing. You sound fairly sensible to me,' and he hung up.

Charlotte turned round and, despite the seriousness of the affair, burst out laughing at the look on the three faces.

Her brother said, 'Sharlie, you goat! You could have antagonized him to start with.'

She shrugged her shoulders. 'I'm a great student of human nature,' she vowed. 'He's off women, naturally enough, and I could see he'd rather have a buxom woman in her forties or fifties, but I'm all he can get. So my waspishness convinced him I'm a man-hater. He's feeling all reassured right now.'

Ivan surveyed her sarcastically. 'You don't even look twenty-five, so how the heck you're going to make him think you're thirty is beyond me. Redheads never look their age.'

Charlotte said, 'Watch this . . .' She scooped back the thick red hair, twisted it into an uncompromising bun, strained away from her face, and held it there. 'See . . . I never did suit my hair pulled back. Makes my face too aquiline by far. Adds a good five years. And I'll use no eye-shadow, and very little lipstick. It will be fun.'

They continued to regard her with the greatest of misgiving. Diana voiced it for them. 'It's just as well Mum and Dad are in the middle of the Pacific. I'd hate to be us when they find out what we've let our little sister do.'

'Let me do . . . try to stop me! Look, pets, it's our only hope

24

of finding out what's really happened. The master of the Forbidden Valley has really forbidden me to come. It's his fault. Phyl's relations have got to stand by – we're the only blood relations the children have. The less Mum and Dad know the better. I'll write them a perfectly ordinary letter tonight, gushing about the scenery here and how perfectly super it is to be with you again and how in two or three weeks' time I'll tear myself away and go on to Amberleigh to stay with Phyl. By then I'll have found out who Phyl has gone with and where she is.

'I must be there, for the children's sakes. It's unthinkable that they should be left alone in such circumstances . . . with a curmudgeon of an uncle as this one sounds. Can you imagine it? . . . those poor kids cooped up with a resentful bachelor! He'll probably feed them on an unvarying diet of mutton and bread, and never think about vitamins!

'We've got to face the possibility of Owen dying, and if he does, the Leighs may not want to keep the children. You really couldn't expect them to. I've got to be there to find out what's happening to them, day by day. Thank heaven they were too young to remember me and that Edmund Leigh will never connect Charlotte Smith with someone he believes to be Lacey Ward.'

In her heart of hearts she added: 'I certainly hope not,' and knew a tremor of apprehension. In what sticky situation was she involving herself?

CHAPTER TWO

CHARLOTTE subdued all such fears as she drove along the next morning. She was not in the Holden. John had pointed out that Edmund Leigh would hardly expect such a new arrival to own quite such a luxurious car and Diana suggested Sharlie should take her Mini.

'You could always say your brother's wife loaned it to you. Good job the farm and telephone are in John Smith's name, and not under Ivan Ward's. You'd better be careful not to mention Ivan's name. In any case, keep pretty quiet about Ivan. New Zealand has such a small population, country folk, even in scattered districts, always seem to know someone who knows someone else.' She looked at Charlotte and giggled. 'I'd never have thought a hairdo could change a girl so much. A centre parting and a severe style certainly doesn't suit you. Darling, you're such a pet. Most girls have too much vanity to trick themselves out like this. It's the measure of your love for Phyl.'

Charlotte grinned. 'I mightn't like my hair like this among the folk back home, but amongst strangers I don't give a darn. I'm determined to find out just what's behind all this, apart from seeing that the children are well cared for and loved. These neighbours won't want to keep the children too long – you know how it is – people weary of well-doing. Two extra children in a busy farming household can make a deal of extra work, and this disruption in their lives may make the children naughty anyway.'

Charlotte forced herself to enjoy the journey through country she was seeing for the first time, because if she worked herself up and entertained too many fears, she might appear suspicious and nervous. She loved the *kowhai* trees drooping their golden pendulous blooms over the Kowhai River, and the massed effect of climbing geraniums smothering the fences of the houses. She guessed from their luxuriance and height that they must flourish outside all through the winter here.

She wondered if the Conway River had been named after Conway in Wales, by settlers homesick for the land they had left. She was fascinated by the steep bush-clad sides dropping

26

down and spreading out to a vast riverbed, threaded by many streams after she had crossed the bridge to the far side, and toyed with the idea that Ferniehurst was probably named for Ferniehurst Castle in the Cheviot Hills, but Parnassus, a delightful little township, sweet with English trees, its gardens blowing blue and gold with English spring flowers, was surely named for the famous mountain of the Muses in Greece.

Further on she came upon a dreamy little town called Cheviot, so perhaps she was right about Ferniehurst. There were downs here and fields, which she must remember to call paddocks now, as John had told her, great spreading paddocks divided now by hawthorn hedges instead of gorse as further north. On her left roads led off, according to their signposts, to bays beside the Pacific, and on her right, rolling hills, green enough, though not as emerald as England's, sloped up towards foothills, the more distant ones grape-blue, and beyond them again the still snow-capped splendour of the Southern Alps that led like a gigantic chain right down this island.

Other names flashed by, places she might come to know and to love if she stayed long enough. Her heart contracted at the thought. She must not allow these doubts of Phyl to creep in. Phyl would be back. She would never desert her children permanently. They must hear from her soon. Trying to even imagine Phyl running off with someone for an illicit honeymoon – on which one could not, presumably, take one's offspring – was bad enough. But surely she wouldn't just leave them to a stepfather? And that stepfather, unknown to Phyl, his wife, was seriously injured, perhaps even at death's door. Oh, Phyl, Phyl!

Amberley, a small township with hills running down to the sea, reminded her of Amberleigh, with a varied spelling, of course. Was this near her destination? No, it was probably named for Amberley in Devonshire. Phyl had said in a letter once that the first Leigh to take up land in Oxford, finding the river that ran through the valley had been named the Amber, had tacked Leigh on to it, for his own homestead. She found it was some little distance on.

She crossed the Ashley River and knew that soon she must look for a signpost to Oxford. 'It's little more than a village,' Ivan had said, adding to Edmund Leigh's instructions, 'and you continue through it towards the mountains and Ashley Gorge. There are two deep valleys here, Lees Valley and Tapuwharua. You'll see a notice by Tapuwharua saying "No exit", just as we say "No through road" back home. It's steep and rough and shingled and you'll get patches of dense bush on either side. The Oxford area is where New Zealand troops do their jungle training. It's not called Little Malaya for nothing! Incidentally, Sharlie, there'll probably be a lot of bush round the property. Don't explore it on your own, ever. But there are big open sunlit patches too, of course, hill pastureland.'

To say it was a steep road was the understatement of the year. Charlotte had imagined, seeing it was called a valley road, that only the approach would have been steep and that the rest of the way would have been along the valley floor, with a pleasant river meandering along the side of it. She got into her lowest gear and began to grind up the first few miles, cautiously sounding her horn at every corner.

Dust rose from the heavily metalled surface and she had to concentrate on driving, not scenery. But presently the road levelled out for some distance along a sort of terrace and she was able to look far below and see the Amber River confined narrowly between great rock walls, canyon-like, running swiftly. Perhaps the snows on the mountains were melting. It was gloriously hot, though, here within the valley walls that rose as high above as they dropped below.

Dragonflies darted and gleamed in iridescent flashes, and butterflies, and now and then above the sound of the engine she could heard birdsong, some undoubtedly the birds she had known and loved in England, some strange to her. The road dipped down, narrowing, and she saw a most inadequate-looking bridge with the water not far from the surface. No wonder they were cut off sometimes. She crawled over it, but found it more solid than she'd estimated, then ground up a terrific slope, gained the summit with the heat indicator rising alarmingly, and found it dropped down just as sheerly and there was a warning to change gear. She crossed another loop of the river at the bottom, a river that certainly bent back and twisted on itself in an endeavour to find the swiftest, easiest way to the plains and the sea amongst these towering and solitary hills.

Where was this village comprised of the store, the church, the petrol pumps and garage? There seemed only homesteads and indeed most of these weren't visible from the road, the only indications being the mail boxes by the drive entrances. Some of these had Maori names for the homesteads, but none said Amberleigh.

Then ahead of her on the right, with the river on the left, she saw a vivid splash of camellia blooms ... did they flank a gateway? Yes ... well, cattle-stops, and a finely gravelled drive led through the camellias and on through a positive tunnel of trees and shrubs. She thought it looked menacing beyond the cerise blooms, and sure enough the white board said Amberleigh and on the mail box: Owen J. Leigh.

She felt her heart thumping madly. Tapuwharua ... the Forbidden Valley. One that, as Phyllis's cousin, she had been banned from by this Edmund Leigh, the man she had already deceived and was about to practise further deception on.

Charlotte shook her head impatiently as if to free it from such thoughts and forebodings of disaster to come, and began to drive uphill through the dimness, but at the first turn she emerged into sunlight ... surely a happier omen ... and smiling acres surrounded a house that was wide and low-set except for some quaint gabled dormers set in its steeply sloping roof ... a house that looked surprisingly hospitable with its threshold set on terraces afoam with frothing alyssum, with ranunculus in scarlet and gold swaying in the slight breeze; where primroses and violets sought shade from the hot sun under trees and cinerarias patched the dark corners with purples and blues. A circular drive led up to that threshold.

She drove up to it, stopped, looked at the open front door. Did that mean Edmund Leigh was home or that doors were never locked in this remote valley?

As she set foot on the first of the six steps that led to the open door, he appeared in the doorway. From his stern voice last night she'd pictured him dark-visaged and hawk-like. He had a broad, Saxon-featured face and almost tawny hair bleached at the ends and the bluest and most piercing of eyes. She somehow shrank from that look. Never in all her twenty-five years had she feared scrutiny, or had anything to conceal. This was what lying did to you ... undermined your confidence. He made no apology for his close appraisal, probably saw no reason to do so. He was summing her up, wondering if she was suitable to be engaged to live beneath his roof, look after his brother's stepchildren.

He grunted, but she had no idea whether it was a grunt of approval or disappointment. It was simply an 'M'mmmm'.

Then he came to her as she reached the top step, crossing the flagged path between that and the threshold, and held out his hand.

'Good afternoon, Miss Smith. I'm Edmund Leigh.'

'Good afternoon, Mr. Leigh. Tell me, what's the news from the hospital?'

His eyes flickered. 'He hasn't regained consciousness yet. They seem to think – from X-rays and so on – that some pressure needs to be relieved. They'll probably operate the day after tomorrow, depending upon his general condition. I'm glad you could come right away, I need someone on the spot for the children. This neighbour is very kind. We've known her all our lives, but she has quite a large family of her own. Besides, the children are so upset by knowing about the accident – they think their mother is at Owen's bedside and they're missing her – I think they need the reassurance of their familiar surroundings. I gather they've not had much stability in their lives. I think my flibberty-gibbet of a sister-in-law enjoyed flitting about the world, joining her first husband at various ports – he was a seaman. Sounds abominably selfish to me, uprooting children all the time. Seems to me that once you bring children into the world you ought to be prepared to make a permanent home for them. But nowadays people don't seem to plan ahead, and children just happen along and are regarded as nuisances that mustn't be allowed to interfere too much with their parents' lives.'

Charlotte had to crush down the temptation to fly to Phyl's defence. Phyl, who had provided stability and love for her children as a solo job, who had given up all she held dear and gone out to Australia to try to save her marriage, to give the children a father . . . a father they'd hardly have seen otherwise. Here was a man of rigid ideas. To him black would be black, and white white. He'd have grown up in this isolated pocket of the hills and bush in a secure family atmosphere, in the place where his pioneering ancestors had begun a home, perhaps had tried to create a sort of Colonial dynasty, where son after son succeeded . . . and ruled . . . and judged lesser mortals by their own rigid standards.

But she must appear to this man as if all this was news to her, as it unfolded, something she'd heard of only last night.

So she said, 'I think this is right, Mr. Leigh, and if I can create some sort of continuity in their daily lives I will – providing you approve my references and take me on.'

He allowed himself a bleak smile. 'I've not much choice, have I? And you look and sound pretty sensible. Come on inside.'

Charlotte subdued a grin. He might as well have said, '*Plain* and sensible!' She felt quite unlike herself with her hair screwed back like this, but at least it would set his mind at ease knowing she wasn't too, too young for the job.

He took her into what was obviously the farm office, hung round the walls with sheets of wool samples, stud records, diagrams of farm machinery, endless papers. This would be to put it on a business basis, she supposed. He motioned her to a chair and went behind the desk, holding out his hand for her references.

He read quickly, looked at her over them. 'These are extremely good. My main worry has been the children, and this is the department in which you're fully trained. I'm afraid I can't offer you any domestic help – I know that in England it's still possible to get in women for the rough, say, but there's just no one round here who needs any work. They're mostly concerned with keeping their own houses. So I'm afraid you're stuck with all the housework and the cooking – that's why I'm prepared to pay well to compensate. Our men and I are used to helping, even to rustling up meals for ourselves, so we'll give you a hand as we can – dishes at night and so on. It may not be what you're used to, but—'

Charlotte held up a hand. 'You may have an exaggerated idea of conditions in Britain. We're not as feudal as once we were, and I was the only member of the household staff on this Welsh farm. I loved it. My employer was just a few years older than myself and Megan worked as hard as any New Zealand farmer's wife, I should imagine. She had five children, though, so having a nanny enabled her to assist her husband outside without neglecting them. I was just like a sister there, pitched in and helped with everything. It was a much bigger and older house than this – this would be easier to run. I take it that – that your brother's wife ran everything herself?'

Heavens! She'd almost said Phyl!

His tone held a wry note. 'She did, and evidently, to give the devil her due, most efficiently. The letters my parents wrote me, when I was in Canada, positively sang her praises. Then when they arrived in Canada, to visit my sister, just before I

31

came home, they continued the refrain. Mother was so happy at leaving Amberleigh, this home she'd loved so well herself, in Phyl's hands. They'd dreamed for years of visiting Rowena, and are looking forward to going on to England when they get back from Alaska. So if I can avoid letting them know about this till they're on their way, I will. But of course, if Owen goes from the seriously ill list to the dangerously, I'll have to.'

He looked thoughtful. 'I've never known Mother a poor judge of character. She loves people, is most gregarious, but is still fairly shrewd. When Owen came back from Australia where he'd been on holiday and announced that he was marrying a young widow with two children, Mum flew over to help her pack, and seemed to think she had to do this for Phyl's sake so she'd not think she was coming amongst strangers, and she fell for Phyl in a big way, and for the children too. With Rowena being in Canada, Mum's missed out on grandchildren, and she adores Mark and Barbie. She missed Rowena too – they were great pals, my sister and mother, a real pair of gigglers, and she said in one letter that Phyl had brought back laughter into a too-serious male household. I was looking forward to meeting her. Oh, lord!' he sighed.

'So there was no mother-in-law trouble. But there must have been slyness under this façade of efficiency and affection. Perhaps this woman was carried away by the fact that we're established landowners – though farming's not what it was – then tired of the novelty. Perhaps this unknown chap offered city life . . . access to theatres, restaurants, shops.'

Charlotte knew she mustn't appear, yet, to probe, yet anyone would ask some questions. She squashed down her reaction to his analysis of Phyl's probable character, because she knew that it wasn't even remotely correct. Phyl had been brought up in the Surrey countryside and positively wilted when she had to live in a city . . . she assumed a most disapproving expression and said, 'I can't understand any woman leaving her children. I grant some can't resist falling for other men, are not content with their own, but desertion of the children one has brought into the world is beyond my powers to understand. Children are so vulnerable, so much at the mercy of their parents. But tell me, have you no idea at all of whom she ran away with? Was he a local man?'

He looked savage. 'I only wish I knew. I just wish it! Because if I did, and therefore knew where they were likely to be,

32

I could and would go after her, and I'd tell her what's happened to Owen because of her outrageous conduct and twist her arm enough to bring her back here – though of course, God alone knows if Owen would want her back. Imagine the state of mind he's going to be in when he comes to!'

Charlotte felt more appalled than ever. But she rallied, looked puzzled. 'Then if no one knows who this man is, how can you be so sure she's gone off with someone? You said she left a letter. What—'

Well, it was hardly likely he'd show a stranger the letter right away, but it had been worth a try.

He said, instead, savagely, 'It was all there except his name. Imagine the sort of homecoming it was for me. I landed at Harewood Airport – that's at Christchurch – expecting to be met. Certainly Owen himself would be there, but I even thought – and hoped – Phyllis and the kids would be, too. It was a Saturday, so they'd be off school. I waited for ages, thinking they'd had a breakdown or a puncture. Rang the house. No answer, so I thought they were certainly on their way. Hours later I hired a car, leaving a message at the airport, should they turn up.

'The men had been given the day off – afternoon rather – so I got in here to find the house wide open, both cars gone, and a rather crumpled letter, flung down on the table. *Her* letter, telling him what she'd done and asking him, quite coolly, to collect the children at some school friend's place, away back near Oxford – presumably they had been asked there for a party and to stay the night. Oh, she had it well planned. Owen must have gone straight after her and, not surprisingly in the state of mind he'd be in, went over the bank. Not that I knew that then. Ten minutes after I got in, still tearing round the house to see if I could find any clues as to where they'd have gone, the phone rang. It was the daughter of a neighbouring estate. She'd come over to see Phyl, she said, found the doors wide open, walked through and found the pages of this letter blowing about. She had a sense of something wrong and read that damned letter. So I've no show of keeping it quiet – her mother's a gossip, though they've promised to say nothing yet. This girl was most helpful. I used to think of her as a very selfish type, but give her her due, she did what she could. Otherwise, on my own, I think I'd have gone clean mad. I'd no idea when the men would be back.

'Shortly after Avis came over – which was good of her – the police rang to say Owen was in hospital. But for Avis I'd not have been capable of thinking what to do next, though all I could think of was Owen. Avis rang the people the children were staying with, said Owen had had an accident and as Phyl would be staying in Christchurch to be near him, would they keep the children till we could make other arrangements – they're at a closer neighbour's now. Only that close neighbour knows . . . Judy Sandringham. Avis stayed here till my men got home. I was at the hospital overnight, then came home. I felt I must be here – but I don't go far from the phone.'

Charlotte's heart was like a lump of lead. If only, if only she had the right to see that letter. But what he had said was convincing enough. How heavily the scales were weighted against her cousin!

She swallowed. 'Have you seen the children? What have you told them?'

'I went over to Oxford and brought them home, told them their daddy had had an accident and naturally their mummy wanted to be near him. They just accepted that. Then I took them over to Sandringhams' when they'd sorted out what clothes they wanted, and some toys and books. Judy's a marvel, and as close as an oyster.' He made a face. 'She seems stunned about Phyl. Apparently they were great friends, and she can't believe it. She vows Phyl never looked at anyone save Owen. Doesn't know of anyone she could have met – either unattached or married – so I showed her the letter, that damning, cruel letter. Gosh, when I think of my brother, the most trusting chap anyone ever knew, reading *that*, I feel sick. Judy had to accept it then – there was no loophole for misunderstanding in it. Yet even so every now and then when we're on our own, Judy mutters that it can't be true and that surely Phyl will be in touch soon – about the children.'

Did that mean Judy was now accepting the man in Phyl's life, but not the desertion – for long – of her children? That must be it.

It was beyond belief for Charlotte too, but she said crisply, as a stranger would, 'Well, these things do happen, Mr. Leigh. We'll just have to cope with the situation as it is. Show me the ropes now, before you collect the children, because I expect that you'll just be telling them that I'm here housekeeping till their mother comes home?'

34

The blue eyes locked with her hazel ones and for a moment he didn't look savage, he looked bewildered and lost. He ran a hand through his streaky hair. 'I keep telling myself that even if she's gone off with another man, she'll not fade completely out of her children's lives. Not in these circumstances. I mean, I have heard of mothers doing it, leaving the children with their fathers, but never of leaving them to a stepfather! Have you? No. Every time the phone goes I think: "This is it," and wonder what the devil I'll do if she wants the children sent to her. What would Owen want? And he's out of this world of consciousness at the moment! Then I realize it could be a week or more before we hear. That she'll be trying to have some travesty of a honeymoon before she sends for them.'

He set his jaw. 'Owen legally adopted the children. That might give him rights over them, and if she's got no more morals than a barn cat, I'm wondering if they wouldn't be best left here. My mother would help when she gets back. But I'm pretty sure that when this sort of thing happens, the courts prefer them to be with their mothers, unless the case is too bad.'

Every now and then a most unreal feeling surged over Charlotte. They must be talking about someone else, never her cousin Phyl. It was going to be even harder than she'd thought. She must keep her masquerade firmly in the forefront of her mind. She must appear a stranger to the set-up, she must give the impression she knew nothing save what he'd told her.

But she responded rather gently to that bewildered look. 'Mr. Leigh, don't let's look too far ahead. I take it things won't be gossiped about – for a while yet. You've asked Avis's mother not to, and Judy won't. Don't let's cross all the bridges before we come to them. Let's take it step by step. Show me round, tell the children I'm here till their mother can leave their stepfather – they'll just accept that. I'll free you all I can to spend as much time as possible with him. What about the men? What do they know?'

'Everything. I couldn't hide it. They're grand chaps.' He stood up. 'Thanks, Miss Smith. You're a godsend. I may have been hoping for someone older, but at least you're not a flibberty-gibbet, and thirty's not too bad. You seem mature – I couldn't have stood a young girl. I'll get your luggage out of the Mini and take you up to your room. It's one of the dormers.'

He led the way into the first one. 'It's all ready for you. One thing, Phyllis was evidently a good housekeeper and very fore-handed. She had a cousin from England arriving and had the bed made up, and everything neat and tidy. Fortunately this girl wrote – she's come out to her parents in Wellington – so I simply answered it right away and told her what had happened and on no account to come here. I don't suppose she'll answer. I think it's quite likely Phyl's been in touch with her by now, telling her the whole dramatic treacly story. She – the cousin – seemed to know something about it. Said she was sorry her cousin was so unhappy, but never mind, she'd be here soon and they could talk it over. Pah! Birds of a feather, I suppose.' A thought struck him. 'If she does write to her cousin – and gives her an address to write to – this cousin just might pass on the news that Owen has had an accident. Surely under those cir-cumstances Phyl would get in touch with Amberleigh!'

Charlotte's thoughts raced. It would never do to have Edmund Leigh banking on that. She said swiftly, 'I shouldn't think she'd write to this cousin soon, though. I mean, if you'd eloped, you wouldn't, not till a bit of the scandal had died down.'

'No, probably not. Anyway, till Owen recovers conscious-ness and I know what he wants to do, I could cope with an-other female of the same type, probably, as my sister-in-law. The children will be much better with a stranger like you than with someone who might want to treat the whole affair differently from the way I do. So I put a veto on the visit. I hope she's got the sense to stay right out of it. I want neither letters nor phone calls from her.'

Unreality again beset Charlotte. Things must have reached a climax – crisis point, in fact – very quickly with Phyl for her to have timed this so badly. If she had planned it ahead, surely she'd have had a letter awaiting Charlotte in Wellington, to stop her coming down here? Not that anyone, contemplating an elopement, would confess what she was doing, but surely she'd have written to say: 'Don't come till you hear from me. I've got to be away for a week or two. I'll be in touch later,' or some-thing like that.

All of a sudden Charlotte's heart felt lighter. It was all too crazy. It was completely out of character. There was something wrong and she was here to find out what, but she mustn't expect to solve it right away. No matter what Phyl had done, under some emotion that had swept away her integrity, her sense of

36

loyalty to Owen, she wouldn't just disappear without trace. Some day, probably soon, they would hear from her, and when they did she, Charlotte, would be here to sort it out.

She mustn't appear moved at the evidence of Phyl's loving preparation of the room for her cousin. There was a desk with airmail paper, envelopes, aerogrammes and stamps laid on it, for writing to Megan and her other friends. There were English magazines beside the bed, even a Surrey County Magazine. Surrey was where Charlotte had been born and brought up, where she had lived with Phyllis and Aunt Sue in that terrible time after Daddy had died.

Edmund Leigh dumped her bags down, moved on to the landing again. 'That's the children's room there, next to yours, the main bedroom is the other side of it. The toilet and then the bathroom is at the end. My room is down below. There's another spare room, a double, downstairs.'

Charlotte was glad he didn't take her into the master bedroom. It could have Phyl's possessions scattered about, her photos and her pictures. It might upset her and she mustn't appear upset.

The house was quite large and, by New Zealand history, old. But all of it had been modernized. There were wall-to-wall carpets, cupboards and shelves numerous enough to delight any housewife's heart, all kinds of aids fitted or supplied, and, given other circumstances, Charlotte would have loved it, particularly the big drawing-room with latticed French windows opening on to a flagged patio where wistaria and clematis twined, framing a view of hyacinthine hills that were only footstools to towering peaks. 'The men have their afternoon tea away with them. I wanted to interview you myself,' said Edmund Leigh, removing a bubbling kettle from an electric element. 'I guess you'll be ready for a cuppa. It's always been a tradition at Amberleigh to have fresh scones or pikelets every day, but it's bought biscuits for buttering today, I'm afraid. But the tins seem well stocked up with fruit cake and cookies.'

'Pikelets?' asked Charlotte, a line between her brows. 'Then that's one tradition you must do without, unless this Judy can tell me how to make them. I've never heard of them. What are they?'

'You cook them on a girdle,' said Edmund Leigh vaguely. 'Or if you do them on an electric stove with a solid plate, on the plate itself. Nice with cream and jam, or just buttered. But not

37

to worry. Scones will do.'

He buttered some crackers, brought out a fruit cake and some shortbread. Charlotte knew a tremor of the lips. The shortbread was cut in playing-card shapes, diamonds, hearts, clubs, spades. Phyl must have brought the cutters out with her, the ones Aunt Sue had used long ago, when they were all children, and so happy. She felt in great need of that tea and felt much better when she'd had two cups, fairly strong and very hot. Then she stood up.

'I'd better unpack immediately, find myself an overall and get stuck into producing some sort of a meal. I suppose you'll be going over for the children?'

'There's plenty of cold meat. I cooked a huge leg of mutton last night. There are jars of preserved beetroot in the larder and lettuces and tomatoes. That will do, with bread-and-butter and bottled fruit. There are loads of bottled peaches left over from last year's preserving. I'd prefer you to come across to Judy's. She's all worked up about who's going to look after the children.' He grinned. 'She was the one who advised me not to get someone too young. Last time she went into the nursing-home, Bill had quite a hectic time persuading a young local, manmad, that he didn't need consolation!'

Charlotte's voice was tart. 'Well, you'll be quite safe with me, Mr. Leigh. I'm not young, local, nor man-mad. I'm only interested in my job. It's an ideal career for anyone who likes the country and doesn't want to be tied to any one place for ever. I've got all of a very fascinating new land to explore. Many of your New Zealand girls come to Britain for a working holiday. That's what I'm here for. My brother thinks I may settle here to be near him, but I hardly think so. But it will be good experience and I'll stay as long as you need me. Something's bound to happen soon and once your brother is recovered, it will be his responsibility . . . deciding what to do about his wife and her children.'

(There . . . that ought to rid his mind of any designs he might suspect her of.)

But immediately Edmund's face became grim. 'Yes . . . *if* he recovers,' he said.

The Sandringhams could scarcely be called close neighbours, but they were the nearest. These hill farms were large and the road wound up and round the Amber, but finally they reached it, a large, new-looking house, white and long and gleaming. There was a tumbled heap on the front lawn that sorted itself into six separate units as the car swept up the drive, and all six rushed to the car as it stopped.

Charlotte could pick out Phyl's two immediately, though that was probably because all the others had hair even redder than her own. Mark had a fair, straight fringe, and sherry-brown eyes, and Barbie was the nut-brown pixie she had been at two except that her hair was long now and confined in a ponytail. What a blessing they'd been so young when last they'd seen her.

Barbie's eyes were grave, too grave for a child, as if the sight of her stepfather's brother had recalled the tragedy to her. Her very stance suggested she was braced for bad news.

'Uncle Edmund, how's my father?'

Yes, Owen had been just that to Phyl's children. She had said so in her frequent letters.

'No worse, Barbie. They're going to operate soon to make him better.'

Mark looked up from under his fringe and his lowered brows and said, controlling a trembling lip, 'When's Mummy coming home?'

'Well, she's got to be at the hospital just now while your dad's sick, so I told her we'd manage fine on our own. Said I'd heard of someone who'd cook for us a darned sight better than I can, and here she is. Her name is Miss Smith.'

Charlotte said, 'I think you'd better call me Sharlie. It's easier than all this Miss business. Aren't you going to tell me the names of your friends?'

They were in the middle of it when Judy Sandringham came running out, looking incredibly young to be the mother of these boys and girls, a slim, grey-eyed, redheaded slip of a girl. Charlotte warmed to her immediately. Here was the girl who couldn't believe Phyl would desert her children or her husband.

She said, 'Oh, aren't your children like you!' and they all burst out laughing because at that moment Judy's husband arrived on the scene and he had hair just as red.

Judy had the children's clothes packed and there was a carton of home-made biscuits to give Charlotte a good start. She wangled a few minutes alone with Charlotte, upstairs, and said how glad she was Edmund had got someone. She said anxiously, 'When children have had an upset, I always find they play up for a day or two . . . they're all confused and upset, you see. So if they are naughty, please don't think they're always like that. They're very biddable, really. They're so attached to their stepfather and they realize he could die.' She bit her lip. 'But oh, if only it was just what the children believe .. that Phyl is in Christchurch at Owen's side. I dread to think what's going to happen – how they'll react – when they know, as they'll have to know, that she isn't coming back.' She pressed the heels of her hands against her forehead suddenly, almost beat her brow. 'It's all too incredible. I still can't believe it's happened. I feel it could have happened with other women – not with Phyl. That won't mean a thing to you, of course, not knowing her, but believe me, she just wasn't that type. Yet we've got to accept that letter she wrote.'

Charlotte said: 'Mr. Leigh said you couldn't accept it till he showed you the letter, so I realized it must have been very definite – no room for misunderstanding?'

'None – and yet—'

Charlotte loved her for that 'and yet'.

She said, 'I wonder what she said to her husband, in that letter, to tell the children. She must have had some thought for them – I mean besides telling him to pick them up?'

Judy nodded. 'Yes, evidently she said, "I don't know what to tell you to tell the children. Perhaps for now they could think I've been called away for illness. You could say Aunt Rhoda in Wellington is ill and I've gone to nurse her." But with this happening to Owen, Edmund used that as an excuse for their mother's absence. He must be nearly out of his mind.'

Charlotte reflected it was just as well she'd only mentioned a brother to Edmund, not a mother in Wellington.

Judy said hurriedly, 'I think Edmund's coming up here. He mightn't like us talking about it.' She raised her voice a little. 'Well, that's about all, they have few likes and dislikes, really. They've been brought up very sensibly. Oh, there's Barbie's Teddy-bear, mustn't get away without that, above all.' She tucked it into the crook of Charlotte's arm. Charlotte looked down on it. She'd been with Phyl when she'd bought it to put into her little daughter's Christmas stocking when Barbie had been too young to know what Christmas meant, and the Teddy-bear had been shiningly golden and austerely new. Now he was lop-eared and shabby and his face was bald of fluff, because

40

he'd been kissed so often, she supposed. A wave of longing for Phyl swept over her, for the Phyl of yesteryear, clear-eyed, courageous, shouldering burdens so often too heavy for her, being determinedly gay for the children's sakes, bearing all Ranulf's misdemeanours and disillusionments without a word of complaint and only after he had been drowned, opening her heart out in her letters.

Well, what Phyl had done, and done recently, couldn't be undone. Although they didn't know it, she was the children's closest relative, so she must do all she could for them and leave the future to take care of itself.

She came down, talking to Judy and Edmund, to find all the children gathered at the foot of the stairs, faces upraised. Barbie said distinctly, 'Sharlie, you talk exactly like our mummy. Our mummy doesn't speak like our daddy, or like us.' True enough, the children had adopted New Zealand accents.

Sharlie said calmly, 'Oh, do I? How funny. Though I think your uncle said your mummy came from England to Australia. Perhaps she was from the South of England, just as I am, though I've been a few years in Wales. I was born in Surrey, in fact, though you mightn't know where that is.'

'Oh, we do,' answered Barbie promptly. 'Mummy was born in Surrey too. In a town called Godalming. She often talks to us about it – about bluebells in the woods and squirrels and robins. Do you know Godalming too, Miss – I mean Sharlie?'

Did she?

'Yes, I grew up not far from there. Now what about—'

Barbie said, 'I hope you stay on for a bit when Mummy gets home when Daddy's better. Mummy would like that.'

Charlotte picked up the Teddy-bear she'd dropped. 'Oh, dear, I mustn't drop Teddy or we'll have to bandage him up. Now I think we'd better get away because you'll have to show me all sorts of things, you and Mark, till I get used to them. Where the dishes are and your clothes, and what you want to wear to school tomorrow. Right?' And they were away.

Charlotte found that having the men there helped. She had to cook for them too, of course, and they all ate together in the big kitchen. Tod was a huge, good-natured chap, loving the tractor work, and Lance was long and lean and more than a bit shy, and loved the animal work best. They made no comments on the situation, so no doubt Edmund had primed them well. They just accepted Miss Smith as a fill-in till the children's mother would get home, told her she was pretty good as a cook, and anyway, anyone was better than Edmund, and all this lightened the situation.

Their quarters were joined on to the house, in the form of a three-roomed cottage that jutted out from the back like a wing, and they had only to go along a verandah to it. It had two bedrooms, a sitting-room and a lean-to kitchen.

Edmund Leigh explained that it had been the original cottage built by his great-great-grandfather, one Alfred Leigh, when all these hillsides had been thick with virgin timber and he had made a clearing, had sawn down his own trees, to build his house. 'Pit-sawn . . . see . . . look at the edges. They simply dug a pit, put the huge trunks across and hand-sawed them over the pit. Houses were desperately needed in Christchurch — stone was scarce in that area — and timber mills sprang up all over this part. My forebear had one of the first mills here. He had it a lot nearer the lowlands than this, though. He'd built a cob cottage — out of sods and tussocks — much nearer the cartage tracks beside his mill, first. But he always hankered to build back in here and finally farm it when some of the bush had been cleared for grazing. These timbers are still sound and every generation has kept it in good order. They like it, the men. They have their own fun in the sitting-room, their own TV, radio, record-player and heaps of books.' He looked at her sharply. 'So you won't get much company in the evenings. Think you can stand it, Miss Smith?'

She looked at him coolly. 'I've always been fond of my own company. I believe even as a child I was self-sufficient, never bored. I'm still the same. I notice you've a fair library here . . . who could be bored in a world of books? I've seen bookshelves in every room and — and your sister-in-law had put plenty of magazines in my — in the room she'd prepared for her cousin.' Heavens, how hard this was. She'd almost said Phyl again.

She got the children bathed, heard their prayers, which nearly undermined her stoicism as they prayed for their step-father, came downstairs, got their clothes ready for the next morning and said to Edmund Leigh, sitting reading beside the fire he'd lit in the living-room, 'I'll make it an early night, Mr. Leigh. It's been a pretty big day. Would it be all right if I made you a cup of tea about nine-thirty, and turned in then?'

He nodded. 'You come and sit down now with a book and I'll make that supper at nine-thirty. The men make their own. I'm immensely grateful to you for filling in like this. I think the children seem more settled already. You're a no-nonsense person, I can see that. Praise the saints for it! I expect their mother was one of these excitable, sort of emotional types, lacking control of herself. Thank heaven I managed to stop that cousin of hers coming here. One of that breed is enough for Amberleigh. More than enough.'

Charlotte picked up her book and buried her head in it, though she read all of the first chapter without taking in a word. How would this man react if ever he found out she was the cousin in question? At first the urgent thing had seemed to get here under any guise, to find out what had happened, to look to the children, but there were uncharted rocks ahead. One she ought to have thought of. When Owen recovered, as pray God he would, *he* might know Phyl's cousin Lacey's name was, in reality, Charlotte Smith. Certainly Smith was common enough, but Charlotte was a little unusual these days. And what if Phyl suddenly rang Owen? She could hardly mean to disappear permanently. Oh, if only she could read that letter, she might find something, between the lines, that the others had missed.

If Phyl rang, she would recognize Charlotte's voice immediately. Even if, by some fluke, she didn't, she'd want to know who she was, what she was doing there. And if Edmund was within hearing, what on earth could she answer? Then too, if Edmund answered the phone, he'd tear strips off Phyl for her behaviour, and would hurl at her the news that her abominable treatment of her husband had caused him to have a near-fatal accident. Yet anything was preferable to not knowing where Phyl was, or with whom, and with her husband lying at what might be death's door! Nevertheless, panic about what might or might not happen rose in Charlotte till she could have screamed, and when the phone did suddenly ring, she jumped visibly.

Edmund went across to the extension in the living-room. Charlotte felt her hands clench on the book. It could be Phyl. It could be the hospital with bad news ... the worst news of all ... then Edmund said, 'Oh, hullo, Avis. Good of you to ring. No, not a word from anyone yet. But they're operating on Owen soon. Yes, I've got someone – sheer good luck. An English nanny, used to backblocks too, was on a Welsh farm for years. A no-nonsense sort of person, not *too* young. Happened to be passing through Kaikoura and saw my advert. She rang, so I asked her to come through.' He chatted on. While he was busy, Charlotte put the kettle on, buttered some bread, made sandwiches, put out some of the shortbread, brought it back to the living-room.

He put the phone down. It had been a long conversation. His voice had warmed as he talked. He said now, 'Oh, thanks. My good intentions caved in re getting the supper. Phone call saved me.' He grinned. 'That was Avis, the girl who found the note. She's reassured me that her mother won't tell anyone. That'll give us time to get Owen better if the surgery is successful. A breathing-space. Then he can decide what to do. Of course I think it's more than likely he knows more about this than we realize, may know who she's run off with. He may have seen this coming. Hell of a mess, isn't it?'

Charlotte's thoughts were chaotic, her mind a jumble, but her last conscious thought before falling asleep was: Yes, a hell of a mess indeed!

CHAPTER THREE

THE next day was a lull in the storm, the day between arrival and the critical, ghastly one of Owen's operation, when Edmund Leigh would know hair-trigger tension.

Charlotte had, to her relief, slept exhaustedly and wondered where on earth she was when she awoke. She crossed to her window and knew immediate and unreasoning resentment that there could be such pain and bewilderment and tragedy in a world so fair. Beyond the confines of the garden stretched limitless lavender hills and where the garden met the paddocks, almond blossom showed rosily transparent against the sun, forsythia showed gold above the budding rhododendrons and azaleas and Iceland poppies danced wantonly in yellows and orange, coral and bluish-pink.

Tulips, with blue forget-me-nots interspersing them, grew in the more formal beds and a patch of hyacinths sent a wave of heady perfume up to Charlotte. In the paddocks beyond, lambs were calling for their mothers, and the contented sound of hens clucking as they moved about on free range added a felicity to the day that, as far as this family situation went, it did not deserve.

Charlotte brought her clenched fist down on the black windowsill in an impotent, sudden rage. 'Why?' she demanded of that uncaring, beautiful world outside, 'Why did this have to happen? And happen now? It could have been so lovely, coming down here for a visit, being with Phyl again, riding round this wonderful property, these hills. Having fun with the children, getting to know Owen. How *could* Phyl do this to everyone?' And, as she realized she was now accepting Phyl's guilt, she clapped a hand over her mouth, to still her thoughts.

But you *had* to accept it. No good battering your head against the proverbial brick wall. She must force herself to believe it and stop feeling disloyal for doing so. Phyl had written to her just when she was leaving England to say that if she – Charlotte – came, she might help her to make a decision. This must've been the decision . . . whether or not to leave Owen for this other man. As if she, Charlotte, would or could have ad-

45

vised such a thing! Phyl must have known she'd have been horrified. Not at the thought of Phyl falling in love with someone else – that sort of thing did happen, even to women of Phyl's calibre, but horrified at the thought of Phyl, whom she'd long regarded as a perfect mother, even thinking of leaving the children. At the thought, Charlotte's inability to – quite – believe it of Phyl smote her again.

What *did* you do under such circumstances? Her question was more in her heart than in her mind. More a prayer than a question, even. And out of her twenty-five years of life came the answer: 'You take it a day at a time and do with your might what your hand finds to do.'

In this case . . . get breakfast, look after Phyl's children, help Edmund Leigh to bear what he must bear . . . anxiety for tomorrow, the dread of perhaps having to tell his parents half a world away that Owen had succumbed . . . worst of all, having to tell them the reasons for the crash. Edmund Leigh who, if he knew who she was, would send her from here at an instant's notice in justifiable anger at her deception. But she must, she must be with Phyl's children at this time. That was the task to her hand, and she, having done what she'd done, must stand by it.

Charlotte brushed out her hair, screwed it fiercely into its little knot, anchored into place behind her ears the straying tendrils that wanted to escape and would have softened the severity, grimaced at her plain tailored navy-blue slacks and shirt blouse, and went into the children's room.

Mark was still asleep, his fair head buried in the pillow. Barbie was lying unnaturally still, her hands behind her head, gazing into space. Charlotte realized the child was hating another day without the matchless comfort of her mother's presence in the home, but at least was resigned to the fact that while her stepfather was critically ill, her mother's place was beside him. At the thought that in a matter of days, probably, the truth could no longer be kept from these children, Charlotte's heart constricted. But she must be ordinary in her manner, even gay.

She said briskly, 'Morning, Barbara, how about getting washed and dressed right away so you can come down to show me where things are? I had a bit of a poke round last night, but I'm sure I'll get in a real tizzy this morning.'

The lost lonely look faded and Barbie sat up, all eagerness.

46

'Right, and anyway, they all like their eggs different. Lance likes his hard but with the sunny side up, Tod likes his flipped over and very hard, and Mark an' me like ours soft. I don't know about Uncle Edmund 'cos he's just come. Lance has cornflakes and Tod has weetbix and they eat lashings of toast.'

Charlotte was glad they were first in the kitchen, with a sleepy and unwashed Mark tumbling after them. She wanted to earn Edmund Leigh's respect, so that even if – ghastly thought – he found out who she was, he'd at least not think her a light-weight, classing her with a cousin who took her marital and maternal duties so lightly, she vanished into thin air.

They had place-mats on the big laminex-covered table in the kitchen, and the rind cut off the bacon before the men appeared, but they came in from outside, having already completed some chores, it seemed.

Barbie said importantly, 'I know how the other men like their eggs, Uncle Edmund, but what about you? Dad's like us, he likes the yolk soft.'

Edmund grinned, 'I take my eggs as they come, Barbie, soft, hard, indifferent. As long as they're fresh-laid it's okay by me. And I didn't ask the men how they wanted 'em yesterday, I beat them all up together and scrambled them. Much easier. What about you and Miss Smith? What are you having?'

It had a feeling of normality and a little of the pain went from round Charlotte's heart. She did stacks of toast in the pop-up toaster and didn't bother with too much fancy serving, just slapped it on the table as speedily as possible. If she were too finicky they'd be impatient. In Wales, it had always been a case of breakfast on the table quickly, and off outside.

The men went out again immediately, not forgetting to thank her, but Edmund stayed. 'I'll take the children to the school bus. Judy put me in the picture for their routine. So I'll help you put up their lunches. Kids, how much do you like and what?'

Charlotte looked at him with respect. These youngsters were no relation to him whatever and he could have been forgiven under these circumstances if he'd been short with them, resenting their presence, their disruption of the farming routine in a bachelor establishment that could have operated nicely without a housekeeper except for the children, but he was evidently a fair-minded man with a good family sense, seeing the children

47

as victims of an uncaring mother. He wasn't even leaving them to the housekeeper. What a super family Phyl had married into. But—

Never mind, an attitude like this would make her position much easier than she'd thought. She'd even imagined having to act as buffer between him and the children.

Mark had taken the opportunity as a golden one. 'I like three choclit biscuits besides the plain biscuits and some shortbread, and cheese-and-pineapple sandwiches, and a hard-boiled egg and some radishes and a cold sausage if there's one in the fridge.'

His uncle looked at him with great respect. 'You're certainly a good trencherman if you can put away all that. But I might tell you, one chocolate biscuit is the ration . . . you'll ruin your teeth otherwise. There aren't any sausages, but I'll slice you off some cold mutton if you like. Want a screw of paper with salt in? And if you're eating sweet stuff don't forget to eat your apple last, young man.'

When the children had gone to get their school-bags, Charlotte said, 'Could I take them down to where they get this school bus? I've a feeling you'd prefer to be within earshot of the phone, because of the hospital or—'

'Or if their mother should ring. I'd certainly like to be on the talking end when – if that happens!'

Charlotte said, 'But she's bound to ring. Even – even the most wayward of women have a thought for their children. I mean, Judy seemed to think she was an exceptional mother. Said she'd had a scoundrel for her first husband and had brought up the children beautifully – mostly on her own.'

'We've only *her* word for it he was a scoundrel. He might have had some excuse for his behaviour.'

Charlotte swallowed. She knew Ranulf hadn't, but dared not say a thing. 'And by the way, Mr. Leigh, you'd better tell me what *I'm* to say to her if she does ring when you aren't here. I mean about Owen. It's going to be an awful shock to her to know—'

His face set. 'I hope it *is* a shock – a horrible shock. I'm not going to try to break it to her gently, Miss Smith. I only hope I'm about. For that reason I'll be staying close to the house today. The men are doing all the jobs that would take me too far away. It will relieve my feelings no end to tell my sister-in-law exactly what I think of her. So if she should ring, Miss Smith, at a time when you have to answer the phone, don't even tell her who you are – keep her guessing. Don't explain that you're the housekeeper – if she thinks we've got someone, it may make things just too easy for her. If she asks *me* who answered the phone I'll tell her it's no business of hers. Oh, hell, I don't know what to think, what to hope for. Will Owen want her back? I mean if, knowing how seriously injured he is, she offers to return. In any case I'd not dare let her see him without consultation with the doctors. I'll have to tell them, of course. They wanted to know his next of kin. Oh, here are the kids coming. They sound pretty normal, don't they? Arguing which apple is the biggest . . . let's try to keep them thataway.'

Charlotte was offered the station wagon, but preferred to drive the car she'd got used to. The children directed her to a place where a minor valley joined this one, where half a dozen other children waited. A good thing they'd be away all day. Much easier to be natural. As Barbie took Mark's hand to help him up the bus steps, she said, 'If Mummy rings from the hospital, tell her we're quite all right and we hope Daddy will be better soon.'

'I will,' promised Charlotte, and swallowed.

But the phone didn't ring except for Judy Sandringham calling to find out how Charlotte was making out. Charlotte was conscious of a great impatience to be able to do something about the situation. She'd come here full of confidence to try to find things out, even hoping things might not be as bad, merely confused . . . but this was a brick wall in her path. Phyl had gone, no one knew where or with whom, and they – Edmund Leigh and herself, a man she'd met only last night – were left to pick up the pieces and do what they could for the stepchildren of a man who, his driving judgment impaired by the knowledge of his wife's betrayal, had all but killed himself. And she, Charlotte, could do nothing more helpful than stand at the sink and peel potatoes!

'What's that huge sigh for, Miss Smith?' asked a voice behind her – Edmund's. He was bringing in a turnip and some carrots out of the cool store.

She decided on partial honesty, still peeling away, but turning a little towards him. 'It's just that I hate situations where one can do *nothing*. If only we knew where Mrs. Leigh is and could contact her and force her to tell us what she intends to do – acquaint her with the whole situation. I mean, it's too hideous, isn't it? The children are bound to ask awkward questions soon. Barbara said if her mother rang to tell her they're okay and that they hoped their daddy would be better soon. But before long they're going to be asking why their mother doesn't ring *them* from the hospital.'

Edmund Leigh nodded, two deeply graven lines grooving his square cheeks, and making him almost haggard. 'That's what Tod said a little while ago. I don't know what to think, what to do. The poor little beggars! They seem so alone.'

Charlotte said uncertainly, 'Except for this cousin of their mother's. Would she know if they had any other relatives?' (If he showed any sign of softening there, she might pluck up the courage in a few days, when he knew her better, to confess her real identity.)

'Heavens, no, I want nothing to do with her. If Phyl had had a mother I might have got in touch with her. It needs someone older. In fact, it needs *my* mother. But I'll wait till I see how it goes with Owen before I contact Mum and Dad. I couldn't say what I want to, by radio-telegraph to their ship, and I'd like to play it along. The situation may alter. That wretched woman may come flying back, all contrition, and I'd just hate to pitchfork Mother and Dad into an affair like that – besides, it's the first time in their lives they've ever been off the farm for more than a month. If this operation relieves the pressure, and Owen regains consciousness, it will give me something to go on. Tomorrow, I'd like to go into Christchurch very early indeed – they're starting the operation at nine-thirty. Miss Smith, could you cope with everything here? I feel I must be there. One never knows. When he regains consciousness someone from the family must be on hand. But it seems terrible to put so much responsibility on to you, so strange to New Zealand, so far from any neighbour.'

She said instantly, 'I was going to ask you if you'd like to stay at the hospital all day. After any operation a patient wants the reassurance of a familiar face, a member of the family, but in this case, the shock of remembering what happened just before is going to be terrible. For him to bear that alone would be unthinkable. And, Mr. Leigh, if it so happens you feel you ought to stay with him tomorrow night, don't worry about me. I'll get the children off to school – and the men are in the house – or very nearly – and I'm not in the least nervous in any case. Often, at home, I stayed with the children on my own, for a few nights, if my employers went off to stock sales.'

It was the first really wide smile she'd seen him give, and what a difference it made to his face. 'Thank you very much, Miss Smith. What a blessing it is to have someone with a bit of grit! Someone who gives, not just takes. Pity my brother hadn't met someone like you . . . who knows the meaning of the word duty. I'll ring you from the hospital tomorrow when the operation's over. And thank you.'

Charlotte looked swiftly down on her potatoes. If only he knew!

He rang the next afternoon, half an hour or so before the children would be off the bus. 'Miss Smith? I'll take you up on that offer. Because of this situation, the doctors are allowing me to sit at his bed all night. The position is a little better than expected. They think there isn't as much damage done as might have been. He's come out of the anaesthetic, but is anything but lucid. He asked for Phyl in a mumbling sort of way and I said, "She's just gone out to get a bit of fresh air for a moment," and he seemed content with that and closed his eyes. The doctors think he's not fully aware yet, that the consciousness of all that happened before the crash is bound to come back, and of course that's what these medical chaps dread. They'd like me to be around then, so that the sight of someone of his own will reassure him to some extent. Some extent! A hell of a lot of use that's going to be, but if they think it will compensate in any way for the loss of his wife, I must be there.'

'Of course you must. Everything's fine here. The men are just finishing their afternoon tea and are going out round the sheep. They said to tell you they'll not take any time off till Owen is well out of the wood. And there was a message from the insurance people to say the car's a write-off, and they'll be in touch.'

'I thought so. Never expected anything else. Jolly good job Dad's station wagon was here. I believe he almost sold it before they left for Canada, but Owen said it could be handy, even though his wife had a Mini. Owen and Dad and Mum gave it to her for her birthday, so she could be free to come and go as she pleased whenever she wanted to go shopping in Christchurch or what-have-you.' His tone was understandingly bitter. 'Perhaps she had too much freedom . . . too much of the "what-have-you". Maybe that's why we've no idea who she could have eloped with. Evidently she had the nerve to stick to the car.'

But Phyl hadn't stuck to the car. Five minutes after Edmund had hung up, there was another ring. From a garage in Christchurch, and a voice said, 'Oh, hullo, Mrs. Leigh, I thought I'd let you know your car is all de-dented, good as new. They've made a fine job of it. Damned shame you didn't know who'd done it. I've got it in for these people who scrape other people's cars in parking areas and don't let on. Will you pick it up soon, or have you got to wait till Owen can bring you into town, because—'

Charlotte thought she'd better interrupt. Naturally he'd taken her for Phyl – their accents were the same. 'I'm sorry, this isn't Mrs. Leigh. I'm just working here. I gather you've not seen in the paper that Mr. Owen Leigh had a bad accident and is in hospital in Christchurch? But I'll see Mrs. Leigh gets the message.' She was thinking rapidly, so added: 'When did she leave the car?'

'Saturday afternoon. She'd spoken to us about it the other week and I said to bring it in whenever she could leave it for a few days. I must have missed seeing about the accident. Where was it, and how is Owen?'

'I can't tell you exactly where, I'm just out from England, but it was somewhere on the main road. Owen's pretty bad. I just had a ring from the hospital, though, to say they operated this morning and he's recovered partial consciousness. We'll hope for a steady improvement. I can't tell you any more than that, I'm afraid.'

'Nasty business! And Owen's a very good driver. First accident he's ever had. Tell Mrs. Leigh how sorry I am, will you, and that I'll just hold the car till I hear from her. She won't want it just now probably. Ed will be driving her in and out, I suppose. Good job he's home, but what a homecoming! I say, are you her cousin? She told me she was expecting her cousin from England?'

Charlotte caught her breath, released it, tried to sound natural.

'No. I'm just the housekeeper they've engaged. Mrs. Leigh will have to stay in Christchurch for some time, I suppose. This farm is so remote.'

'That's so. Well, we'll hope for better news soon. Just pass on that message, would you? Thank you, good-bye.'

She sat staring at the phone, long after she'd replaced the

receiver. Phyl hadn't taken her car. What did it mean?

Did it mean the man she had run away with had a car of his own? Yes, that must be it. You didn't want two cars on an elopement. Phyl must have used the car to reach him in Christchurch, and, using the excuse of the panel-beating job, have calmly left it at this garage, knowing that when it was done they'd ring Amberleigh. Once more incredulity swept Charlotte. This was the sort of thing you read about, but not something you'd associate with Phyl. Not that sort of callous, calculated behaviour. It buzzed in her mind till she was almost distracted, then she rang Judy Sandringham. 'I thought I'd tell you this – an odd thing has just happened. I wondered if you'd advise me on whether or not to ring and tell Mr. Leigh tonight. Owen is through and has recovered a bit of consciousness, but his mind must be still clouded, and it was very brief, so he asked for Phyl. Mr. Leigh told him she'd gone out for a breath of air. He seemed satisfied and went to sleep – or lapsed back. I suppose the poor beggar will remember suddenly, later, as he becomes fully aware. Oh, it's too horrible. I do trust that the shock doesn't set him back too much. But I had a ring just now from a Christchurch garage. Phyl left the car there for some panel-beating on Saturday. I–I think she must have needed it to reach whoever she was meeting in Christchurch, then gone on with him.'

Judy Sandringham's voice sounded tired. 'That must have been it. I've got to make myself accept it. I mean, there *was* the letter in Phyl's own handwriting. *You'll* probably find it easier to accept because you don't know her, but I did. I know one's got to accept facts, but, although Phyl's been here just over a year, she's my best friend, a real kindred spirit. My mind tells me I've got to admit she's run away with someone, apparently deserting her children too – though surely she's bound to send for them later – but my heart keeps up a sort of refrain, it says over and over: "Not Phyl – not Phyl!" '

Charlotte was glad they were not face-to-face. She'd have given herself away for sure. She would have wanted to hug Judy for her loyalty.

She swallowed, said as might this Miss Smith say, who knew nothing of Phyl, who wasn't her cousin Lacey, 'Mrs. Sandringham, the fact that you speak this way of her makes me more than ever sure we're bound to hear of her sooner or later. Mr. Leigh has left me strict instructions about what I'm to say or not say, if she rings. I'm to say – very bluntly – that Edmund Leigh has left her a message to say that on receiving her runaway note, Owen took after her and has smashed himself up, and is seriously ill in hospital. And what does she intend to do about it, and the children? That she's to give me her address, and she's to ring him at a certain time and at whatever cost, at a time to be fixed by herself, allowing him time to get home. And I'm to say if she doesn't give the address and doesn't ring that he'll contact the police to trace her. I'm jittery at the very thought.'

There, she thought, that sounded just how a stranger would feel at having to relay a message like that. Though if it so happened she was alone in the house when Phyl rang, Phyl would recognize her voice and the subsequent conversation would be very different, though she'd have to say, at the last, what Edmund had said. But she prayed she'd be alone, with the men outside, and that she could reason with Phyl, plead with her.

The next moment, to her dismay, Judy said crisply, 'It's terribly tough on you. I know what I'll do. Immediately I've got my brood settled with their homework tonight, I'll drive over and spend the evening with you. No, of course it isn't too far. I often drove over to spend a night with Phyl if she was on her own and Owen off to a Young Farmers' Club meeting or something. Bill will be in tonight and I'd love to come over, it will stop me brooding on this. It does me good just to hear your voice, it's so like Phyl's. No, I won't hear any more objections. I think you're a brick to take on something like this, away out in the backblocks in a strange country. I'll be with you about seven-thirty.'

Charlotte put the phone down and groaned. All she wanted, if Phyl should ring, was solitude. Time alone with her on the other end of a telephone wire. She looked at the time. She must go down and meet the children.

She rather wished the village had been larger. She could have taken her mind off things by exploring it. There was the store, a very old-fashioned one, nothing like the supermarts she'd seen in other townships as she came south, but fascinating too with its mixter-maxter of goods, and, at the junction of the Small Gorge Road, where she met the bus, a garage with petrol pumps, surrounded by farm machinery in various stages of repair. She couldn't see the church, but coming home they passed the lych-gate, half hidden in huge English trees, and with a path winding up to a little church, quite old for this country, set among more trees on the crest of a hill. 'That's the Church of St. Francis. Our daddy's ancestor built it when he first came to the valley,' said Barbie proudly. 'He started it as soon as he got his house built, before ever there was another house here, because he believed that some day this would be a big farming centre. He felled the trees and sawed the wood in a pit and he learned how to split shingles – wooden ones – for the roof, and it's a tradition in our family that the eldest son always carries on, that the roof must never be tiled, or done with corrugated iron, always repaired with wood shingles. But they send to Canada for them now.'

Charlotte knew a pang that was almost physical as she realized how these children had identified themselves with Amberleigh. After all the disturbed, restless years of their early childhood they had come to a permanent haven here. And now their mother had thrown it all away for an infatuation that, in all probability, would not last. She looked down on Barbie, with pain. She was so like Phyl . . . Phyl had looked like this at twelve when Charlotte had been four and had adored her older cousin.

Barbie was rattling on. 'The Vicar comes to take a service here every other Sunday, but we have Sunday school every Sunday morning, of course. Mummy's one of the teachers. I expect they'll have to put two classes together on Sunday, or will Daddy be better enough for Mummy to come home by then, Sharlie?'

'Oh, I think it'll take a bit longer than that, but Uncle Edmund rang and said the operation had been a success. He's not as badly hurt as they feared and he opened his eyes and spoke to them. Isn't that good? He'll get a bit better every day now and be awake longer each time, I should think.'

Mark controlled a quiver of his lip, then, with an assumed stolidity, said, 'I expect Mummy will do the ringing next time and . . . and speak to *us*.'

Charlotte kept her tone light. 'Well, I expect that for the next few days your mummy won't want to leave your daddy's side even for the phone, in case he wakes up and wants her, so don't count on it for some time. I made a steak-and-kidney pie for tonight, and I had some pastry over, so I made some little pastry-men, with currants for eyes and a bit of cherry for a mouth and little green buttons on their jackets from angelica. You can have a couple each as soon as you get home, and you can have some in your lunch tomorrow. How's that?'

They were soon diverted.

Charlotte was relieved when Tod reported Phyl hadn't rung. He added, 'If either Lance or myself are about and she does, we'll get the kids out of the way somehow. You could stall, say: "Just a moment, someone wants me," to her, and tip us the wink. If we aren't about you'd better invent something. Say it's a friend of yours and you can't hear and tell them to play outside.' So that took care of that. But it was the chance of Phyl ringing when Judy Sandringham was there that bothered Charlotte. But she was spared that, because there was nothing but a continued long and uncaring silence as far as Phyl and the phone were concerned.

But chatting with Judy helped. Charlotte realized the long evening would have been well-nigh intolerable without her. They talked about the happenings so much, Charlotte realized it was relieving Judy's feelings too and felt she could ask a few questions.

Judy had said, five minutes after she settled down, busy knitting a pullover for one of her boys, 'I simply can't go on calling you Miss Smith. Can I make it Charlotte? And do call me Judy. We've been thrown together in this misfortune, and we never stand on ceremony, anyway.'

Judy added, 'It's going to be terrible for Owen knowing so many people have read that letter. It's like an intrusion on his privacy. Of course, he'd just flung it down and rushed out after her. He'd been out, and was coming home to get Phyl to go to meet Edmund. I can't understand her picking such a moment. As for Avis Weybourne reading it . . . I felt quite sick. None of us have ever been very fond of her. That will upset Owen more than anything, I'd think. She had a fancy for Owen years ago, but he had no feelings for her at all. She said some very nasty things about Phyl before Owen brought her here, even.

'Said she was probably a widow with an eye to the main chance, wanted to dig herself in for the sake of a home for the children, and so on. But Owen's mother soon squashed that — said Phyl was the daughter-in-law of any mother's dreams, with the sweetest nature, and that even her own grandchildren, if Phyl and Owen had any, couldn't be more to her than Barbie

56

and Mark. But I do wish she'd not been the one to find the letter.'

Charlotte said slowly, 'Mr. Leigh said she'd been very helpful and sympathetic, even if when she was a kid he hadn't liked her at all. But he thought she had improved a lot.'

Judy made a face. 'Trust Avis! She'd make the most of the situation with Edmund. With any man, if it comes to that. She always puts the men off finally, because she's malicious. In time they see through her. She may have appeared sympathetic, but believe me, she'd be secretly purring inside!' Judy stopped short, laughed, said, 'Oh, dear, talk about the pot calling the kettle black . . . hark at me! If that's not being catty, what is? Though I don't care. I mean it. So I won't apologize.'

Charlotte said, consideringly, 'It was a pretty strange thing to do, wasn't it? Reading a letter a wife had left for a husband. I mean, even if the pages of this letter were blowing about, as Mr. Leigh said, if a stranger – well, a non-member of the family – picked up a letter starting: "Dear Owen" as presumably it would, it seems very odd and unethical to me, to read it . . . a letter from a wife to a husband. I mean, that sort of letter is hardly likely to begin: "Dear Owen, I've had to go into Christchurch ahead of you . . ." or "Darling, I'm over at the stables . . ." so why read it? It's horrible.'

Judy said, also slowly, as if reluctant to admit there might have been an excuse for Avis's behaviour, 'Edmund said, when he saw the look on my face, because I felt it was pretty poor too, that when Avis walked into the house – having found the door open – the pages were blowing madly all round the room, because the windows were open and a vase smashed. I suppose Phyl had anchored her letter down with a vase of flowers. The curtains had caught them. So to be fair, if you chased the pages round, you would look down on them, even just to make sure they were all there . . . and the words would rise up and hit you. The only thing I know was – from Edmund – that he said savagely, and I don't blame him, the state he was in, "Well, at least she said she was sorry . . . sorry to do this to me, especially when I'd just got home." She rang, you know, just after Edmund got in, then came over.

'I keep telling myself it's just some horrible dream. I keep trying to imagine the details. I think Owen had to go away over past Oxford that morning, for something. Then he was to collect Phyl and take her to the airport with him to meet Edmund.

I remember Phyl saying what a good thing it was the children had been invited to that party, that it'd give the two brothers an uninterrupted chance of catching up on two years' conversations. She seemed so ordinary about it. If only we knew what Phyl intends doing eventually! Then we'd know how long we have to stall the children. How it will affect Owen when he regains his full senses and remembers, I don't know. I expect, really, that's why the pages were blowing about. Even though that vase had been tipped over, it might have been upright when he first got home, and he must have flung the letter down once he'd read it, and rushed out, leaving the door open, to try to catch her up. Though she didn't mention a destination. Odd, that – I mean here, you could go either south or north on the main road. I wonder if that means he knew the chap. He'd go like fury, and in his car, if she'd not been gone long, he'd have had every chance of catching her up, if he hadn't crashed.'

When Judy left she kissed Charlotte. 'I feel I've known you for ages. Look on me as a friend, won't you, and if you want me at any time, no matter when, just ring.'

Charlotte sat on, comforted by Judy's friendliness, still willing that phone to ring. At eleven she decided to ring Kaikoura and let John and Diana and Ivan know what was happening. They were glad to hear from her, sorry she had no progress to report, and relieved the masquerade had succeeded and she'd been accepted by Edmund Leigh as Miss Smith, and that he seemed glad of her assistance. She promised to ring them if there was any word from Phyl. She'd no sooner hung up than the phone rang again. She jumped, rushed to it, but it wasn't Phyl. It was Edmund Leigh again.

He said quickly, 'Has she just rung?'

'No. Sorry, Mr. Leigh, no one's rung.' (True, in a way, since she had done the ringing.)

'No one?' His voice almost squeaked with surprise. 'But I tried to get you a moment or so ago, and the phone was engaged.'

Charlotte just managed to clamp down on a dismayed gasp. Instead she said quickly, 'Oh, that. It was just a wrong number. You must have rung at that very moment.' Heavens, when one departed from the truth, it was very dodgy. Honesty certainly was the best policy. Less nerve-racking.

'Everything okay?'

'Yes, Judy Sandringham came over. She seemed to think I

might need company. It was very nice. She's just gone. Has your brother said anything more?'

'Not of any significance. I sat on holding his hand, giving it a little pressure whenever I thought he was coming to the surface again. Once he muttered an endearment, so he must have thought it was Phyl's hand, then he lapsed into heavy dozing again. They're making him comfortable for the night at the moment – their way of putting it, not mine. He moans a fair bit. I expect coming to after surgery on one's head is very painful. Thank goodness for you, Miss Smith. At least I know the children are in their own home and well looked after. I'm rather hopeful now that Owen will make the grade. The doctors seem reasonably pleased, but it's going to be a long night. Of course what I dread most is his asking for Phyl as he becomes more lucid. I can't stall indefinitely by saying she's having a spell of fresh air. What on earth can I concoct next in the way of an excuse?'

It came to Charlotte in a flash. 'Mr. Leigh, why not say she's gone down with a heavy cold and the doctors won't let her near him for fear of infection?'

His tone became admiring. 'Miss Smith, I hand it to you, you're quick on the uptake. That's first-rate and it may reassure him for a little longer, till he suddenly remembers, as remember he must, in time. Then there'll be the devil to pay. Delayed shock and reaction, I suppose. What it will do to him in the state he's in I dare not think. But every moment gained will mean another one towards recovery, I suppose.'

Charlotte said, 'Mr. Leigh, I hope you won't think I'm uttering a lot of platitudes, but don't keep that dreaded moment before you all the time. Meet it when it comes. If he's like you, he's got a good physical constitution and may take it better than you think. It will be a great blessing if he doesn't remember all of it at once. Play it along – if that's what the doctors advise – on the grounds that she has this heavy cold. From what Judy's told me of Owen tonight, he's a grand chap and he may surprise you by drawing on some reserve of the spirit you've not guessed at.'

There was a moment of silence, then Edmund Leigh said, 'Thank you, Miss Smith. What a relief it is to have someone so mature to help us at this time. I'll do just that. Owen *has* got what it takes . . . even for this. I'll go back to his bedside now. I'll come back tomorrow night if they report him out of

59

danger.'

Charlotte felt a wave of warmth at her heart. She had been right to come, right to even deceive him. She could never have helped him like this, if he'd known her for Phyl's cousin, even supposing he'd let her stay. He so desperately needed help, so did the children, so did Owen and . . . so might Phyl yet!

But if only she could have seen that letter, in case anything might have given her a clue. If she could even have read a difference in Phyl's nature, that could make her realize how she had changed. She took a look round the room, then hesitated as she caught herself doing it. She'd been scathing about Avis Weybourne reading it. It had been meant for no one's eyes but Owen's. Then she stiffened her resolve. She wasn't doing it out of curiosity . . . she was trying to reach a woman whose children thought she'd be coming back to them some day soon. But where to start? You could see all the Leighs were great readers, and they seemed to do a fair amount of correspondence too, apart from the farm office. There were overflowing bookshelves in every room, and two desks in here, one a secretaire type that probably belonged to Owen's mother.

Charlotte turned the key and pulled the flap down. Phyl had quite evidently used this. At the sight of her loved writing, Charlotte caught her lower lip between her teeth. She began searching in the pigeonholes. It was just the sort of thing Edmund Leigh might have done after he'd shown it to Judy, thrust it quickly into one of these.

She worked quickly and methodically, shuffling through the papers and going from left to right and then down. She closed the flap, began on the drawers. There were letters to Phyl from Owen here, written while she was still in Australia, before they married, carefully tied up with blue ribbon in the accustomed lovers' way. Charlotte put them aside quickly, without untying them. She felt sneaky. It ought to be on top, but there was just the chance that Edmund might have thrust it under everything, so the children couldn't come across it. Nothing came to light.

The more masculine-looking and massive desk held a lot of family letters. Charlotte's cheeks grew hot, though she just glanced at their headings. The top right-hand drawer was the only one locked, though every one had a keyhole. Undoubtedly the letter would be here. She remembered seeing a bunch of keys in the office, went through, brought them back, but none fitted. Edmund would have it on his personal key-ring, to stop the children seeing that fateful letter. Well, that was that. Only one faint chance remained ... when Edmund got to know her better, if she could contrive some situation, he might show it to her. At present it would seem like offensive curiosity from a stranger.

It was past midnight. She made herself some tea and went to bed. As she turned the landing light on, she saw that the door of the main bedroom was open. Owen's and Phyllis's. Would there, could there be anything in there to give her a clue to Phyl's whereabouts? Any letter hidden under clothes, from this man? Could be.

She went in quietly, shut the door, in case the children woke and saw the light. She crossed to the wardrobe and on opening it saw it was just full of clothes, lovely clothes such as Phyl had deserved long ago.

Why on earth hadn't Phyl taken these with her? Or most of them? Charlotte reached in, began diving into coat and suit pockets. There could be an overlooked note from this man, an address, a telephone number. There were two garments that were brand-new. One was a frilly cotton evening dress with a square bodice, embroidered, very modern, in lovely turquoise and purple patterning, the other was the loveliest spring suit in bright orange with a silky, pearl-coloured fur collar and cuffs. This even had the price ticket on. Now why would any woman leave an outfit like that? But nobody would know what Phyl *had* taken. The children couldn't be asked. It took Charlotte over an hour to go through every drawer, Owen's and Phyl's. This just wasn't the room of a woman who had run away. Her brushes and combs were there and a fair range of cosmetics. It wasn't the room of a woman who wasn't coming back. There was that pearl brooch that had belonged to Aunt Sue, Phyl's cameo ring, and an evening watch, which Owen must have given her, tiny, in gold, encrusted with stones.

All of a sudden Charlotte felt frightened ... and lonely. There was something here she couldn't understand ... and the house was just too silent. Silent as if the very walls were listening for a message from a woman who had gone, leaving no trace. The men were away out at the back of the homestead, and the hills were lonely in their immensity ... they went back and back in fold after fold, clothed in almost impenetrable bush, to where high cold mountains reared up ... the bush crept close to the house on this side, too, and she wished that owl, with his strange cry, would stop his mournful note.

She wished, most of all, that Edmund Leigh were here. On that thought Charlotte pulled herself up, went along to the children's room, peered at them in the light of the landing globe. There they slept, Mark with the lovely abandon of childhood, a hand under his cheek, his fringe slanting to one side; Barbie, with her Teddy-bear carefully garbed for the night in striped pyjamas. Charlotte tiptoed out, went to bed.

CHAPTER FOUR

EDMUND LEIGH didn't come home till long after the children were in bed next night. The men were in their own quarters and Charlotte could hear their TV going full bore with some musical show. She'd turned the one in the living-room off and was ironing the children's things for school next day. She heard the car sweep up, drive into the stables, then Edmund Leigh's footsteps. She thought they lagged.

He stood in the doorway and looked at her and Charlotte knew an instant fear. He had aged years since she'd last seen him. The lines were deeper, the eyes lack-lustre ... loss of sleep, she supposed, and yet was it only that? His clothes, of course, were crumpled from sitting up all night. But it was the look in his eyes that made her stand the iron up, walk round the ironing-board, grasp his arm.

'Edmund, Owen isn't—?'

'No. Oh, no, not that. He's actually showing a great improvement and is quite clear in his mind, but—'

He stopped, seemed to search for words. Charlotte, distressed, said, 'Oh, I can imagine how he's feeling. He's distraught, beside himself, remembering all that happened just before. Oh, Edmund, sit down and I'll make you some coffee. This kettle's boiling. You look all in.'

He put out a protesting hand, walked away from her, leaned on a sturdy table the children used for their homework, said, shaking his head, 'No, that's not it. That's not it at all. I just don't know where we go from here. He just doesn't know about Phyl at all. Doesn't know that she's gone ... that there's anything wrong at all.'

Charlotte stood staring, then she clicked. 'Oh, I get it ... you mean he's suffering from amnesia? I believe that's quite usual – that it often ties up with shock, especially if a person has had an emotional upset. Oh, what did I read about it not long since? Something about nature putting up a defence mechanism and blotting out what one doesn't want to remember. But what do the doctors say? How long do they think it might be before he recovers his memory?'

Edmund said slowly: 'There's nothing wrong with his

memory. We've been on the wrong track all along. He wasn't rushing *after* Phyl. He was merely coming home *to get her* – to meet me. The car skid marks must have been due to its turning right round. Not that I know about that, I never questioned it, just accepted what I was told.

'There were no witnesses. Another motorist noticed a car down the bank. Oh, my God, it was awful, trying to think one step ahead of his next question. We were so well prepared for other questions. Miss Smith – Oh, look, I can't under these circumstances go on calling you Miss Smith – Charlotte, I can't tell you how grateful I was for your suggestion about the heavy cold. He looked horribly disappointed but just accepted the fact that the hospital dared not expose him to any infection.

'Thank heaven the doctor was there at that moment! He was little short of magnificent, helped me out on two or three counts. Owen opened his eyes, focused them with some difficulty, then said, "Ed, you old son-of-a-gun . . . you got here! Gosh, what a homecoming! Did I kill that cow?"

' "Cow?" I said. "What cow?" and just boggled.

'He seemed to think we should have known about it. "It leapt down from that bank – fell against the car – I swerved, of course, and next moment I knew I was going over the bank. Gosh, it must have upset Phyl. She'd be frantic. How long before she knew? And who met you?"

'I said, rather feebly, because I didn't know where to go from there, "There was no sign of a cow. You couldn't have hurt it much. It must've cleared off." Then I waited for him to volunteer more, and I was in a nervous sweat for fear I'd say the wrong thing, but his doctor is quite pleased. He seems to think the longer we can stall, the better shape he'll be in to bear – what he must bear – when more time has elapsed. He wanted to know where she was, said, "Don't tell me that when I come to properly, she's off for fresh air again?" so we trotted out the bit about the chesty cold. He got very anxious, asked me was I quite sure it wasn't bronchitis, because she had a touch of that last winter, and had she seen the doctor and so on.

'We managed that, assuring him it was only a cold, then I had to improvise rapidly, but kept it fairly simple – I was terrified if I embroidered the story too much that he'd trip me up another time. I never realized before what a memory a liar has to have. I said Phyl had got frantic when he was delayed, but hadn't dreamed of an accident, just that he'd probably had a puncture or engine trouble or something, some distance from a farm and phone. So she'd rung the Millensens, people we know in Christchurch, and asked them to meet my plane.

'I said that when they did, I rang Amberleigh and by then a passing motorist had seen his car over the bank, the ambulance had taken him to hospital, and Tod had said Phyl was in there now. It was ghastly, because even though the doctor was there, and helped me out on several counts, he was as unprepared for this as I was, of course, so I couldn't ask him how to treat the situation, but had to play it by ear. He asked after the kids, sent them all sorts of messages. You'd think they were his own.

'Well, I've got to go along with what the doctors want me to do. No doubt it will give him a relapse when he has to be told, but day by day he may gain strength to meet it. Fortunately, the doctor, knowing what thin ice I was skating on, said, as soon as Owen seemed pretty satisfied, "Now, Mr. Leigh, that was a pretty bad crack on the head you had, so no more talking just now. You can see your brother again, in, say, a couple of days, and he can give you all the news about the family then. But we'll keep your wife away from you till she's germ-free! You've had more than enough to cope with as it is."

'Owen was asleep again almost before we left the room. The doctor knew it had been a frightful strain, so he took me away and gave me a stiff brandy. Boy, did I need it! He said he'd told Owen that – about my not seeing him for a couple of days – because that would postpone the evil day and be less tough on me. Every day gained is a tremendous help in Owen's ultimate recovery and his resistance. At this stage, news like that could send him into serious shock. And it just might be that in the interim, Phyl may ring. If she does, I'll get her back here if I have to go after her and kidnap her, and force her to Owen's bedside and make her act as if none of it has happened. Later she can make another decision. But that all depends on whether or not she rings.'

Charlotte folded up the ironing-board. 'I'll bake you some supper. I guess you've had very little.'

Edmund nodded. 'Mainly just cups of tea or coffee. I felt as if food would have choked me. Yes, I'll be glad of something savoury. Have some with me. I hate eating alone.'

Charlotte grilled bacon and tomatoes, fried eggs, did a pile of golden toast, put out what was left of the daily batch of scones, some rhubarb-and-fig jam out of a jar labelled with

Phyl's neat printing. Pain stabbed her afresh.

Wonderful what a difference food made. Edmund's face looked more relaxed immediately. They were sitting at a small round table she'd moved nearer the fire. The evening had turned cool, though in any case they had fires most nights here at this time of year, because even though the days were warm, the distance above sea-level crisped the air.

He held his cup out for more tea, the blue eyes looked straight into her hazel ones. 'Thank heaven you were here, Charlotte. It would have been ghastly to come home to just the men tonight. We're all camp cooks, no more, but apart from that it needed a woman's touch.'

Charlotte felt a warmth spread through her. She had been right to come. She had done it for the children's sakes, but she'd helped Edmund Leigh too, a man bearing an unthinkable burden. He wasn't the curmudgeon she'd expected.

Edmund grinned, 'I feel I can sound off about my brother's wife to *you*. Imagine if that cousin of hers had arrived – I wouldn't have been able to give vent to my feelings. What a complication it would have been – she might have insisted on staying to take care of the children. It was such an odd letter she wrote. She certainly seemed to know what was going on, because she spoke of helping Phyl to a decision. They must be frightfully irresponsible people. Just as if there was any decision to come to! I reckon if this cousin had been mature and well-balanced like you she'd have told Phyl that there was only one thing to do – stick to her husband and children.'

Charlotte said, 'Perhaps she didn't know what she was advising on. I mean, perhaps your sister-in-law only hinted at a problem.'

Edmund looked at Charlotte appreciatively. 'You'd find excuses for the devil himself. Mother's like that. She sees everyone's problems, understands what makes them tick, excuses them on the grounds of what's happened to them in childhood, and we admire it tremendously, even if at times we get scared she'll be let down. Yet somehow she never is – she seems rather to bring out the best in people. Except in the case of Phyl. But oh, how I'd like her here right now!' He chuckled, 'Does that sound sissy? A man over thirty wishing for his mother?'

She shook her head and a couple of pins fell out from in front of her right ear on to the table. 'I think it's endearing. It's the

66

sort of situation that does need an older woman's hand and experience. But I can also understand your not wanting to break into their trip till Owen is much improved and we know something of what his wife intends to do.' She smoothed the escaped tress back and began to anchor it again.

Edmund Leigh's hand came across the table, caught hers, made her stop. 'Don't pin it back. That style's so severe. What makes you want to skewer your hair back like that, anyway? I don't like it.'

Charlotte said coolly, 'Sorry about that, but it's less bother this way – I haven't time to be eternally fussing about my hair. This is easy.'

He grimaced. 'You're an odd creature, Charlotte Smith. At times you sound about ninety. Yet the other day when you were chasing the kids up the hill, from the back you looked about seventeen!'

She said lightly, 'Thank you, Mr. Leigh. When you're over thirty, that's quite a compliment. Now, you look all in, as well you might. You ought to turn in. I'll wash up. There was a parcel of books today from some firm in Christchurch. The men wanted something to read and opened it. I think a shower, then a read in bed would relax you. Don't mull over this. Sometimes things turn out better than you think, take an unexpected twist. Take a day at a time, you may be guided in a way of procedure by some incident or influence as yet unknown.'

To her surprise he burst out laughing. 'Charlotte Smith, you make me laugh! Tell me, did you ever read Patricia Wentworth's mysteries?'

She blinked. 'Yes, why?'

'Well, you remind me for all the world of her Miss Silver, the prim governess turned private detective. What did that police detective call her? Oh, I know . . . revered preceptress! She was always trotting out little maxims, or quoting Tennyson for his benefit and comfort.'

Charlotte had to laugh with him. 'I guess I did sound a bit that way – and do you know what?' Her eyes danced with mischief.

'What?'

'I'm very fond of Tennyson. Oh, I read modern poetry too, but at certain times in my life when I've needed comfort, I've turned to the poets of earlier generations.'

He leaned forward, elbows on table, his chin in his cupped

hands. 'Have there been many times like that? When you've needed comfort, I mean? You know I've been so selfishly concerned with all that's been happening here, telescoped into such a short space of time it seems like months, I've not thought about you much – and your former life. You came out because you have a brother here. Does that mean you're orphans?'

She thought the truth, or near-truth, would serve. 'My father is dead. My mother married again, very happily. I'm not exactly joining my brother. I think married couples should be on their own, but he thought he'd like to have a relative of his own here. He thinks there are great opportunities; that it's a good life in an under-populated country. If I like it, I'll stay. I paid my own passage out, so I'm not tied. About needing comfort . . . after my father died, my mother was ill for a long time, worn out by the nursing. She was magnificent till it was all over, then she collapsed.'

'You would be too young then, though, perhaps, to fly to poetry for comfort?'

'In a way, yes, though my love for it was born about then. My aunt looked after us and she was wonderful. She was so concerned for us that after living all that time in the shadow of my father's impending death, then the collapse of our little world when my mother took ill, we might develop some complexes, that she set herself out to give us a sense of security and gaiety. She had one daughter of her own, rather older than we were. Every night, after tea, we had a reading-aloud session. I think being read to is one of the most comforting and tranquillizing exercises. It gives you a feeling of serenity, of not being bustled, or a nuisance, of being loved and wanted. I was younger than my brother and nearly always fell asleep before the end, but it gave me a love of words and rhythm.'

'Is that why, even on your first night, you made a point of reading a story to the kids before you tucked them down?'

'Yes, besides, they told me Mark is just starting to read for himself. They need more time than teachers can spare to each child. It increases their vocabulary, gets them used to the shape of words. Last night I got both of them to read to me too. I think it's important.'

Edmund's teeth looked very white in his tanned face when he smiled. 'Do that reading downstairs from now on – some of it, anyway. Beside the fire. Don't think it might create even more security for the children if their uncle shared that time too?'

Something stirred in Charlotte, a sort of sweetness, like a tide.

Edmund said slowly, 'When you spoke of comfort, I thought you might have had some sort of – of setback – in adult life. Oh, sorry, it may sound too curious. I meant you might have fallen in love and had things go wrong . . . and have emigrated because of it . . . for fresh scenes to take your mind off it?'

Charlotte gave him a very frank look. 'I've known only passing fancies.' She giggled, and, had she known it, looked very young. 'I've even tried to imagine myself feeling more than that. But it was only kidding myself. One likes to think one is capable of a grand passion, but I've just not met anyone I'd like to spend the rest of my life with, yet.'

He grew sombre instantly. 'That's what it would mean, with *you*? The rest of your life? Not like my brother's wife . . . little more than a year!'

In a flash, after the brief time of kinship, fellowship, their problems were back with them again. Phyl, who had taken vows and then broken them, whose husband, a man chivalrous enough to shoulder the responsibility of two children not his own, for love of her, was lying recovering from a serious operation, all unknowing his wife had run away. If this man knew who she was, he would banish her too, away from the children she so dearly loved, away from this fair valley, Tapuwharua . . . the Forbidden Valley. Her stay here was precarious. It would last only till she knew what Phyl was going to do about the children, or – till this man found out her secret. So there was nothing – nothing – to be gained by allowing oneself to grow fond of . . . fond of *what*?

Fond of the *place*, of course, Charlotte Smith! Fond of the lavender hills, the sweep of green pastures, the tantalizing glimpses of the alpine heights, the murmuring of the streams, the forest-clad sides of the gorges, the sunlight dappling the willows . . . it's just the place you're getting fond of, just the *place*. It's time you went to bed!

Edmund was himself again next morning. He made the children chuckle at breakfast, telling them stories of Owen and himself getting into pickles, getting walloped by their father for doing dangerous things; of the time they'd been snowed up in the valley for three weeks in one of the hardest winters in living memory, of the time when he and Owen and their father had been treed by a wild boar that had been making terrible depredations among their young lambs.

'We weren't hunting for it, so didn't have the pig-dogs with us. We'd just gone into Wheka Gully to get Mother some special tree-ferns she wanted for decorating the church hall with for a local do. This boar was a massive fellow . . . shoulders like armour plates and great gleaming tusks, and we didn't hesitate. We all shinned up a tree. It wasn't the best sort of tree either, it was gnarled and old.

'The sight of that boar below was enough to give us nightmares for weeks. His snarl was the most ferocious I've ever seen, and one rip from one of those tusks could have laid a leg open from ankle to knee. We were in a real flap. Dad didn't minimize the danger. I said to him that we were bound to be missed sooner or later and someone would come looking for us.

'Dad's face was grim. "Yes, but what if it's your mother? She could saddle up and come after us, find our horses tethered further down and come up here on foot, same as us. If we hear her coming we'll have to yell like mad to tell her to get away out of it, and to bring the men in with the dogs and weapons. Our only hope otherwise is that he'll get tired of this and go away, and if he goes far enough, we can get down and go for our lives. I wish to goodness there was more cover here – thick stuff, to impede him a bit. But if we do run for it, we'll have to keep an eye out for likely trees to scale as we go – and mind, you boys aren't to wait for me. Go up the first tree you can. But let's hope he trots off out of earshot and doesn't return."

'We were there for an hour that seemed like a year. Then the most extraordinary thing happened. Dad was in a very narrow crotch, Owen and I were in another. Dad got cramp in his hip, tried to move out on to a branch to ease it, slipped, crashed down on a lower branch which must have been rotten, and the branch, plus Dad, fell with a thud clean on the old boar *and knocked him out cold*! I'll never forget our horror when we saw Dad falling. We thought he'd injure himself and then get attacked. Boy, did we shin down! Dad had slid along to the leafy part after the impact with the boar, made a wild scramble to get up to turn to face the animal, and then we all just boggled. He was lying as still as if he were dead.

'Believe me, we wasted no time at all. We didn't want to be there when he came round. We bolted, got the horses, galloped back home, and went out again with the men and the pig-dogs. But there was no need for slaughter. He was as dead as a door-nail. We got headlines in the paper and Dad still gets pointed out occasionally as the man who could knock out an old man boar single-handed, but he wasn't the same man for weeks!'

Charlotte's eyes were as round as the children's, rounder in fact, because they, at least, knew there were 'Captain Cookers' back in the bush. 'We've got most of them cleaned up,' said Edmund, 'but we still get a few. Wild pork is delicious. I don't care for it as a sport, myself, but when you see a lamb after it's been attacked, you know you've just got to get the brutes. Captain Cook released a lot of pigs when he realized how little this country had in the way of animals to provide meat. The Maori diet was largely fish and feathered game.'

Mark was brushing his fair fringe back in a way he had when excited. 'I've got to give a morning talk this week . . . I'll use that, Uncle Edmund. I like exciting stories. Do you know what? Some clunky girl gave one yesterday and said: "A very exciting thing happened the day before yesterday . . . we got a new baby!" Exciting! Gosh, girls are stupid things. I thought something bad must've happened!'

His uncle laughed, 'Does it have to be bad to be thrilling, Mark? Well, get your lunches out of the fridge and I'll take you down to the bus – after you've done your teeth.'

When he came back Tod and Lance were away out, and Charlotte was just finishing the beds. She heard him bounding upstairs two at a time. He stood in the doorway, filling it, one hand on the jamb. 'I say, you were on a Welsh mountain farm . . . can you ride?'

She laughed. 'For sure. We bred Welsh ponies. Do you want some help outside? I can spare the time if you do, long as it's something I'm used to.'

'No, not a job, just I'd like some company and I reckon a break from the house would do you good. You've been a Trojan, never even asked when you're going to have a day off.'

She flushed with pleasure. His appreciation might soften his fury, his censure, if ever it had to be revealed that she was Phyl's cousin. She said, 'I'm hardly likely to be looking for days off in an emergency like this one. Besides, it's all so novel, so different, it's been almost a holiday.'

'Glad you said almost or I'd have suspected you of hypocrisy. You've worked blamed hard, getting used to this house, neglected for days, faced up to managing strange children, with nothing normal, only strain and worry. You've identified yourself so much with our problems you deserve to be treated as one of the family now. We can't stay for ever tied to the house for a phone that never does bring us word from the children's mother. She may never ring – or write. I'm inclined to think she's gone for ever. Unless she does come back a bit to sanity when she finishes this pseudo-honeymoon and remembers she's a mother, and perhaps writes to make arrangements for the children to be sent to her. But if so, Owen will have to be told. He's their adoptive father.

'Anyway, if she rings when we're out, she'll ring again, perhaps at night when someone's bound to be home. I want to inspect this property Owen was able to buy in. We're just using it for grazing dry cattle just now, but I want to look over the buildings. It was in the family once, and during the Depression we lost it. There's a bungalow on the place that the last owner built, but I'd like to see if the old homestead could be restored. It was built for my favourite ancestress, Dorothea Leigh. She married Jonathan, old Alfred's son, so she's my great-grandmother. She didn't mind going further back in than any other woman had been before . . . right to the end of the road. Which was only, in those days, a rutted track in dense bush. Yet she came from the East End of London.

'Of course it's all right having these plans, about restoring it. But if Phyl doesn't come back, I'll have to keep Owen company at Amberleigh. That'd mean I'd have to put a married couple in the bungalow. Owen would go mad alone, otherwise. However, we'll have to meet that when it comes to a decision. Could you put up some sandwiches and fill a flask? We'll have to have a lunch snack over there. We'll see Tod and Lance as we go. They can just hot up that soup for their lunch, and fry themselves some sausages.'

The phone rang. It was the doctor. 'I've just seen your brother. He's vastly improved this morning. Seems satisfied with the story you put up, so we'll stick to that meanwhile. How about sending him a message – I'll get a nurse to tell him you phoned – that you're very busy on the estate, can't get in till nearer the end of the week, and that his wife's better but still in bed? That'll stop him worrying about her and give us a bit more time. He said he expected his wife would write to him

72

soon, so I said I'd rather she didn't, that paper might carry infection. He probably thought that was carrying precaution too far, but he accepted it. That'll stop him smelling a rat.'

Edmund swung round from the phone, reported to Charlotte. 'What a relief! A break of two more whole days from the strain of wondering what Owen will ask next.'

'And it could be,' said Charlotte, 'that his wife will be in touch with us by then. Edmund, if she hears from you that Owen never received her letter, that he's been lying in a critical condition, she might come back to stay . . . *never* tell him. I mean, could you bring yourself to act out the deception, keep him in ignorance, always?'

Their eyes met in a long, reflective exchange, wondering.

He said slowly, 'I've no idea. Would it be altogether fair to Owen? And could it be kept a secret? The Sandringhams would never breathe a word, but I'm not sure about Avis Weybourne or her mother. Well, it's all in the lap of the gods . . . or rather on whether or not we ever hear from Phyl. Sometimes I can't believe it's happened, especially to Owen, he deserved better.'

Charlotte sketched a helpless gesture with her hands. 'I suppose you wouldn't have her traced?'

His voice went harsh. 'No, it's the last thing I'd do. It's for Owen to instigate anything like that. I dare not make it public in any way. Sorry, Charlotte, but the thought of that horrifies me. Imagine if it got into the news. Woman deserts her husband and children while he lies at death's door, unknown to her! Oh, no! Oh, sorry, Charlotte, I ought not to have spoken so sharply to you. You just spoke the thought that's been in my own mind all along. Oh, to hell with this. Let's get out and into the saddle. If you've not ridden for some time you'd better take Floss, she's very reliable.'

It was wonderful to be in the saddle again and on this rolling country. They took the easiest way through the hills, almost on a terrace-like plateau. 'Quicker than going round by the road,' said Edmund. 'This property is as far into the valley as you can go. It ends where the Amber falls down the cliffs where they narrow into a V. And even that's nearly a mile from the old homestead. It's not quite as old as Amberleigh, of course, but was allowed to fall into disrepair by a former owner. Dorothea – the wife of Jonathan, the first bride there – loved it, but one or two later brides found it a little too remote, which it is, yet it

73

has something.

'It was always a dream of mine, as a little boy, when other folk were farming it, that some day I might buy it back. I'd like to bring it back to some of its former glory, because in its day it was a show-place. The first Leigh loved his trees, and so did his son. Even as they felled the ones they had to fell, to build the houses of Christchurch, they culled them knowledgeably, not greedily as so many did, when there was such a demand for timber, with more and more emigrants arriving on the Canterbury plains.

'Old Alfred was a man of dreams as well as being intensely practical, and he set English trees among the native ones he preserved in what he called his park. And he imbued in Jonathan the same ideas, so his place, Te-iti-rangi, is planted and preserved on the same lines. Both places in autumn, which is April here, are pictures, because Alfred brought the glory of an English autumn into the leafy Eden of a New Zealand bush setting.'

'How strange to think of April as autumn . . . to me the very sound of the name conjures up violets and primroses. I find it fascinating. Edmund, when the pioneers brought out their plants and trees, how did those living saplings react? Did they continue on for a year or two, trying to bloom, or turn colour at the right seasons, or what?'

Edmund looked at her with respect. 'I've never thought of that before. I expect climate would force the changes on them, I mean the seasons. Because if frosts come early, leaves change colour early. If they don't, autumn colours are late. There must have been a lot of casualties, of course, and some setbacks, but I guess most would survive after the first struggle. I must look up the old diaries to find out if there's any mention.'

The horses picked their way carefully now, as the terrace narrowed above the Amber. Gradually it sloped down. 'Is there a bridge for us to cross on, Edmund?'

He shook his head. 'Not for the horses. There's a sort of swing-bridge, for walking across only. Not that anybody except us ever uses it. Other people come to it by the road that dwindles to an end above the house. We walk the horses through the ford. There are times when it's too deep, but not at present. I'll lead Floss if you like and let you cross on the bridge. It sways a bit, but Owen's kept it in good order and it has netting sides.'

She shook her head. 'I'd love to go through the ford. I always think it's idyllic, taking horses through water. We used to do it on the farm, through mountain streams, on the ponies. Oh, Edmund, how truly beautiful, look at the sun shining through the willows!'

They were almost at the brink. They reined in their horses. To the right, down the golden-tinted cliffs that gave the Amber its name, splashed the stream that, near its source, was narrowed to the width of the cleft. The water fell musically into an enormous pool that brimmed over to form the river on the shingle bed that widened out into the valley. Above the waterfall towered the New Zealand bush, glossily green as if enamelled, aromatic, humid, luxuriant. It was a case of Nature abhorring a vacuum indeed; from every tree crevice of the trunk and twisted mossy roots sprang its own ferns and fungi, rioting over the entire area; and fallen logs of hundreds, in fact thousands, of years had contoured the valley floor with an undulating mossy carpet like an emerald sponge.

Matai, the black pine, with dark trunks and symmetrical boughs, lancewoods, spiky and straight, silver beeches, red beeches, flourished here, with leaves much smaller than their English counterparts – something which had caused the early settlers to dub them birches, Edmund explained. There were *kowhais* showing yellow blooms, *kotukutukus*, a variety of small-flowered fuchsia, but with great apricot-tan coloured branches twisted and colourful, and the graceful pendulous green needles of the *rimus*, the red pines.

But on the far side, on a magnificent sweep of green sward grazed close by the cattle, lay an old, old garden curving up the bank in a succession of terraces to where a weatherbeaten house, built in the same early colonial style as Amberleigh, sat against a background of exotic trees brought from all over the world. The house had a green corrugated roof, broken by dormers, and its sills were black, against what had once been white weatherboard walls, deepened by years of neglect into a soft grey. Creepers that had no doubt been lovingly pruned and restrained once, and trees that had been espaliered against the stone walls that sheltered the house, had now run riot, but soon the whole house would be plumy with purple wistaria and clematis, and in summer it would be a glory of cottage roses and lavender.

Daffodils were still blooming in the turf and a tangle of

75

japonica was a mass of coral flowers. Little pansies that must have seeded year after year, still made a brave struggle amidst the encroaching grass. The access drive must wind round behind the house, out of sight, so the old house appeared to dream on its past, remote from any link with the outside world, its face to the river and the hills, its back to civilization.

Charlotte let the reins fall on Floss's neck and clasped her hands in delight. 'Oh, it's like a little world of its own, remote and lovely. A miniature paradise.'

She brought her roving gaze back to Edmund and surprised a strange look on his face. She couldn't read it. He looked away quickly, as if embarrassed, then back, and said lightly, 'You must be psychic, revered preceptress. A miniature paradise! That's just what Te-iti-rangi means. The Little Heaven. *Iti* is used as a diminutive, and *rangi* is heaven or the sky.'

Charlotte said in a dazed sort of way, 'Fancy those other brides not wanting to live here. They must have been out of their minds.' Then she flushed. 'That's pretty stupid of me. Access is no doubt easy now. Then it would have been the ends of the earth to those women, with doctors so far and the only access by horse. I suppose the road would be a porridge-pot of clay in winter.'

'Yes, and they were often cut off by flood and snow, perhaps when their time was upon them, or when their children were gravely sick. And someone had to ride for the doctor before he could even set out. Even if at times now we still get cut off, there are always helicopters.'

They allowed the horses to drink. It always fascinated Charlotte to see the animals delicately blowing on the water with their nostrils, to clear away any debris, or insects. Then they came up the overgrown paths, Edmund leading, and tied their horses to the hitching-rings still firmly embedded in the verandah rail.

'Step carefully here. If ever this is lived in again, this whole verandah will need renewing – the floorboards, anyway. The rails are *totara* and solid.'

Naturally the house was musty, so they left the front door open. The hall floor, as one might have expected, since Alfred and Jonathan had designed it, was of parquet, native timbers lovingly matched and polished, under its veneer of dust. On the right was the old drawing-room that had been the scene of many Colonial reunions, of shipmates and pioneers. It ran two-thirds of the breadth of the house and had three sets of French windows in it, small-paned and elegant. At the far end one led out into a tiny walled garden, overgrown, but the eye of the mind could picture its former charm. The little fountain in the middle, raised up so it could spell no danger to toddlers, had long since ceased to play and it was covered with birdlime, but the stone cherub that crowned it, looking down into the bowl, didn't look forlorn and deserted, rather just as if he waited for the sound of footsteps. On the far side of the wall, an espaliered apricot tree was covered with blossoms, and under their feet were the brown shrivelled rose petals of a score of forgotten summers.

On the left of the hall at the front was a guest-room, with still a faded carpet on the floor and lace curtains that would disintegrate at a touch. Behind this was the living quarters, a dining-room, a smaller room that in these days would surely be turned into a TV room, the kitchen, a vast larder, a dairy, a laundry, with, across the courtyard paved with river stones, all sorts of outbuildings.

They went upstairs on creaking boards. The dormers were very large, and with the exception of the two single ones, all boasted three window recesses and looked out on such shining beauty of mountain and river, Charlotte was moved by envy. 'Though you'd never get your chores done here ... you'd always be sitting on the window-seats, dreaming.'

They went downstairs. Edmund found a duster in a cupboard and flicked it over the ancient kitchen table that was so huge it must have been built inside the room, and had their flask of coffee, their sandwiches and pikelets. Charlotte had chuckled when she found out what they were. 'We call them drop-scones in the South of England, and in some places, Scotch pancakes.' They were simply a sweet thick batter dropped on to a hot greased girdle and browned both sides She'd found the men could demolish a batch at a sitting, with jam and cream.

Edmund inspected thoroughly, tapping, measuring, estimating an effect he might aim for, through narrowed eyes. She realized that a love of trees and wood had descended through all the generations. She thought it was taking his mind off his domestic problems.

'Why did you say Dorothea was your favourite ancestress?'

He smiled. 'Perhaps because she'd had the toughest time of all, even exceeding Margaretta, the pioneer bride, her mother-in-law. Because Margaretta had known a happy childhood and a girlhood full of gaiety, and been within the circle of a loving family. But Dorothea was a London waif who came out here to Christchurch under some scheme, to supply the ever-increasing demand for servants.

'Trouble was, women, single ones, were so scarce, they were snapped up as wives very quickly, almost as soon as the settlers' wives got them trained.

'Jonathan, my great-grandfather, was courting, in Christchurch, the daughter of one of the early surveyors – moneyed family. He was infatuated with her. She was an exquisite girl, from the early photos. But she had a vixenish temper, though she'd never shown it to Jonathan. Then unfortunately – I mean unfortunately for Olivia – Jonathan came in one day, unexpectedly. As he came up the drive on foot, and stepped on to the verandah, he heard Olivia berating Dorothea, her maid. Her voice was a screaming fury, her language unrestrained. Through the French windows he saw her snatch a crop off the wall and beat Dorothea about the shoulders. He rushed in and intervened.

'It was all over then, though Olivia tried to excuse herself, tried to force Dorothea to admit she'd tried Olivia beyond endurance. And Dorothea, though obviously terrified, knowing she'd be turned out on the streets, refused to do this, because, as she said simply, it just wasn't true. Jonathan took Dorothea back to Amberleigh, to his mother, and later – much later – married her. Dorothea thought she wasn't good enough for him. But Jonathan's mother talked her out of that, said even if she was a foundling, even if she might be illegitimate, there was breeding in every inch of her. There was, too. Jonathan had a portrait done of her. I'll show it to you some time. It's in at Christchurch having the glass renewed. Tod told me. They had an accident with it at spring-cleaning time. She had golden-brown hair and an oval face and sweet grey eyes, and her hands were the hands of a gentlewoman – by then. And she worked ceaselessly to educate herself up to Jonathan's standards. My great-grandfather used to say Dorothea was the most wonderful thing that ever happened to him. My own grandfather, their son, Henry, told me that. Dorothea learned to play the piano and the violin, she was a born musician, and she could

78

paint and embroider – and keep house in a way that came up to the standards of the day, which were very exacting.' He fell silent, then looked at Charlotte, standing at the window, looking into the little walled garden. He added, 'Our family has a great tradition of love-matches. There's never been a broken marriage, till now.'

Charlotte came back from dreams she'd scarcely analysed ... dreams to do with imagining that fountain working again ... of sitting here, in summer, under the shade of the huge mulberry that overhung the wall, the sound of children's laughter echoing in the courtyard ... what had dreams like that to do with her, who was the cousin of the woman who had broken the tradition of this family, who had flouted her marriage vows and brought terrible sorrow and perplexity to this household?

She moved abruptly, the spell broken. They went out to the stables, found a rotting phaeton in one and an ancient trap, relics of the transport of yesteryear. Then through the shearing-sheds which Edmund inspected with a satisfied eye, said they'd been modernized so well he'd have more to spend on the house, then rode across to the bungalow, quite near the road entrance, a tidy, well-kept house, unfurnished now, of course, but in excellent order and, as far as Charlotte was concerned, without an atom of charm or magic. But, as she said, ideal for a married couple, or a pair of bachelor workers to live in and manage. They rode back along the road, fringed with aspen and lombardy poplars, because it was quicker than riding back through the valley, and one of them must pick up the children.

It wasn't till after supper that anything was said to mar the day that had so refreshed them both.

Edmund had been reading in a big wing chair by the fire, Charlotte studying an old book on trees she'd found in the bookcase. It had given her a queer sort of thrill because Edmund's great-great-grandfather must have brought it out from England, as the flyleaf bore the inscription: 'Alfred Leigh, from his loving mother' and had 'Knott's Farm, Farnham, Surrey', on it, and a date, '1837'. Heavens, the year Queen Victoria came to the throne!

Edmund looked round as she exclaimed over it. 'I hadn't realized your ancestors came from Surrey too ... no wonder they loved trees. Surrey is just a maze of trees – even today, just an hour's journey from London, there are all these lanes arching over and aching down with trees in full leaf, and with sheets of bluebells under the trees in April and May. I can see them now, with the public footpaths meandering across fields and through copses, acres and acres of trees. All part once of the great forest that spread right from Windsor.'

Edmund nodded. 'I'd love to see it some day. This time I only got as far as Canada and the States. I was working in Canada for experience and meant to go on to Britain to see where my forebears came from, but when the way opened up, with Owen marrying and taking over the farm, for Mother and Father to have this break, Owen seemed to want me to come home.'

Charlotte said, 'Alfred Leigh, 1837! And we enjoy the trees he planted or preserved today. Quite a link with the past. I'll never forget that first sight of Te-iti-rangi. The Little Heaven. Even with all the hardships the remoteness may have imposed, I can't imagine anyone not wanting to live there.'

Remembering, she leaned forward, her chin in her hands, her elbows resting on the table. Her hazel eyes, amber-flecked like the river that ran through the valley, were clear and shining, starry and full of dreams. She still had the golden scarf, tied triangular-wise, at her throat, that she had worn for riding.

Edmund Leigh made a strange sound in his throat, then said, harshly, 'It's easy enough to wax lyrical over the beauty of a place whose remote conditions you'll never be called upon to suffer! That's the whole trouble – girls are so sentimenal, rave over a place one moment, can't stand the isolation the next!'

Charlotte brought her chin out of her hands, stared at him, then stood up. 'Mr. Leigh! You're the moodiest, most impossible man! You don't have to be cynical about all women just because it seems as if your sister-in-law has let your brother down! That's about the most illogical thing I've ever heard! I *loathe* sarcastic people.' Suddenly her eyes narrowed. 'Oh, I get it! How could I forget what you said to me on the phone that night! Just because I waxed lyrical over the beauty of Te-iti-rangi, you've got it into your conceited head that I fancy the owner! Of all the vain men! Some men *are* like that, I believe . . . think every single woman wants to get married. Well, we don't. I'm perfectly content with my state as I am. Believe me, I'd rather be single than have to cope with any man's moods, especially yours. I'm not Women's Lib, either. I just don't have strong feelings one way or the other. If I happened to meet someone I could fall for, plus having respect for him, I'd marry . . . but I can tell you this, Edmund Leigh, I'd certainly never marry because I'd fallen in love with a very beautiful homestead . . . and especially marry a great, conceited *lump* like you!' Charlotte clenched her teeth together, glared at him, was horrified to find herself stamping her foot, and, completely humiliated by her show of temper, turned to flee.

But she wasn't quite quick enough. He caught her at the door. What a giant of a man! She was quite helpless. He pinned her there, his grip biting into her arms. 'Oh, no, you don't, Charlotte. No, you don't!' She found, to her increased fury, that he was laughing helplessly. 'Oh, my dear, prim Miss Smith . . . nothing of the revered preceptress about you at this moment . . . you're more like a spitting fury! Oh, no, you don't,' as she tried to twist away from him, 'you needn't think you can free yourself. Stay still, or you'll be bruised. Now listen. I don't blame you for reacting the way you did that first night I spoke to you on the phone. I was sore and – frankly, after what Bill Sandringham went through with that girl they had housekeeping when Judy was in the nursing-home, I was terrified.

'I mean . . . put yourself in my position, landing back home into a situation like this. I'd *had* women. But I simply couldn't do without one to look after the children and the house.'

Charlotte stamped her foot again, not caring now about any exhibition of temper, because it was maddening to be held here against one's will. It came down on his foot and he jumped, saying, 'Ouch!' but he relaxed his hold for only an ineffectual moment as far as she was concerned. She said between her teeth, 'I'm not talking about *that* night. I realized why you felt that way *then*, but to react like this tonight because I was stupid enough to drool over the perfection of that setting was unbearably insulting. It sounded vain and it *was* vain, and I *wasn't* setting my cap at you. I wouldn't, anyway, not if – not if – not if—'

He was laughing uncontrollably. 'Suffering from an impediment, my dear Miss Smith? Surely not . . . and I was so admiring your fine flow of invective! Let me help you out . . . you'd not set your cap at me if I were hung from top to toe with diamonds . . . that it?'

'Exactly!' said Charlotte. 'Ohhhhhhhhh!' She gritted her teeth with sheer rage.

He said, with irritatingly soothing tones, as if humouring a cross child, 'Of course you wouldn't, there, there . . . Look, I haven't the faintest idea what prompted me to say that. It was one of those things that just get jerked out of one. I know it sounded sarcastic. I grovel, I grovel, oh, how I grovel, only don't stay mad at me, my dear Miss Smith. I couldn't bear it.'

To her annoyance, Charlotte felt her anger just slipping away from her and she felt a giggle rising which she sternly subdued. She said, and even to herself it sounded childish, 'You – you're just afraid I'll walk out on you. That's all you're grovelling for.'

Then she looked directly up into the blue gaze so close to hers. Her eyes tried to flicker away from that look. It was still a puzzled one, she thought, as if he couldn't understand his own behaviour.

Finally he said gently, 'It's not that, you know, Charlotte. I'm genuinely sorry I've hurt you,' then, just as she was about to accept that graciously, a mischievous light shot into his eye, and he bent his head and kissed her. She was entirely taken by surprise, and his grip had tightened again, so she could not twist away. Nor, to be quite candid, did she want to, as she realized later. She'd never felt – quite – this way in her life before. No other kiss had meant anything like this. At that moment she felt all the pins fall out of that inadequate knot at the nape of her neck and the loosened strands fall free.

Edmund, still holding her, lifted his mouth from hers, a rather quizzical smile lifting the corners of his mouth and he blinked, then pulled her more upright so that her hair swung softly about her face, shoulder-length, tawny and waving a little, curving up at the ends.

His eyes narrowed. 'I get it . . . I put my foot in it that night on the phone, didn't I? And you wanted this job. It was right up your street . . . with children and in the country to boot, so you advanced your age and screwed your hair back to make yourself look older. Confess now . . . didn't you?'

She hesitated. Oh, it wasn't fair that a man should have such charm. That smile of his! But he answered for her, 'Yes, you did, and I don't blame you. How old are you, Charlotte, twenty-two, twenty-three?'

'Twenty-five. Yes, that's why I did it.' Then she gave him a stern look. 'Now let's forget all this silly nonsense . . . kissing and all that. It happened simply and solely because we were struggling. We don't want any of these capers! Even if I am younger than I said, Mr. Leigh, you're quite safe from me. Thank your lucky stars I'm not one of those designing house-keepers you dreaded, because you've got about as much idea of how to keep them at arm's length as a babe unborn! So we'll just forget this.'

The smile was lingering round his mouth. '*Can* you forget it? That kiss?'

Her eyes sparked. 'I can. We both can. It was just horse-play. But anyway, we know where we stand. And I can admire that house and its setting without you thinking I have designs on it . . . and you! I don't suppose I'll even stay in New Zealand. A few months might see me back in Britain.'

When he didn't answer she had to look at him. His look was direct.

'Do you really think so? I think New Zealand has already cast its spell upon you.

She hunched an impatient shoulder, turned to go, said as casually as she could manage, 'Good night, Mr. Leigh.'

He said, 'It's a bit stupid, surely, to revert to formality. Don't be so daft, girl. And another thing, leave your hair loose. It's a crime for anyone with such lovely hair to torture it into a tiny bun the way you've been doing. Its served its purpose. And you were right . . . if you'd looked the way you look now I might not have engaged you. Not in the mood I was in that day. Well, here's hoping you sleep well.'

She turned, said over her shoulder in crushing tones, 'I cer-tainly hope you don't think that — that anything that happened tonight will keep me awake. I assure it won't.'

Strange then that she did not sleep, that feeling she'd been a stranger to till now kept flooding over her. In a way never before known, she was conscious of her own femininity, of desires till now dormant. One moment she would tell herself it did not, could not, must not matter, that she was here for only a short time, till Owen came home to take up his shattered life, or till Phyl came up with some idea for her children's future . . . or till her unmasking; the next moment she'd be lost in a sea of impossible dreams and hopes.

But deep down, she knew with horrible certainty that though Edmund Leigh was a much more pleasant man to deal with than she'd imagined at first, she didn't dare to think of his reactions if he discovered how she had deceived him.

CHAPTER FIVE

CHARLOTTE was relieved to find she got back to normality next morning more easily than she had anticipated. Of course, having the men in for breakfast helped and the children's chatter and arguing dispelled any hint of constraint in her manner and Edmund's. She made no issue about his command about her hair. Because it *had* been a command. Better to let it go. But she slipped an emerald green band about it to confine it a little.

Tod and Lance emitted wolf-whistles when they saw it and told her she must have been mad to wear her hair any other way. She just laughed and said lightly that it was less bother the other way. 'Well, this is certainly easier on the eye,' said Tod. 'You just leave it that way. After all, *we* have to look at you.'

The days slipped by. Edmund said once, to the three of them, when the children were at school, 'I feel as if I'm in a state of suspended animation — as if all I can do is carry on, waiting for the blow to fall, when Owen suddenly realizes something is up.'

Tod said, 'But Phyl's bound to make some sort of contact before then. She'll have had her fling by now. No mother, least of all Phyl, as we knew her, would simply cut herself off like this.'

Charlotte gave him a grateful glance, then checked herself, glowing inside and blessing him for his perception. She said cautiously, 'Everyone seems to say that of her. She seems to have acted completely out of character.'

'That's just it,' said Tod. 'You see, Edmund didn't know her. If he had, he'd have felt as we do, completely numbed with the shock of it. Not quite believing it.'

Edmund said, '*Someone* believes it,' and to their look of inquiry he said, 'Avis. She vows she's not surprised at all, that she felt with my brother's wife it was a case of still waters running deep.'

Charlotte had to swallow her mouthful of bran muffin very quickly or she'd have choked. Then she managed: 'What is that supposed to mean? Does having depths have to be suspect?

Seemingly the alternative to that would mean being *shallow*! Isn't that the antonym of *deep*?'

She spoke unwarily and with heat.

Tod said, 'Good on you, Sharlie, sticking up for someone you've never met.'

Edmund said sourly, '*I've* never met her either, but I've enough gumption to know what Avis means. She means deep in the sense of being sly . . . and sly Phyl must have been to deceive Owen like that.'

Lance, who was younger and shyer than Tod, surprised even himself by saying, 'But sly was just what Phyl wasn't! I'd stake my oath on that.' They all looked towards him and he crimsoned to the roots of his ginger hair. Charlotte expected Edmund to crush him, but he didn't. He was unexpectedly kind. It was obvious that he was not wishful of setting the boy back when he'd actually ventured an opinion of his own. 'Lance, I'm working in the dark, having never met her. What was she really like, in your opinion? That's a beautiful picture of her on Owen's desk. I'd think too, looking at it, that here was a woman of character. But one can be so mistaken – in looks.'

Lance spoke again. 'I heard your mother say to Owen once, not long after she came here, "Oh, I *do* like your Phyllis, son. There's no shilly-shallying about her. She's a yes-no person, the kind I've aye liked best." They didn't know Phyl and I were in the scullery, and Phyl burst out laughing and called out, "Thank you for the compliment, Mum, but that sort of nature carries a drawback with it – my own mother always asked me to tone things down a bit, not to be so blunt! She said I sometimes hurt folk by telling the truth and shaming the devil." It doesn't add . . . *Phyl* sneaking off like this.'

Two of his listeners knew how true this was. Edmund, of course, didn't. He said, 'Well, I imagine when a woman first finds she's attracted to someone not her husband, she's hardly likely to be brutally candid about that. It's one of the situations that almost always goes hand in hand with deception. I'm handicapped, I know, with not knowing her, and the fact that you and Tod and Bill and Judy find it hard to credit puzzles me. But against that, I've got to put that letter of hers. There's not an ambiguous word in it. Just a statement of fact. Therefore, I have to give some credence to Avis's opinion.'

Tod set his jaw. 'Avis would believe the worst of Phyl even without the evidence of that letter. *How* she must have gloated when she read it!'

Edmund looked up quickly. 'You can't mean Avis is still carrying a torch for Owen? Surely, once he was married, she'd drop all that? None of us ever liked her much – she was such a mean, spoiled kid, even in play, but once Owen was married—' He broke off as Tod said quietly: 'She was livid when Owen announced that he was going to marry an English girl living in Australia. And she never, when Phyl arrived, lost the chance of sly digs. Every time she said: "Poor Owen," I could have choked her.'

Edmund said heavily, 'And now it *is* poor Owen!' He looked across at Charlotte. 'And even you, who've never as much as set eyes upon her, seem to want to fly to her defence. Why? You've never met Avis either, so you can't, like the chaps, hold her in aversion and want to hold a contrary opinion from hers!'

Charlotte's colour rose. She said spiritedly, 'But I do hold her in aversion. I detest people sneaky enough to read other people's letters. Oh, she may have read a line or two automatically, when she gathered up the scattered sheets, but she'd no business at all to read the lot. That, to me, was unforgivable. Anybody decent would have thought "How awful . . . nobody's eyes but Owen's ought to see this!" and she should have put the sheets together, weighted them down, and left the house, determined never to tell what she'd seen. After all, Phyl had expected Owen back . . . Avis didn't know then that this accident was going to happen. Most people wouldn't have wanted to get involved. But you said once she read right through a couple of pages.'

Edmund said, 'I didn't like it much myself, but at least she didn't hide what she'd done. She came straight out with it, and seemed to have a genuine desire to help.'

Tod looked scornful. 'Pigs *may* whistle, but they've poor mouths for it!' he said. 'Well, I'd better get back to the job. Come on, Lance.'

Charlotte sought him out later when he was on his own. 'Tod, you don't think Avis interfered so much she drove a wedge between Phyl and Owen? She might have turned for comfort to someone else? I mean, Phyl seems to have been such a likeable person that it would take external pressures to make her act so out of character.'

Tod shook his head. 'She made no mischief between Phyl and Owen. Owen put a stop to Avis's capers a month or so before Phyl left home. He saw through her and he thought she was getting under Phyl's skin a bit. Phyl had lost a bit of weight and was rather quiet. She seemed to sigh a lot. Avis was over here one day, made some snide remark, and for once Owen boiled over. I heard the tail end of it. Owen's a great chap, very placid, but when he does lose his temper, we all go for cover till the show's over. I was as pleased as punch – don't mind admitting it – that she'd got her come-uppance for once.

'You know what a shy bloke young Lance is, but very kind. Avis isn't popular in the district . . . he saw her on the fringe of things at one of the local hops, so he asked her to dance. Gosh, I could have wrung her neck! She drawled: "Hardly, sonny, you're not even dry behind the ears yet!" '

Charlotte burned with indignation. 'Oh, I loathe her for that even before I've met her. What an effect that must have had on Lance!'

Tod grinned reminiscently, 'I got the shock of my life. I could have cheered. For once Lance hit back. He drawled in return: "Oh, sorry. I'll get back to my own age group. Perhaps wallflowers have only themselves to blame!" '

Charlotte gave a gurgle of real merriment. 'Oh, how I wish I'd been there! Oh . . . the phone,' and she sped inside. It wasn't Phyl. It never was Phyl, despite the belief some of them still held in her.

She could well imagine this Avis . . . past the first flush of youth, one of the girls with a grudge against the whole male sex simply because she'd not happened to get married. Getting married or not was largely a matter of chance anyway . . . the right man coming along at the right time, when you were seventeen or thirty-seven. But some carried burdens of inferiority complexes that spoiled some of the best years of their lives. And it was so stupid . . . you had only to look round on the scores of charming unmarried women to realize that, to say nothing of the wives who made you wonder how they had managed to marry! Even if Avis was as plain as a pikestaff, she probably neutralized any charm she might possess in spite of that, by resentment and sullenness.

Therefore Charlotte didn't for a moment imagine Edmund was ushering Avis Weybourne in, when he was preceded by a tall slim girl with the palest gold hair lying in swirls on her shoulders, a girl with eyes as blue as forget-me-nots, and an apple-blossom complexion. She didn't look twenty-seven, or a shrew capable of saying what she'd said to Lance. She looked ethereal, dream-like. Who could this entrancing girl be? A neighbour? A relation? ...

The girl anticipated Edmund's introduction as he started, 'Oh, Avis, this—' by putting out both hands in a seemingly spontaneous gesture of welcome. 'You must be Charlotte Smith. I've been nursing my mother or I'd have been over before. Ed's been telling me all you've done for us during this difficult time.' *Us.* How odd!

Avis continued, 'I'd expected to pitch in and help, of course, but my mother sprained her ankle very badly. She's not a good patient – she loves people, and dashing hither and thither – very sociable type, so to have her confined to a couch is terrible, though she's keeping in touch with all her friends and neighbours by phone.'

Charlotte felt disquiet flowering within her. Keeping in touch by phone ... and with a piece of gossip such as this to relate! Would she have been able to keep it to herself?

Avis tossed back a swirl of hair. Charlotte found herself wishing she could think that the colour came out of a dye pack, but it didn't, it glistened naturally golden clear to her scalp. No disgruntled plain spinster here. She was a golden girl, with charm.

Avis said ingenuously, 'You know, when Edmund described you first, I imagined someone so different ... plainer and older ... isn't it odd, the impressions one gets?'

A slightly dry note crisped Charlotte's tone. 'Oh, we all get different impressions ... or give them.'

Still the ingenuous tone. 'Yes, like everyone does thinking Owen's wife a model of rectitude, but somehow I just couldn't go all the way with that. I just felt there was something!'

Charlotte felt her hackles rise. 'You mean you instinctively recognized her for a husband-deceiver?'

She glanced briefly at Edmund and saw a hint of laughter lurking in his eyes.

Avis fluttered her beautiful hands. 'Oh, no. But there was just something I couldn't – quite – trust. To me she didn't seem quite right – for Owen. Know what I mean?'

Charlotte shook her head decidedly, made her tone indifferent. 'Not knowing either of them I couldn't possibly pass an opinion. Though one often feels like that about a couple and it doesn't mean a thing. I still hope she'll ring soon and come flying back before Owen has to know she'd ever gone. We aren't beyond hope of that yet.'

A strange expression flitted so quickly through the blue eyes, Charlotte thought afterwards she might have imagined it. A sudden shrinking, a flash of – what? Fear? Dread? Some sort of shrinking, anyway, yet not just a shrinking from the thought of Owen and Phyllis being reconciled, as you might expect. But almost a guilty shrinking.

Charlotte decided to press it. 'That would be a truly marvellous solution, wouldn't it? If she rang before he regained consciousness and we could get her back?'

Avis said, 'I expect so – only—'

Charlotte barked out, 'Only what?' She thought Edmund was watching Avis very closely for her reaction.

'Only it hardly seems fair to Owen. He'd be living in a fool's paradise.'

Edmund came in, 'Wouldn't it be a case of ignorance being bliss, Avis? After all, Judy and Bill, or Charlotte, would never divulge a word about that note . . . neither would you, or your mother . . . would you?'

Again the pretty, helpless gesture. 'Of course we wouldn't. But do you really think she'll ring . . . *now*?' Again that slightly furtive look. Charlotte told herself she was looking for it. But that was the whole cruel question . . . would Phyl ever ring? Or write? How long could they go on enduring this nightmare of not knowing?

Charlotte offered hospitality, 'A cup of tea?' Avis accepted and watched while Charlotte buttered her fresh, crisp cheese scones, cut gingerbread and a cake the children loved with a topping of brown sugar, chopped walnuts and pineapple, but contrived an air of surprise when Charlotte set it out on the kitchen table. 'Oh, we're having it in here? Well, it saves work, I suppose.'

The slight insinuation that standards at Amberleigh were slipping a little was there. Charlotte said smoothly, 'Oh, I thought you'd be in and out so often there'd be no formality.' But she did not offer to take it into the living-room. Again she saw laughter lurking in Edmund's eyes. Charlotte felt wrathful and deliberate and as watchful as if Avis had been a declared enemy of her own, and she must weigh up every word, study every move.

Avis managed to drop several nasty remarks about Phyl's

conduct, things only she had noticed, and looked sad over her apparent perfidy, till Charlotte could have screamed. She had to be so careful to display no undue partisanship, no real resentment, and all her efforts to change the conversation failed.

Avis very cunningly managed to convey that had Owen only married a local girl none of this hoo-ha would have happened. By the time Edmund escorted the golden girl to her car and waved goodbye to her, Charlotte felt exhausted.

Edmund came in rather silently and made her jump by saying, 'And what's that huge sigh in aid of?'

'Oh, it's been a tiring day. And I had nightmares last night – not a good quality of sleep at all.' True enough, but it was only an excuse.

Edmund picked up the towel and began drying a cup. He cocked a quizzical eyebrow at her. 'Or is it just that our visitor rubbed you up the wrong way?'

Charlotte dashed her hair back impatiently, 'Well, she added to the feeling of strain we're all labouring under.' She swung round on Edmund. 'You didn't help much! You left it to me to carry on the conversation. And you were amused!' This last was an accusation.

He chuckled unrepentantly. 'It wasn't so much a conversation as a fencing match. You make me laugh, Sharlie. You get on the defensive as soon as Phyl's name is mentioned. Why?'

Charlotte grew very still. She'd given herself away. She closed her eyes, standing at the sink with her back towards him. Then she achieved a chuckle. 'Well, it's sheer contrariness, I suppose, but no matter what your brother's wife has done or not done, that girl is just revelling in the fact that it's happened. Evidently she fancied Owen herself. It must have been just a fancy, not love, or she'd be concerned for Owen, sorry he might have to suffer disillusionment and heartbreak as soon as he's strong enough to bear it. She looks like an angel, but it was quite horrible to see her – to see her—'

Edmund burst out laughing. 'To see her licking her chops over it all. I think that's the expression you're after, revered preceptress! It's such an elegant one . . . right in the Tennyson tradition.'

Charlotte waved a hand. 'Well, it may not be elegant, but it expresses exactly what that girl was doing. Thank you for putting it so aptly, Edmund Leigh! There may have been pressures on this marriage we've not dreamed of. Tod told me that Owen told Avis exactly what he thought of her not long since — yet here she is, sort of worming her way in, and I'm convinced, utterly convinced, she's just trying to make a bad situation worse. Now you can think *I'm* being catty . . . and so I am. But I don't care. This situation is bad enough without that one making it worse!' Charlotte wrung her dishcloth as if she'd like to wring Avis's neck. Edmund took it off her. 'O, revered preceptress, who'd have thought that under that prim and smooth exterior . . . of the Miss Smith I first engaged . . . lurked such a bonny fighter!' He peered into her eyes. 'You've got tears of real rage brimming up. Sharlie, I find it endearing!'

Her cheeks grew hot. 'Find what endearing?'

The teasing light left his eyes. 'Endearing that in some way I don't profess to understand, you keep on going to the defence of someone you've never seen and who's probably not worth defending. Pity there aren't more women like you in the world, ready to believe the old tag about there being so much good in the worst of us . . .'

He took her face between his hands . . . they felt gloriously cool against her hot cheeks, then he dropped the lightest of kisses upon her forehead, turned and went outside.

Charlotte was left knowing she didn't deserve that tribute. She wasn't flying to the defence of an unknown woman, she was doing it for a loved and dear cousin . . . and she was a deceiver in Edmund Leigh's household.

Nevertheless, she tasted the compliment to the full. She had an idea that Edmund Leigh, once he gave his friendship, would be a friend to the end. If she won his respect and admiration, he might, when the day of truth came, not resent her masquerade as much as if she had been unmasked immediately. Because come it must, some day. How or where she did not know. If Phyl suddenly returned, having heard of Owen's accident from some outside source, or if she rang or wrote and they told her. Suddenly Charlotte bit her lip as a strange longing rushed in on her awareness.

Oh, if only, if only she had met Edmund Leigh in an ordinary way. If, when she'd come here as his new sister-in-law's cousin from England, he'd been here, part of the household, newly home from experience in Canada. If only they could have met, and liked each other. *Liked*. Suddenly Charlotte's cheeks were burning again. It wasn't just *liking* she wanted from Edmund Leigh. She flung her dishcloth down and rushed upstairs to her room – her only retreat, somewhere to sort out her chaotic, unwelcome thoughts. But if she had been in a different situation they wouldn't have been unwelcome. Because she knew very well that Edmund Leigh had the beginning of a *tendresse* for her. That it would take very little for this feeling that was flowering between them to blossom into a full, delightful maturity.

Charlotte flung herself on to her bed, buried her face in the pillow. Oh, Phyl, Phyl, what incalculable harm you did us all when you ran away! She did not allow herself to shed a single tear. It would show, and Edmund was astute. He might press for a reason.

When she felt she had calmed, she went across to her window, flung wide this glad October day in New Zealand to the spring air. Everything shouted to her of Edmund. He had walked her round this garden of his mother's in the lengthening twilight. He'd said, 'I'm always very conscious of my forebears here. Because they made this garden out of a wilderness. There were still the same rolling contours of these lovely hills to remind them of the rolling hills of Surrey, but there weren't any bluebells under the trees, so they planted some ... see, they're just starting to fade.' He'd held up the branches of an English beech to show her.

Charlotte had felt a swift warmth that Edmund's forebears too had loved those woods of Home where bluebells lay like a lake flung down from the sky above. Now she leaned out and saw with enchantment that the hawthorns were rose and ivory on the hedge beyond the garden confines, that on the hillside in a triangular bed devoted to nothing else, azaleas were glowing in saffron and pale yellow, apricot and salmon, that the cinerarias still flaunted their deep, jewel-like colours under the trees, pale pink clematis rioted over the trellises and side by side the native *kowhais* and their English cousins, the laburnums, hung their pendulous golden blooms. She watched a bellbird swing upside down beneath a *kowhai* flower to dip its brush-tipped tongue deep into it, in search of the honey it so dearly loved. Then it perched among the branches and dropped silver chimes into the silence. The old world and the new world had blended beautifully here. The world of flowers and trees and birds anyway.

But Phyl's world and Owen's world hadn't, seemingly. And

92

because of that, perhaps her own and Edmund's never would. It was too snarled a situation. Only a miracle could unravel it.

Nevertheless, in some way, the loveliness of the garden Margaretta Leigh had planted and tended more than a hundred years ago soothed Charlotte into a measure of happiness. She was here, and Edmund was here, and no matter what happened in the future, she was glad, glad, glad she had met him. She would enjoy the present.

The very ordinariness of life here, apart from the anxiety about Owen, and the wild speculations about Phyl, lulled one into a false sense of security. That night Tod and Lance came in for a game of Chinese Checkers and Charlotte had a strange sense of belonging, as if this was what she'd looked for all her life . . . this farm tucked into a forested valley threaded through with a river that looked golden as it rippled over the yellowish rocks of its bed, far down in the Southern Hemisphere.

They paused in their game to switch on television and listen to the news. There was some report of wheat-growing and on the frozen lamb market . . . suddenly a police message was relayed across. Passengers on a certain plane that had touched down at Hongkong and Singapore recently had been contacted and put in touch with local health authorities, as one passenger was ill in an Auckland hospital with suspected typhoid. Only one passenger remained to be found – a Miss Charlotte de Lacey Smith, believed to have gone to the South Island, possibly in the Kaikoura area. Anyone knowing her whereabouts was requested to get in touch with her immediately to ask her to report, or to get in touch with the local police if they could not make personal contact, if they had any clues as to her whereabouts.

Charlotte felt a suffocating feeling rise in her throat. She put a hand up to it. Her hand was icy cold, but she felt a rush of hot blood to her cheeks. It was all over. It was horrible news, doubly disastrous for her, because as a second name de Lacey was so uncommon. Edmund would tumble to it immediately. Lacey Smith . . . whom he had thought to be Lacey Ward. She felt turned to stone, but now she moved her head to the right, looked at the men, who were staring at her.

Tod spoke first. 'It *is* you, isn't it? Charlotte Smith . . . is it another Charlotte Smith, or were you on that plane?'

Charlotte swallowed. 'No, it's me, all right. That was the date we flew into Auckland.' Her eyes fastened on Edmund in an imploring sort of look ... not to bawl her out in front of his men.

She felt bewildered when his reaction was so different. He stood up, pushed his chair back, reached out for her hands, said, shaking them a little as if to stir her out of her trance, 'Don't look like that, Charlotte ... typhoid isn't the dread thing it was once. They bring down the fever in record time now with antibiotics. And you may not contract it, anyway. That's why when going from New Zealand to Britain these days, they don't immunize you against typhoid ... and it's not as if we're a dairy farm. We don't do Town Supply milk. It could have been worse – smallpox, for instance.'

Charlotte snapped out of her fear that Edmund would have leapt to her relationship with Phyl, and plunged into a worse dread. 'Edmund, how can you be so casual? Mark complained of a headache tonight. And he was hot. Remember how he took off his jersey and was very thirsty? Oh, do you—'

Edmund laughed, 'Charlotte, you're letting your imagination bolt with you. You know perfectly well he's just catching that cold Barbie has had.'

Charlotte stood up, her voice crisp again instead of wavery. 'I shall have to get in touch with the authorities right away, then I'm going to call the doctor about Mark. We'll take no risks. I could be a carrier.' She looked so appalled and distressed at the idea that they all, even Lance, rushed into reassuring speech.

She brushed aside their comforting. 'I feel horribly guilty. I've brought this risk into this household, at a time when everything's at sixes and sevens anyway. When tragedy has already stuck once – though Owen seems to be on the mend. But we still don't know where – where the children's mother is. Oh, is there no end to the list of complications?'

Edmund shook her again, this time by the elbows. 'Don't whip yourself, girl, this could happen to anyone. Think of all the others in the plane ... they'll be back with their families if they were coming home or if they were visiting New Zealand relations, will feel they've brought risk to their hosts. Some will feel even worse ... they'll be touring with some group or at hotels. Here we're a fairly isolated community. In a city you could have had endless contacts, with no chance of checking everybody. Now, snap out of it. *We* aren't going to blame you. It's unfortunate, nothing more, but it's positively masochistic to whip yourself about coming here – in fact, it's plain stupid. You needn't feel the slightest hint of guilt!'

Charlotte knew why she felt so horribly guilty . . . because she had no right to come here in the first place, because this valley homestead, this family, had been forbidden to her, as Phyl's cousin. But she had wormed her way in here under false pretences, under a name Edmund Leigh hadn't dreamed could belong to Phyl's cousin . . . and look what had come of it . . . she had exposed them all to the risk of typhoid.

Edmund was already looking up the number of the Medical Officer of Health in Christchurch, and dialling. As he waited for an answer, he said, 'I wanted to get this quickly before we get deluged by phone calls from the folk round here who know Charlotte is here and want to know have we heard the message and is it really her?'

Charlotte sat with her head in her hands while he did it all. Arrangements were made for the farm to be visited, instructions given, precautions advised. Edmund copied everything down meticulously. As he put the receiver down other calls started. People were sweet . . . concerned for them, and sympathetic and reassuring; probably nothing would come of it at all, they were sure.

Then Avis rang. She had a thin, high voice with a carrying quality. They all heard her opening remark. Tod and Lance looked murderous. Edmund looked embarrassed. Avis said, 'Well, that girl has certainly landed you – and us with you – in a nice mess!'

Charlotte froze. Then she relaxed a little as Edmund said, 'Oh, come, it could happen to any of us. That chap could have been on the plane *I* flew in by. No need to get in a flap. It's not even dead certain this man *has* typhoid. So far it's only a suspected case, but rightly enough they take no chances. You can imagine how Charlotte feels. Now, don't let your imagination run riot. There'll be a bit of inconvenience – nothing much more. No need for anyone to be alarmist and carry on as if a raging epidemic is about to hit the district. I've been on to the authorities. I'm to check on all contacts. I'll just tell you what they want us to do. Charlotte's not been abroad at all, so it's a small circle.'

They didn't hear the rest of Avis's conversation. It seemed as if Edmund, to spare Charlotte further embarrassment, had pressed the earpiece firmly to his ear. When he replaced the receiver Charlotte said miserably, 'I'm afraid quite a lot of people will think it would have been far better for you if I'd never come here.'

She looked up and saw a peculiar look on Edmund's face. His blue eyes held hers for a moment, he started to say something, looked over at Tod and Lance, still sitting by the checker-board, and Charlotte wished them a hundred miles away – she very badly wanted to know what Edmund had been going to say. The phone rang again.

'*Now* who?' muttered Tod. 'I thought everyone who knew about you had rung by this time! I'd like to finish the game.'

Edmund answered it. 'Where from? Oh yes, sure. She's right here.' He had a line between his brows. 'A call from Kaikoura for you, Charlotte. Will that be—'

She felt her heart give a thump. It would be John. Naturally, a brother, hearing news like that, would want to reassure himself about her. Besides, she'd have had to ring him – they would all be contacts too.

It wasn't John, it was Ivan. 'Sharlie, did you hear the news on TV half an hour ago? You did? I tried to ring you then, but your number was engaged incessantly. John and Diana are out. Have you been in touch with the health department?'

'Yes, Ivan, immediately. Mr. Leigh has got it all in hand. Oh, shall I give you your instructions, or will yours be a different district? M'm. Well, no harm if I do give you what we've been told. What was that? I didn't quite catch it? . . . No, he doesn't.' (Oh, horrors, Ivan had asked if this meant Edmund knew she was Phyl's cousin.) 'No, the situation is still as it was. Yes, Mr. Leigh's brother is steadily improving, but—' Charlotte could have screamed. If Ivan didn't stop asking questions soon, she'd reveal more than she should. He must imagine the phone was in the hall, and private. It was terribly hard to answer in a non-committal way. She had to rapidly pre-judge her every answer. Her brain was whirling. In any case, apart from this conversation, Edmund could put two and two together at any moment. He could think: 'de Lacey . . . oh, yes, Phyl's cousin was Lacey . . . of course!' Charlotte managed to rally and began to talk rapidly and nervously. She mustn't allow too many pauses, for Ivan to get in any more questions.

She repeated what Edmund had said about modern treatment of typhoid, and finished up by saying she would keep him informed. It was a great relief when Ivan finally said, 'Well, bye-bye, dear. Look after yourself and call the doctor at the slightest sign.' She'd begun to take the receiver from her ear at the second word, her relief was so great. And though the men probably heard his last words, they didn't give anything away.

All Edmund said was: 'We'll go up now and look at Mark. That might set your mind at rest. I peeped at him before and he was sleeping like an angel, didn't look a bit flushed. We'll take the torch up.'

They crept upstairs. Normally an earthquake wouldn't have wakened Mark, but they'd take no chances tonight. The beam of the torch shone out, touched the pillow, centred on the little face. He lay in complete and relaxed abandon, the fair fringe slanting across his forehead, one little arm hooked round . . . not a Teddy-bear, but a very muddy Rugby ball! They both laughed silently.

Charlotte put a hand against his brow, his cheek, and found them just warm. No fever there. His breathing was rhythmical and gentle. Edmund took her elbow to draw her away. She felt a sweetness sweep over her. A man and a woman, bent above a sleeping child. Edmund's son would look like this.

Downstairs Tod and Lance were carefully putting the checker-board on the dresser. 'We'll finish that game tomorrow night. We certainly won't be going anywhere, we'll be in quarantine. We'll turn in – goodnight.'

Charlotte went out to the kitchen, brought the kettle forward on to the hottest plate of the fuel stove, put out some biscuits.

Edmund bit into a gingernut, said, 'Who is Ivan? I'd not realized you had anyone as near as Kaikoura. I thought when you rang about the job you'd been on a tour of the South Island in your car, had seen a paper and thought our job might suit you. But it sounds as if you might have been staying – with friends?'

Charlotte tried to sound nonchalant, not evasive. 'Oh, it wasn't quite like that. I came over to Picton from Wellington, went on and stayed for a night or two with relations.'

Edmund said a thought impatiently, 'Why didn't you tell me you had relations there? It's no distance. They could have run down to Amberleigh to see you.'

'Oh, that's very sweet of you. I didn't think of it. I seem to have been here no time at all yet.'

Edmund persisted, with the faint impatience of tone that a

man uses when he is aware he is having to drag out information he thinks ought to be volunteered: 'You said you had a brother in New Zealand. Was that him? Or have you other relations? In that case, where—'

'Oh, Ivan's not a relation. He works for my brother.'

'I might know your brother. What's – oh, of course his name will be Smith. Well, that doesn't help much. What does your brother do? Does he live right in Kaikoura?'

'Not really. He's farming. I don't know if I could pinpoint it, Edmund. It's just a rural mail delivery address.'

She didn't want to say where Huntress Hill was. Edmund could know other farmers on the Hundalee, put two and two together, because it just could be, if Owen had corresponded with his brother in Canada, he might have said his wife had relations farming there.

Edmund said slowly, 'That chap had an English voice. Did you know him before you came out here? This Ivan?'

Charlotte tried to sound nonchalant again. 'Yes, known him since I was a youngster. He came out to work on my brother's farm because of that.'

Edmund was just as casual. 'Nice for you to have some folk here.'

She decided to keep quiet still about her parents. She had no idea how much Phyl might have told Edmund's mother about her cousin's people, how much Mrs. Leigh might have passed on. It could suddenly fit together in Edmund's mind, especially this night, when her unusual second name had been blared out from the television.

But the feeling of closeness, engendered by Edmund's understanding of her plight and her feelings with regard to the typhoid contact, plus his warm defence of her to Avis, was gone. She could only remember that she was here in a very awkward and possible indefensible position.

It had seemed, at Huntress Hill, so much the right thing to do, utterly convinced as she had been that there must be some good explanation of Phyl's behaviour. Under false colours she'd met the only man she had ever wanted to spend the rest of her life with, and she'd brought the possibility of dangerous illness into a household already overburdened with a faithless wife and an unknowing husband, who had been too close to death to be told. Now they were penned up together in the homestead till the safety margin of quarantine had been reached.

98

Charlotte felt tired to death as she crept quietly up to bed, with a mind so full of unease she would probably be past sleep. She was suddenly and devastatingly homesick for the Welsh farm where she had spent so many happy years, for things known and familiar, for the uncomplicated existence that had been hers, for a mind unburdened by guilt. It seemed quite incredible that less than a month ago she had been looking forward to joining her parents and her brother and stepsister and stepbrother in New Zealand, knowing a zest for a new life, for fresh adventures, anticipating with joy visiting her cousin on this farm Phyl had described so lovingly. Phyl. It always came back to the defaulting Phyl.

CHAPTER SIX

How strange that no matter how desperate one felt the night before, morning always brought a resurgence of energy, of faint hope that all might yet be well. The four of them always met at breakfast with the thought – unspoken in the children's presence – that today might bring a phone-call, a letter.

Charlotte knew that Edmund's reaction to Phyl would be more savage than ever if she rang. He would not spare her any details, even to the fact that now they had the threat of typhoid hanging over them, all due to Phyl because she'd been unable to resist temptation! If Phyl had not run away, he wouldn't have needed to engage a housekeeper. Nevertheless, anything would be better than this continued and nerve-wearing silence.

The children thought it was fun not to have to go to school, and rather excited about the fact that Charlotte had been the subject of a police message even if, they regretted loudly, they hadn't been there to hear it. Barbie rang up Judy's children and talked at length about it. When she hung up she turned round and said, 'I've just thought . . . isn't it a good thing Mummy's not home – that she stayed in Christchurch – else Daddy wouldn't have had any visitors at all?'

Edmund said, 'Yes, it is. He'd have been pretty lonely, wouldn't he? Now look, kids. Tod's going round the sheep in the jogger cart this morning, so you can go with him – but you'd better scram, he's about to start off.'

To Charlotte, after they'd rushed off, he said, 'I fixed that up with Tod. I'm ringing Owen's doctor about it.' He gave a wry smile. 'I expect one can see some good in every disaster. This does give us a bit more breathing-space. Owen can't be stalled off much longer, yet I feel each day he grows more fit to face what he must face.'

Charlotte gazed at him. 'Oh, heavens, I've just realized something. What *is* Owen going to be told about this? I mean, *why* you're in quarantine for typhoid. He'll think Phyl's here.'

They gazed at each other in utter consternation. Edmund's brow was knotted. Then it cleared. 'I'll say Judy had a friend on that plane. That she came here to stay, that Judy brought her over to see us, and consequently we're all in quarantine.'

Charlotte looked at him with great respect. 'Edmund, you'd make a very good writer. You can always come up with something.'

He pulled a face. 'I've made a very good liar. I don't particularly like it. I expect the end justifies the means, but—'

Charlotte hugged that thought to her. Would he then, when he found out, forgive her? Concede that her intentions were equally laudable? Or, if not laudable, understandable?

Suddenly she wanted to get back to the closeness of those moments last night when she'd realized first that Edmund was being very sweet about the fresh complication she'd brought into their lives.

She smiled at him, said, 'Edmund, I want to thank you so much for not making me feel the cuckoo in the nest last night. Any man could have been forgiven for thinking of me as the last straw.' His expression, to her dismay, was shuttered. What was wrong? She made another attempt. 'And it was very sweet of you to take up the cudgels on my behalf when Avis said that.' She added, when he made no answer, 'I think we all heard her opening remark on the phone. We were so near.'

Edmund's tone was dryly derisive. 'Don't you think it's a bit much to put it that way . . . taking up the cudgels? I merely tried to be fair. Perhaps I was too sharp with Avis. I daresay it was only her way of expressing sympathy with me.' He turned, said over his shoulder, 'After I ring the hospital to see if I can get hold of Owen's doctor, I'll be in the wool-shed. You can get me on that extension when the Office of Health chappie arrives. And beat the gong to summon the others then.'

Charlotte stood staring after him. She felt exactly as if someone had doused her with cold water. Then she pulled herself together. No doubt Edmund, after his first amazingly tolerant reaction, was feeling bad about this further setback this morning, about the inconvenience to other contacts in the district Charlotte's presence here had caused. Some of them might have sounded resentful. And ever-prominent in his mind must be dread of the moment when Owen must know his wife had left him for another man. She must make allowances.

What a day! Everyone was immunized, but the moment that was over, things started to happen. Charlotte decided if she made a caramel cake it might sweeten Edmund's mood a little.

She put a double quantity of condensed milk, butter, and golden syrup into a pan, set it on the fuel stove, heard a cry from the barn and rushed out to find Mark had fallen on to a piece of iron covered with loose hay, and gashed his leg quite badly. By the time she got back to the house, the caramel had blackened, boiled over, run into the fire-box, and burst into flames all over the top of the stove, which, naturally, had got red-hot. On the electric stove it would have been a simple matter to turn off the heat, but this, even though she tipped a whole salt-box of salt over it, was going to bubble for ages, smelling out the kitchen to high heaven.

She got Mark soothed and plastered and found that when she'd rushed him inside, she'd done the unforgivable, left a farm gate open, and Marmaduke and Alphonse, the children's two pet lambs, which by now, in the way of all pet lambs, were nothing but nuisances, had eaten down all the remaining spring bulbs, and the hens on free range had scratched up every single lettuce seedling that had been transplanted only that week.

Barbie left the wash-house tap running and the plug in, and the whole floor was awash when Charlotte discovered it, and it took ages to mop up, which made morning tea very late, and because of all this there were no fresh scones or pikelets, so she had to butter some gingerbread that had lasted longer than most, because for some reason it was very dry.

The men tramped mud in and out, made teasing remarks about the smell in the kitchen, and had a field day on asking for things Charlotte couldn't find. She could have screamed. She found herself wishing viciously that things would start going wrong in their domain, not hers, because it would serve them jolly well right, and then felt terribly remorseful when they came in to say one of the horses had got tangled in some loose fencing wire and they were having a devil of a time trying to cut him free. He must have been trapped all night, and had threshed around so much in the ditch under the big macrocarpa hedge it was cut deeply into his foreleg and he was resisting all efforts to free him. He lashed out with his iron-shod hoof every time he saw them reaching out with the cutters.

Charlotte went out to see, and was terrified one of them would suffer real injury. Finally she said, 'I remember something happening like this in Wales. Lloyd finished up blind-folding this mare so she couldn't see what we were doing, therefore she couldn't lash out with the same deadly precision.'

Tod was greatly impressed with this and said so, though Edmund only grunted, but they managed to tie a strip of cloth over Romeo's eyes. They all had to chuckle as his ears twitched round suspiciously, trying to follow their movements. But suddenly Edmund, making a quick and sure plunge, managed to get the wire-cutters under the loops and cut it free.

Tod said, a few minutes later, 'You sure knew what you were doing, boss, when you engaged Sharlie.'

Edmund's tone still held that dry note. 'She has her uses, I'll admit.'

Charlotte's tone matched his. 'Compensation for my nuisance value, which is high, you mean.' Tod and Lance stared, then exchanged a glance which said they thought the two of them had had a tiff, and they grinned in a most maddening fashion and walked away.

They were all glad when the day was over. Charlotte hoped desperately that no one would have a bad reaction to their immunization, or develop toothache, when it wasn't permitted to visit the dentist, and Edmund said, when she remarked on this to Lance, rustling his paper in an aggressive and irritated fashion because they were chatting when he wanted to read, 'Charlotte, *must* you go on croaking like a Cassandra? We've had enough befall us now without *anticipating* further disasters which will probably never happen!'

Charlotte stood up, tossed back her auburn locks, said furiously, 'I don't particularly think *you're* doing much to improve the situation by behaving like a bear with a sore head. I thought you reacted pretty well last night to the shock of knowing I was a typhoid contact ... but your tolerance wore off mighty quickly, didn't it? You've been snarky ever since. I've been worrying like mad about all sorts of things ... well, I'm damned if I will any longer. I'll just take what comes and cope with it at the time. Thank goodness the children are in bed and asleep. I'd like to relax myself, but I've been trying to catch up on the chores. I'll take a bath and read in bed and enjoy the solitude. You can make your own cuppa!'

As she flashed out of the door she heard the irrepressible Tod say: 'Oh boy, Edmund, you sure asked for that one! If I were you I'd go on my bended knees to put that right. We'll be in a dickens of a mess if Charlotte walks out on us!'

She didn't stop to hear any more. She had a bath up to her chin, revelling in the scented water and lying back in it, towelled herself vigorously, brushed her hair till her scalp tingled, finding sheer relaxation in that, slid into a deep teal nightgown with a frilled yoke that looked, as modern ones often did, like an Elizabethan bedgown, and climbed into her bed warm from its electric blanket. She was going to read Margaretta's diary. Edmund had fished it out for her from a glass-fronted bookcase with a key, a couple of hours before that horrible announcement on the television last night; then the men had made her put it aside to play Chinese Checkers with them. It seemed an age ago.

Margaretta's writing was easy to read, even if the ink was brownish with age. It was a bold, firm hand, full of character. At first Charlotte couldn't concentrate. She was so angry with Edmund that the words wouldn't register. But presently the sheer courage and fortitude of those early days gripped her attention and impelled in her an admiration that swamped her own feelings and made them seem so petty, they faded.

The hardships of the voyage on that sailing ship, with her husband, sounded frightfully daunting to one who'd flown across the world recently in thirty-six hours. Imagine being becalmed for thirteen days, then lashed with storms, tormented by seasickness, revolted by sour food, pinpricked by close contact with uncongenial fellow-passengers, driven miles off their course twice . . . more than three months at sea in all. It seemed incredible.

There had been measles and scarlet fever running rampant among children and adults, mothers weeping for the little children who had been consigned to the cruel deep in canvas shrouds. Men weeping too. Margaretta had championed the cause of one of the seamen she had felt to have been too harshly treated. 'I had to grit my teeth,' she had written, 'and plead his cause, when I really wanted to storm at Captain Jakes. He only gave in because I was a woman – and he rather likes me – and I despise having to use woman's wiles. But anything rather than have that poor man have to endure confinement any longer. A ship at sea can be a small, hateful and cruel world, giving the captain powers that can be used wisely or violently. There is far too much tradition. It breeds such injustice. I'm told that out in this New Zealand Colony there is more independence, less of the lingering traces of the old feudal system. I sincerely hope so. While I revere history, not all of it is good. Maybe I'll find more freedom for women there too. I hope so. I despised myself today for acting as I did to Captain Jakes, saying I could so admire a man who was masterful, yet so clement . . . that I was just filled with admiration of him when I heard he was going to free Wilberton. I'd like to live in a community where a woman could express an opinion as a person and have it respected, not just treated with contempt, or indulgence. But meanwhile I'll have to play the part of a sheltered little creature who can't bear the thought of a man in solitary confinement!'

Charlotte felt she'd have loved Margaretta, would have liked her for a friend. She was glad this wife of long ago had come out to a little new country, making its own traditions – sometimes, admittedly, one that swept away the good with the bad, but in the main bringing a fresh vigour into living . . . a country that had given women the vote before the turn of the century! A little new country, one that Charlotte de Lacey Smith was beginning to love.

She sat up, hugging her knees, gazing into space with eyes that did not see the sprigged wallpaper, the gilt mirror over the bureau, only the green acres outside that now dreamed in darkness, the lilac hills, the air that was like wine, unpolluted and clear. She grinned to herself; she had an idea New Zealanders mightn't like it being called a *little* country. It was as big as Britain, with a bit extra thrown in for good measure. And in that size it held less than three million people. Charlotte drew in a deep breath as if she couldn't get enough of this air, from her open window.

She returned to the diary, reading on absorbed. She was with Alfred and Margaretta every step of the way . . . their early life in the growing city of the plains, Christchurch, tales of the men who fared further afield, braving the still unknown, the greater horizons, men the mountains lured, fording rivers that were unpredictable and hazardous, piling all their possessions on drays and plodding through tussock and ravine to grants of land that in their mind's eye would some day yield riches in harvest and in animal husbandry . . . men who, had they stayed home, might have always remained farm labourers, never landowners with smiling acres to hand down to their children's children.

But Alfred had been one who had known all there was to be known about felling timber, milling it, and when his chance came to establish a sawmill in North Canterbury, he took it.

What an opportunity was here, with so little building stone in the area round Christchurch, and a great dearth of trees as yet on the trackless plains there.

Alfred turned his face towards the foothills and the native forests. He wanted to leave Margaretta and the baby Jonathan who'd been born to them in Christchurch, till he had established himself a little, till he could provide a proper rooftree for them, but Margaretta had been adamant.

'I will not allow him to go alone,' she had written. 'Other pioneer women have lived under canvas and so will I. Alfred will so quickly build us a house of timber. I've told him he's a splendid forester but a very poor cook. Why, when I had a feverish cold recently, that man tried to cook an egg in a dry frying-pan! I have a camp-oven, I can swing it over a fire and make bread in it, and roast in it. I have tried it out, even producing an excellent "Colonial goose" – it is a leg of mutton, boned and stuffed, and is delicious. I believe there are plenty of fat wood-pigeons in the bush, and some of the early settlers there will provide us with our mutton. I am gathering together as many seeds and plants as possible. I do hope they survive the journey in the dray. I have my laburnum seeds in a little box. I did not plant them here. I knew this would not satisfy Alfred for long. This is to be a city. Alfred wants his great-great-grandsons to inherit wide pastures and rolling hills, not city plots.' Not only his great-great-grandsons, thought Charlotte dreamily, but endless generations after them ... Edmund and Owen Leigh's sons and grandsons. That brought her up with a jerk. Would Owen ever have a son of his own? How idyllic it all could have been ... Owen at Amberleigh, and Edmund at Te-iti-rangi, the Little Heaven. She snatched her thoughts back from wondering who would bear Edmund Leigh's sons, and read on.

'... and some day my laburnums will shower golden petals by some little stream. Alfred laughed when he saw me looking at the seeds the other day. "There are *kowhais* growing in plenty back in the foothills," he said. But I would like them to grow together, as a symbol of my old world and my new world ... my world and my children's world!'

And outside, this lyrically beautiful springtide, the laburnums and the *kowhais* spread a carpet of living gold on the green turf about the shallow little stream that wandered in musical rivulets about Margaretta's imperishable garden.

Margaretta was so proud of Alfred. 'So many of the men, mindful of the prices timber is bringing in Christchurch, are felling without thought of future years. They fell everything within easy access. Alfred is trying to imbue the men who do not know trees, who do not understand forestry, with the knowledge of how long forests take to regenerate, even here, in this rich, fertile soil. He wants them to cut less ruthlessly, not to leave great tracts of ugly stumps, and huge areas devastated and exposed. Some heed, some learn and are grateful. Others are not. Alfred is quite fearless about it, even where he meets up with opposition and ugly tempers. He says we are here to nourish the land, not exploit it.'

Day by day there were fresh reports. 'Alfred has made us a wooden floor for the tent and erected me a rough shelter where I can cook when the weather is inclement, and now, when it rains, I do not have to move everything into the middle of the floor. I have to remember not to touch the canvas of the roof, though, for then the rain, in little pools on the surface, seeps through. But before winter is upon us, Alfred will have a snug cottage built, with a gabled tin roof and walls of logs chinked with clay and tussock, and a fireplace with a swee on which to hang my kettles, my camp oven, my griddle. Best of all it will have two rooms and little Jonathan will be able to sleep in peace, though he has been so good and has become accustomed to sleeping through all manner of disturbances. How strange it seems to think that now, the end of March, we are into autumn, but there is never a sign of a yellowing leaf in this land of evergreens. But we are planting saplings too, just as they did in Christchurch, where already they have a little autumn.

'These saplings of ours were brought out by a recent ship, poplars and sycamores, plane trees, birches, chestnuts ... all round this little clearing I have buried my acorns deep, and they will lie there, almost forgotten, till out of this leafy bush mould will spring a bit of England. When we have done milling in this area, Alfred will transplant some of each into his valley property. Some people think we are mad for going further and further into the foothills, but Alfred is looking to the years ahead. He thinks that this, here, may in time become a great fruit-producing area, and he wants grazing land. All the men here talk of nothing but sheep. So we are going into Tapu-wharua – that means the Forbidden Valley, but Alfred has no time for superstition, and says he'll make it known in time for welcome, for hospitality.

'I have already ridden into it with him, on a smiling day, with sunlight spilling through the leaves and making a dappled pattern on the ground. There is a natural clearing there, on a sort of plateau, backed by a curving hill, that would provide magnificent shelter for my little saplings, for my roses, my daisies, my pinks. A river runs through the valley, not a big river just now. It comes down from quite a height, cutting a deep cleft in the hills as all these rivers do, but ours has an unusual feature. It falls over browny-golden rocks, spills into a big pool that brims over and then meanders through the folds of the hills, widening and levelling out, till it joins the Ashley River on its way to the Pacific. Because of this golden brown colour the Maoris call it Waipungapunga. *Wai* means water, I'm told, and *pungapunga* is yellow. But the settlers simply call it the Amber River. So Alfred thinks he'll join our name on to it and call our homestead Amberleigh. I think that's very pretty. He's rather ambitious. What they call homesteads here are large houses.

'I'm glad he's ambitious, yet I'm even more glad that in his desire to build a home here for future generations, he will not destroy trees indiscriminately whatever prices timber is bringing. He says he will never want so much land that he has to farm it out, just enough for our sons' and daughters' needs. Oh dear, this candle is completely melting – and smelling! I fear I have not yet quite mastered the art of making them. But I will yet.

'Alfred is already in bed and is calling out in a whisper that I will strain my eyes and that the light is attracting huge moths and that if one does get in, I know perfectly well he'll have to get out and kill it for me. I'm terrified of them – especially when they get in my hair. Ugh! I must try to do more of my diary in the daylight hours – the nights are drawing in. But Alfred wants me to keep this journal faithfully – he says that in another century or so an account of these days will make interesting reading for someone. That I must put in all sorts of details I don't much care about, the prices of tallow and butter and corn and mutton … but I like to write better of how my tiny roses are faring, of the big harvest moon we watched to-night, the singing of the *tuis* and the bellbirds and the dancing flight of the friendly fantails that precede us into the bush as we walk. How odd to think of one's descendants reading these words when one is dust and ashes. How impossible to believe that one can ever cease to be. Drat this candle ... look at that!'

'That!' had evidently been the complete collapse of her home-made candle, for the rest of the page was hugely smeared with a greasy circle. Charlotte touched it almost reverently. That candle-grease was still enduring, yet Margaretta, who had been so full of the joy of living, delight in her husband and son, her roses and laburnums, had been dust and ashes for nearly seventy years. The tears welled up in Charlotte's eyes and spilled over. She dashed a hand at them at the same moment that a knock sounded on her door and Tod's voice said, 'Sharlie, we've brought you up a cuppa. All right to come in?'

Her voice was warm. Dear, thoughtful Tod! 'Oh, rather,' she said, 'I'd just love a cup of tea.'

The door opened a little, a crease marked her brow as she heard Tod's laugh and *retreating* footsteps, and in came Edmund Leigh, bearing a tray of hot, steaming savoury toast!

She was furious. 'I said *Tod* could come in. Not you!'

He cocked a quizzical eyebrow at her. 'I know you did ... crafty of me, wasn't it? You'd never have let me in. You were too mad with me.'

'Mad? Of course I was mad. You were like a—'

'I know. Like a bear with a sore head. Snarky. You told me. I was. I apologize.'

Charlotte said rather unwillingly, 'Well, of course you've had a lot of worry. One thing after another. I suppose my being a typhoid contact was the last straw. It suddenly got on top of you.'

Edmund arranged the tray on her knees. 'Don't be stupid. That wasn't what I was mad about.'

'Then what—'

Edmund didn't answer. Charlotte felt intensely irritated. She said sharply, 'Then I know what it was. You thought when I thanked you for – for taking up the cudgels on my behalf, that I was making things too personal by far. You've got a thing about women coming to work at a homestead and setting their caps at the station-owners, haven't you? Well, let me tell you—'

She got no further. He grinned in the most infuriating

fashion and finished it for her. 'I know. You said that before, too. You wouldn't marry me if I was hung with diamonds . . . of course I don't think that. And I'm not the station-owner, Owen is. I only own Te-iti-rangi, a derelict old house falling down.'

Only Te-iti-rangi. *Only* a small heaven.

She had to sweep her thoughts away from that. 'Then *what* did make you mad? I hadn't done anything.'

The blue piercing eyes seemed to examine her. 'No, you hadn't done a thing. Remember that phrase in church? . . . the place where we pray for forgiveness of two kinds of sins? For the sins of commission and the sins of omission? Yours was the second kind. I was mad clean through with you.'

Charlotte gazed at him in utter bewilderment. 'I haven't the faintest idea what you mean. What have I failed to do . . . omitted? I think I've done most things I should. Perhaps you should draw up a list of duties. If I'm slipping up on anything, I—'

His voice was impatient. 'Of course you haven't. We were darned lucky to get someone like you. It was—'

She broke in hotly, her eyes narrowed to hazel slits, with green sparks in them. 'Oh, I get it. As I left the room Tod said you ought to ask forgiveness on your bended knees, that you'd be in a right mess if I walked out on you, so he persuaded you to come up here to apologize! He got you to the door, and called out so I'd think it was him – and now you can't even apologize in a wholehearted way . . . you've turned the tables on me. It's *my* fault *you* lost your temper and got so snarky. Don't worry, Edmund, I won't walk out on you. But not because I want to stay and look after *you* . . . oh, no, far from it. I'll stay here till I'm not needed any more, simply and solely for the children's sakes!' She glared at him.

He steadied the tray, which had rocked, said, apparently unmoved by this outburst, 'It was nothing of the kind. I simply said to Tod, "I'm taking Charlotte up a cup of tea," and he said, chuckling, "Better let *me* knock. I don't reckon she'd let you in – and serve you right!" '

'I should think so, and—'

She was interrupted. The blue eyes went serious. '*Would* you hear me out? I was hurt. That's why I reacted the way I did. Hurt by your reticence, your reserve. Your omission!'

It didn't make sense.

He continued, 'Sharlie, you got pitchforked into a peculiar

110

situation here. I had to tell a stranger more of our family affairs than one would normally. Only you didn't seem a stranger, even though I didn't make you welcome at first. I was scathing about girls on the make and so on, because of Phyl. But with her clearing out like this, we've had to talk very intimately indeed about family affairs. But you, now, you've been so secretive. Apart from the little mention of living near Godalming and working on that Welsh farm you've hardly said a thing about yourself.

'Last night, when that fellow Ivan rang, you seemed so cagey. I'm pretty sure you gave me the impression when you first rang that you were just passing through Kaikoura like any tourist. When I asked you about Ivan, you retreated into your shell immediately. Is that any way to treat a friend? I thought, well, damn all, if she wants to keep her own counsel, let her! But I was sore about it. You even made me feel I was prying when I asked about your brother's farm. Why?'

Charlotte flushed painfully, looked down, said fumblingly, 'Well – well, perhaps English people are more – more reserved than New Zealanders, more reticent. I – I didn't realize you wanted to know much about me. I – I mean, you're just my employer. I—'

He was sitting on the edge of the bed now. He thumped it so that the china rattled on the tray. 'Just your employer! How ridiculous *can* you get? As for being reserved and reticent, that's rubbish too. Redheads are never reserved and reticent.'

Charlotte said heatedly, 'And *that's* nonsense! I hate all this labelling of people. It ties up with preconceived ideas. Redheads are supposed to be – er – ardent – and quick-tempered. Well, *I'm* not!'

Again the quizzical glance, the lifted eyebrow. 'Aren't you, Sharlie. I don't agree.'

A flake of colour appeared in her cheeks 'I wasn't the one who was snappy and irritable, who lost my temper. *You* were!'

'Was I referring only to temper? I wasn't. You said two things, not one. You said, also, that redheads are supposed to be ardent and that you aren't. I just can't agree with that.'

She looked at him wide-eyed. Then realization came. She choked. 'You – you mean . . . oh, now I *am* mad!'

He laughed in the most maddening way, grabbed the tray, put it on the floor for safety's sake. 'Yes, I mean that when I kissed you I didn't find any lack of ardency.'

Her tone was scornful. 'Sheer rot! *And* vanity – thinking you'd evoked some sort of feeling. I told you at the time I just looked upon it as horse-play.'

He pulled a mock-serious face. 'So you did. Seems as if *you* can label things too. Even kisses. You docket them in your mind and push them into some dusty old pigeonhole where you think you can forget all about them. Oh, Charlotte, you make me laugh ... you're trying to behave like a shrew, and pretend you're still cross with me, and you look so adorable in that exceedingly feminine garment ... though fair go, it looks more like a ballgown to me than something to sleep in!' He stood and surveyed her till she felt the colour rush into her face again, her hair bright over the deep teal blue velvety-looking night-gown.

He bent to the tray. 'Look, our tea is getting cold. Let's have it.'

'*Our* tea?'

'Yes, seeing we'd got pippy with each other I thought it would be a grand idea to smoke the pipe of peace ... or do I mean break bread together? I'll pour out. And don't cut your nose off to spite your face by refusing it. When you thought Tod was bringing it in you said you'd love one.'

He handed her a cup, put the plate of toast near her and peered at her. 'Good lord, you've got tears in your eyes. I didn't mean to upset you. Look, I'm—'

Her tone was scornful. 'How vain can a man get? I wasn't crying over you. I'm crying because of Margaretta—' she indicated the old diary she'd put down at his entry.

He boggled. 'Because of Margaretta? I don't get it.'

She picked up the diary. 'Listen. Alfred told her she must put in the price of mutton and tallow and corn and so on, and then she says this: "But I like better to write of how my tiny roses are faring and the big harvest moon we watched tonight, and the singing of the *tuis* and the bellbirds and the dancing flight of the friendly fantails that precede us into the bush as we walk. How odd to think of one's descendants reading these words when one is dust and ashes. How impossible to believe that one can ever cease to be . ." and suddenly, Edmund, I found myself crying because Margaretta was dead. That she must have been gone before my own mother was born. And I could never know her. And she was just the sort of person I'd have liked for a friend. I couldn't bear to think of all that vitality and love of beauty being just a little heap of ashes.'

Edmund didn't look up for a moment. Then he said, 'Yet out of ashes fresh beauty springs to life each year ... out of the bonfires of autumn.' He picked up the volume, read over what Charlotte had just read aloud, said, 'I think by the time you've finished reading all her diaries, you *will* know her. She kept them up till 1905. Her Alfred died that year and Margaretta followed him just one month later.' He paused and added, 'I think Margaretta would rather have liked to think that someone, more than a century later, would look back and wish she had known her. Even shed a tear for her. Good night, Charlotte,' and he picked up the tray and went out.

Perhaps if he hadn't gone then, if he had pressed the point about her reticence, her evasiveness, she might have told him the reason for it.

She smiled as she heard Tod's voice raised downstairs. 'Well, made your peace, did you?' and Edmund's carelessly natural answer, 'Too right I did. Not to worry, Tod, you'll not have to go back to my cooking.'

Charlotte switched her bedside lamp off and snuggled down. Perhaps it was just as well that Edmund had gone when he did. What lay between them was as yet too intangible, too frail, to withstand any stress. He might understand. He might not. He had resented her reticence, her caginess, he might resent her deception even more. And while this quarantine was giving them a respite as far as telling Owen was concerned, other issues must be put aside. Nothing must be allowed to place the children's welfare in jeopardy. She really didn't know Edmund well enough to be sure of his reactions. She dared not risk being forbidden this golden valley.

CHAPTER SEVEN

NOTHING was more annoying than the way Avis drifted in and out. She covered the miles between the two farms far too often for Charlotte's serenity. She brought over messages from her father, hints from her mother, tried to advise Charlotte on how Edmund liked things, from cooking his meals to making his bed. She kept telling Charlotte how it cheered Edmund up just to see her, in this boring time of quarantine. 'He said how marvellous it was that I'd been a contact too.' Charlotte bore it all with no outward sign of it mattering in the slightest.

One morning it was because she vowed she'd not been able to get them on the phone and she just had to find out how Owen was. Charlotte was pretty sure there was nothing wrong with their instrument.

She said dryly, 'Couldn't you get the hospital either?'

Avis looked hurt. 'Of course, but if you aren't a close relation you get nothing but: "He spent a comfortable night." I wanted to know more than that, naturally, and,' turning to Edmund, 'I thought you'd get news straight from his doctor or the Sister.' True enough, but—

She had brought a fruit cake over. 'Owen said time and again no one could make a fruit cake like me. Not too dry, not too soggy.'

It was a pity that Tod was there and that derision rasped his tone. 'Pity Owen's never tasted Sharlie's. That's a joy in store for him.'

When Avis had gone that day, Edmund said mildly, 'Tod, you'd better stop baiting Avis. I've always believed in living at peace with one's neighbours. And Avis's father is a great friend of Dad's. You know that. She's very concerned about the situation . . . you've got to hand it to her. She never fails to ask has Phyl rung or written. She often rides across if she sees me, just to ask that.'

Charlotte pursed her lips. That was true. She always did ask, and always with that same look of dread, or unease in her eyes. Well, as much as Charlotte detested her, perhaps she really had suffered badly from unrequited love, and thought that if Phyl never returned she might just have a second chance with Owen. Even if he had dressed her down for her criticisms of Phyl, sheer persistence might batter down his resistance, if his marriage was irretrievable. How lonely Owen was going to be, how emotionally confused, at a time when, physically, he was least able to bear it. Charlotte knew that she herself was now accepting the fact that Phyl might never come back. And what would happen to the children?

Charlotte felt as if her thoughts went round in a ceaseless treadmill. When it was all over and things tidied up as well as could be, when Owen came home from hospital, what would happen to her? Charlotte would have to confess who she was before that day, because it was more than likely Owen knew his wife's cousin Lacey was really Charlotte Smith. He'd probably even mailed letters to her, for his wife.

But if she could stay here, undiscovered, as long as possible, at least she was with the children. Beyond that she dared not think. Owen had legally adopted them, but might his attitude change? Would they, if so, and they didn't want the children there as a reminder of a faithless wife, allow her to take the children up to her mother's home in Wellington? But that problem had to be left to the future. She could only play it along from day to day.

It would have been less complicated if her own feelings hadn't been so involved. If every time she looked at Edmund, the clean fair length of him, his nuggety stockiness, his dependability, his kindredness, the bleached short hairs on the backs of his hands, she hadn't been swept with intolerable longing for a different set-up. So foolish to wish to turn back the clock, for things to start again, for things to go to plan, the dreams she had dreamed as she flew in from England, looking forward to the reunions with Mother and Dad, Ivan and John and Diana, her dear, dear family, and the long stay with Phyl on a farm that had sounded just the sort of place she loved best, a place of sweepingly wide acres and dimpled hills and valleys ... well, that at least had exceeded her expectations ... the Forbidden Valley, with, at its apex, the Little Heaven, was the place in which she would like to spend the rest of her life. With Edmund. With Margaretta and Dorothea, the kindly pioneer ghosts, with all the others who had contributed to the Leigh tradition of happy marriages. Oh, if only she had met Edmund in that uncomplicated way. Oh, she ought to hate Phyl for what a mess she had made of all their lives.

As always at the thought of her, the feeling of incredulity hit Charlotte like a physical blow. She turned away from the pain sharply, saw a pile of Edmund's farm socks she'd paired up last night after airing them, and decided to put them away. She went along to his room.

What a mess Edmund had made of this drawer! He must have been looking for something. It was all stirred up and certainly wouldn't hold this bundle of socks unless she tidied it. She pulled the drawer right out, put it on the bed, scooped up the contents and dropped them on the bedspread. She'd start from scratch.

And there, at the bottom, lay a key!

She knew instantly that this was the key to that locked drawer in the desk. She also knew she was going to use it to look for Phyl's letter. There might just be something in it that would give her a clue, or some hint that she, as Phyl's cousin, would be able to understand, which Edmund, not knowing her, wouldn't. It was sly, unethical, horrible, but the situation was unbearable, having to hear it all secondhand.

She seized the key, marched along to the living-room, and across to the desk. She mustn't give herself a chance to change her mind, to let her conscience take over, to have all the things she'd lived by rise up to tell her not to do this thing. Besides, it was so ideal a time. Tod and Lance were concocting some bit of machinery at the blacksmith's forge, and Edmund had said he was off to the far boundary, to inspect some fencing.

The key fitted.

The drawer was a deep one, filled with family papers. Charlotte riffled quickly through those. Last but one she came upon Phyl's letter, recognizing her handwriting immediately. Yes, it bore signs of having been blown about the room, in its crumpled condition, that had been smoothed out.

Everything in Charlotte seemed to be stilled as she read, her lower lip caught between her teeth. There it was, in uncompromising black-and-white, in terms that couldn't be misunderstood, even if they didn't state enough to provide any clue to her whereabouts, or with whom she had gone, forsaking Owen and her children. . . .

It had been dashed off in great haste, her writing was less neat than usual. As well it might have been.

'Dear Owen,

'I'm afraid you'll have to meet Edmund yourself. Please forgive me for doing such a thing to you at this time, but I'm quite desperate, have been for weeks. If I don't go now I never will. I've fought against having to do something. I wasn't brave enough to tell you, but I can't hold out any longer. I'd hoped to wait till after Edmund arrived, but just after you left for the Parkinsons, something happened that left me in no doubt as to what I must do, or lose everything I hold most dear.

'I ought to have told you long since, but I couldn't face it. Night after night I tried to tell you, but the words would stick in my throat. But now, with not much time to spare, I must go before you come home. It's best this way, anyway, because you wouldn't let me go.'

Charlotte threw that page down and rushed on with the next.

'It's a strange and terrible situation – one you can never imagine yourself involved in. It's like something on a TV play. I can see nothing for it but to go to him. I can't do anything else. All our happiness depends upon it. Thank goodness the children are away for the weekend. I don't know what your people will think of me for involving you all in such a situation. But there must be a way out of it. I feel trapped. We'll have to get a divorce. I must be free. And now I must fly. There's so little time. Love, Phyl.

P.S. I don't know what to tell you to tell the children. Perhaps for now they could think I've been called away for illness. You could say Aunt Rhoda in Wellington is ill and I've gone to nurse her. Don't forget to pick the children up.'

Charlotte felt as if she was turned to alabaster and she was certainly just as cold. She stared stupidly down at that signature, 'love, Phyl'. *Love.* How crazy could a woman get? It must have been sheer infatuation to render her as unfeeling as that. *Love!* And to drop the bombshell of her departure, in a letter like that, into an unsuspecting husband's lap just when he was setting out to meet his brother after a two-year separation, was cruel indeed.

And such a husband, one who had given her children his own name, because Phyl had known Ranulf's name was a tarnished one.

Had Owen been entirely unsuspecting, though? They couldn't possibly know that. When Owen was told, it might not be the mystery to him it was to them. He might know to whom his wife had gone, and where.

Why had it been so imperatively sudden for Phyl to go to this man? Had he rung up and issued an ultimatum, tired of weeks of waiting for Phyl to make up her mind?

Charlotte knew a heaviness of spirit that was beyond hope. No wonder Edmund was bitter. What he had to face his convalescent brother with was beyond bearing. Anger against Phyl rose up in her, swamping all other feelings and causing a mist before her eyes.

When it cleared she began reading the letter again, searching it sentence by sentence, phrase by phrase, trying to make sense of it, looking for a reason, a hint of whereabouts. It was extremely incoherent. Perhaps that was understandable. Or had she known Owen would guess at what she'd not said? Not that anything could help. She knew that now. Nothing could.

She was so engrossed, so horrified, that none of the usual sounds of people approaching reached her consciousness. Then Edmund's voice, in tones she'd never heard from him before, demanded of her:

'Charlotte, what in hell do you think you're doing?'

As she swung round she felt the blood leave her face, and her cup of humiliation was full when she saw not only Edmund, but Avis too, in riding kit, standing with him in the doorway, palely gold and triumphant.

Charlotte couldn't speak for fright. Her throat muscles seemed paralysed, her mouth parched.

Edmund's voice was almost expressionless now, simply stating a fact, heavily. 'You're reading Owen's letter from his runaway wife! What a despicable, mean, prying thing to do! And *what* a hypocrite you are. You said you detested people sneaky enough to read other people's letters. That if Avis had read the first line or two automatically when she gathered up the blown-about pages, she had no business to read the lot. Why, you sanctimonious humbug! You said it was unforgivable – that anybody decent would have thought how terrible for other eyes to see them, replaced them, weighted them down, and never let on to a soul she'd even been near the house that day!

'How deceitful *can* women be? You sounded so ethical, so scornful of Avis's action, but believe me, it was nothing to

118

yours, you prying busybody! *She* simply gathered up the pages, appalled to see what was on them ... *you've* deliberately searched for a hidden key to a locked drawer. I keep our most private papers there. I suppose you've even gone through my tax papers and decided how much we're worth!'

Charlotte swallowed as he paused, got control of her voice. 'I did *not* look at any of the other papers. They were no concern of mine. I was simply trying to see what your brother's wife had really written. Trying to see if a woman's intuition might have read between the lines, found some clue as to where she's gone, or who she's with.'

Avis uttered a sound of pure scorn. She laid a hand upon Edmund's arm and laughed. 'Edmund, don't listen to her. There's no excuse for what she's just done. None. Women's intuition? ... why, I'm a woman, but I've enough logic in me to accept that letter at its face value. She's just one of these prying housekeepers you read about. You'd better get rid of her, Edmund.'

Charlotte felt sick at the pit of her stomach. He would, he would! Edmund had reached the end of his tether.

There was a long, horrible silence. Edmund looked down at his feet, evidently thinking furiously. Charlotte hardly knew what she was doing. She looked down on the page she was holding, that second page, and, quite automatically, peeled off from the top of it a triangular fragment of paper, evidently from a discarded page, that adhered to it. She dropped it on the desk, looked up, but not at Edmund, at Avis.

She came out of her frozen state to stare at the girl. What a peculiar expression she was wearing! Charlotte blinked. Once more it looked like fear, a sort of fearful fascination, then as she realized Charlotte was looking at her in a startled fashion, the look disappeared. Charlotte gave herself a mental shake. Wasn't it stupid how unimportant things registered at a time like this?

Avis turned to Edmund, gave him a little shake, said, 'Send her packing, Edmund. You've got enough trouble on your plate without having someone like this in the house.'

Edmund lifted his head and looked at Charlotte, who quailed at his look. She braced her shoulders. At that moment Tod's voice from the doorway cut in. 'Send *who* packing? Not Charlotte, surely? And what the devil's it got to do with *you*, Avis? More mischief-making? Edmund, if she's been saying anything against Charlotte, surely you won't believe it? She tried to drive a wedge between Owen and Phyl, and it looks as if she might have succeeded there. Don't let her do the same to you two.'

Charlotte expected Edmund to annihilate Tod. Merciful heavens, she might lose Tod his job too. But Edmund looked at Tod without anger, only a great weariness, and said, 'Avis didn't do or say a thing. I came in to find Charlotte had pinched the key of the locked drawer in my desk and was going through my papers. How about that, Tod? She's not the paragon she made herself out to be.'

Charlotte came to life. She tossed her bright hair back. 'Tod, I *wasn't* going through his papers. I just couldn't bear this situation any longer, dreading the children asking about their mother not phoning them ... expecting her home as soon as this quarantine is over, dreading the thought of Owen coming home to a house without his wife, not knowing where she is, the scandal that's going to result ... everything! I felt desperate, and thought I might unearth some clue. That a bit of womanly intuition, a bit of reading between the lines, might just have helped.'

Tod said stolidly, 'Sounds a jolly good idea to me. Perhaps it's a pity you hadn't just asked Edmund if you could see it. That would have saved all this bally-hoo, but—' he swung round on Avis, 'but trust *you* to make a bad situation worse. And another thing – I heard Owen tell you to keep off Amberleigh property. Edmund doesn't know that – but he does now. And he'll be a mug if he allows you to influence him against Charlotte. She's been a brick. What those kids would have done without her, I don't know. She might well have picked something from Phyl's letter that Edmund didn't.'

Avis said icily, 'As you know, *I* read that letter and didn't pick up a clue from it, and I daresay I've got as much intuition as Charlotte, but I certainly would never have dreamed of breaking into locked desks to see it. Charlotte knew I'd read it, so her excuse about wanting to read between the lines sounds pretty thin to me. I think she *was* prying into Edmund's personal papers, trying to find out what the estate's worth. She's probably got an eye on him herself.'

Tod beat Edmund to it again. 'Avis! Only you would say a thing like that, and as far as the letter's concerned, *you* would only have read into it what you wanted to read into it! Let's be honest. You're just revelling in the break-up of Owen's marriage. Why the heck don't you go away from here? Do you all the good in the world to go overseas as you've often said you would – meet new people, new men – instead of staying round here making mischief. You've got the looks – if only you had a nature to match you'd be more popular. And let me tell you this ... if you as much as suggest going into see Owen when we're out of quarantine, or coming over here making a bad situation worse when he comes home, I'll see your father about you and tell him the things you tried to insinuate to Owen about Phyl, the day he told you to get out. Your father's one of the best fellows alive, but he'd soon put a stop to your caper if he knew what I knew. Now scram, or I'll tell him anyway!'

Avis scrammed, but at the outer doorway she turned and said, smiling in a thin-lipped sort of way: 'But now there aren't just insinuations about Phyl, are there? There are facts, far worse.' She disappeared.

Edmund looked at Tod. Charlotte flinched for him, but the vials of his wrath did not fall upon her champion. Edmund merely said, tonelessly, 'Thank you, Tod. Gosh, if I'm not sick of women and their devious ways. Believe me, if it weren't for the children I *would* send Charlotte packing!'

Charlotte's head came up, her eyes flashed, colour ran up into her white cheeks. 'Why, you magnanimous prig! You'll suffer me for the sake of the children – how noble! What you really mean is you hate cooking. You'd better be careful, Edmund Leigh ... I don't have to stay. I could walk out on you this very second!'

Edmund looked at her with utter contempt. 'And you were pretending that your prying was for everyone's sakes, not just beastly curiosity. If you don't stay for the children's sakes, I'll think you even more despicable. But please yourself. Only tell me within ten minutes, because if you are going to walk out on us in a temper, I'll want to ring the labour exchange in Christchurch, pronto.'

They measured glances, waited. Then Charlotte said in a gritted-teeth sort of way, 'I'll stay. Does that satisfy you?'

His voice had a whip-flick in it. 'Not entirely. I only want you to stay if you promise me none of this will show in front of the children – that you won't vent your spleen on them. Those kids are due for a big upset when we can't keep the truth from them any longer ... till then I don't want them to face any emotional upsets, such as getting used to another house-keeper.'

The hazel eyes that glared into the blue ones had fiery flecks in them. 'I would like to tell you, Edmund Leigh, that I'm only staying because I feel I must protect the children from *your* temper. I can well imagine the aftermath of this will be a sub-conscious resentment and snappiness on your part. Under these conditions I feel I must remain here to act as buffer!'

Their glances held, both of them breathing deeply. All of a sudden Tod burst out laughing, strode in between them, flung out an arm each side, pushed them further away with his hands and said, 'Now, come on, break it up, both of you. Honestly, I could bang your heads together. You're just like a couple of kids fighting. Look, we're all feeling the strain, but I'm darned if we've got to go on like in a comic opera. Lance will be in with the kids any moment.'

Charlotte said stiffly, 'I don't see anything *comical* about it. But if your boss would stop behaving like a stern grandfather in a Victorian *drama*, I'd be prepared to carry on as before ... even to the extent of pretending a friendliness towards him in front of the children which I certainly don't feel.'

Edmund said icily, 'That goes for me too. How anyone who's just been caught rifling someone else's private papers can put on such an outraged act is quite beyond me, but for the kids' sakes, all shall be sweet harmony,' and he walked out and slammed the door.

'Phew!' said Tod, getting out his handkerchief and mopping his brow in exaggerated fashion, hoping to make Charlotte laugh. 'Blessed are the peacemakers ... I don't think! I feel just as battered as if I'd been at Waterloo!'

Charlotte managed a weak laugh. 'Poor Tod! I thank you, Tod,' and she burst into tears.

Tod put an arm round her, took out his handkerchief again and pushed it into her hand. 'Never mind, Sharlie. It will all come out in the wash. Edmund's not one to sulk, never bears a grudge. He'll come round. In a little while he'll give you credit for only wanting to help.'

He kept patting her back till she felt soothed and relieved, some of the tension disappearing with the tears. She mopped up, sniffed, said, rather shakily, 'Tod, you're so sweet ... and it was so courageous of you, sticking up for me against your boss. Thank you.' She reached up, took his face between both hands and kissed him.

The door opened and Edmund stood there, surveying them sardonically.

'Well, well, well, sorry to interrupt this touching moment, but in case you were having a post-mortem on the late scene, I thought I ought to inform you I can hear Lance coming across with the children.'

Charlotte surveyed him stormily. 'Tod was being sweet to me. I could do with someone being sweet to me just now. I – I – I – just–'

Edmund held up a silencing hand. 'My dear Charlotte, I'm not in the least interested in your reasons for kissing Tod.' He transferred his angry gaze to Tod. 'But you'd better watch she doesn't make a fool of you too, lad. She may be investigating *your* financial papers before long.'

Charlotte said quietly but intensely, 'That's about the most caddish thing a man could possibly say. I was interested in nothing but the letter. I have no more personal interest in your affairs than you have in mine, and I think you ought to apologize.'

Edmund considered that in the most coolly maddening manner possible. Then he said, 'Yes, I think I ought to apologize for that. I think it *was* just the letter you were after. Most women like spicy titbits. It would be a sheer love of scandal. The bit about you thinking you might fathom something I hadn't was too, too feeble.' He turned to go away then looked back over his shoulder. 'But you were wrong about one thing. I was *very* personally interested in you. I hope you'll notice the tense I used. The *past* tense.' And he was gone.

'I have a feeling,' said Tod pathetically, 'that lunch is not going to be a really enjoyable meal.'

Charlotte shrugged. 'For the children's sakes,' she vowed, 'it just mustn't be any different from usual.'

So it proved, though no one but Tod noticed the two protagonists had very little appetite.

The rest of the quarantine dragged on. Charlotte had a lump of lead for a heart. Edmund was very taciturn, rousing himself only when the children were about. Tod had said he never sulked, but apparently this was an exception. Charlotte was meticulous in everything she did, careful not to anger him. Edmund treated her with a cold courtesy. He seemed to spend long hours away from the house, and she wondered sometimes if he spent them across at Longbanks, the Weybourne homestead. She didn't care, she thought drearily. Though sometimes she felt that if they didn't hear from Phyl soon, about her plans for the children, she'd go screaming mad.

One lunchtime Edmund announced he was going over to the Sandringhams' to help Bill with some paperwork and would the kids like to come with him. Barbie was all for it, but Mark elected to stay. He was building himself a hut in the copse above the stables and wanted to go on with it. It was a dreamy afternoon, and as the men were away out on the opposite hill, Charlotte thought it a good time to get on with some baking. She liked cooking, but it was a constant and losing battle here keeping the tins filled. Batches of cookies and biscuits just melted like snow in a heat-wave.

She went up twice to make sure Mark was all right. He was an adventurous little boy, and she was terrified he might suddenly decide to explore the bush that so soon here became featureless and dense. But he was also an obedient boy, and Owen, and since then Edmund, had dinned it into him that he was never to stray beyond the fences, on his own.

The last time, he looked up from hammering a box to a tree-trunk to serve as a seat, beads of perspiration on his short upper lip, his fringe pushed all awry because he'd been mopping his forehead in true workman style. 'Sharlie, how about bringing afternoon tea up here? It would save me stopping. I hate stopping in the middle of a job.'

'All men do,' said Sharlie gravely. 'I'd like a break myself. Think you can fix another seat while I'm getting it ready? I'll have to wait just a few minutes till my banana loaf comes out, that's all.'

Mark looked up, licked his lips. 'Could we have a slice, hot, with some cream on top, Sharlie, like we do with gingerbread? Don't you think it would be nice?'

'I believe it would. Good idea. Well, get cracking on that other seat, Mark boy. I'll be about ten minutes or so.'

She set out a large tray with scones with blackcurrant jelly, a mixture of the biscuits she'd made, including Mark's favourite marshmallow ones, and spooned whipped cream over the hot banana loaf in two dessert plates. She didn't bother to make tea. She would share Mark's favourite drink, pineapple juice and grapefruit juice added to dry ginger ale. She put it in a huge jug, added ice-cubes, picked up the tray.

How idyllic it all seemed ... if only things had been different. If Phyl had been sharing the fun of this, if Edmund had been there, with no friction between them, no burden of intolerable worry sitting upon them as the day of truth for Owen drew near.

There was no stock on the hill, so she could leave the gate open. It would be easier for carrying the tray back, even if, no doubt, it would be appreciably lighter! She put the tray down, picked up a piece of wood, blocked it open with that, picked up the tray again and was carrying on up the slope.

At that moment she heard a blood-chilling scream from Mark that rooted her to the spot, then out from the knoll of trees he came, terror in every line of him, flying downhill towards her. What on — then she saw a huge ugly shape break cover from the trees and come after him, a hairy, low-set animal with vicious white tusks gleaming ... a wild boar.

Charlotte threw the tray from her, raced up towards Mark, who was now quite near her, held out her hand, caught his as she turned to race down with him. They went helter-skelter, aware that the boar must be gaining on them, but they must get through that gate and secure it ... oh, thank God she'd propped it open! Their speed was amazing ... but so was the boar's ... they shot through the gate, their impetus carrying them on, and Charlotte swerving to a turn to slam the gate shut, shouting to Mark to run on, run on ... She got a hand on the gate, gave a terrific swing to dislodge the block of wood, and it crashed to just as the boar charged at it ... she had been a split second too late. It was flung back, splintering, before the catch could connect ... the huge fellow came thundering through, making the most horrible noises, shaking his head from the impact with the gate, then he hesitated ... one quarry was further on, one to the left of the onrushing path.

Charlotte screamed at the top of her lungs, 'Mark, get into the house — go for your life — I'll dodge!' but he had stopped, looked back for her. The boar decided to go for her ... Charlotte zig-zagged madly, and rather effectively, and it brought her nearer the garden, and some cover. She screamed at Mark: 'I'm coming after you, down the path, quick!' and he turned to obey.

Charlotte made a sudden sideways dash ... she must keep between the animal and Mark. They ran down the path ... she saw Mark trip, was near enough to catch him up, and save him from falling, pulled him into the rhododendron bushes on the left; the boar rushed on, stopped, foiled, and they could hear it coming back.

Charlotte yanked Mark along, down this side path, fled with him straight through the herb-garden, saw with horror that the boar was nearly upon them, leapt on to the verandah, realized she had no time to slam the kitchen door behind them, flew straight through the kitchen into the hall, and into Edmund's bedroom, slamming the door behind her just in time. Idiotically she turned the key. Any moment that colossal weight was going to be hurled against the door. She picked up Mark, flung him on to the bed, rushed to the window, which, praise be, was on the catch, pushed it wide, turned to grab Mark, who was silently terrified, thank goodness, because she was sure yelling would incite the boar still further, when she realized the boar had rushed on into the drawing-room. The sounds of crashing indicated disaster there.

The door was right opposite this one. She whispered to Mark that he was to stand on the windowsill, ready to drop out of the window if the animal chased her into here, and beat the big gong on the verandah to bring Tod and Lance rushing, but to shut the back door first. Mark nodded, his eyes wide, implicitly trusting her to do the right thing.

Charlotte stealthily turned the key, and the handle, got one glimpse of the boar charging the window-seat at the far end of the drawing-room, was across the passage and had the door slammed shut before he had time to turn round. She flew back into the bedroom, snatched Mark off the windowsill, and rushed out of the house with him, shutting the back door safely behind them!

She seized the hammer and beat the gong till the very hills reverberated. Relief at their personal safety was superseded by a sickening awareness of the horrible damage that boar was going to do to the lovely old furniture in that darling room. Pieces that Alfred and Margaretta Leigh had brought out from Surrey with them, other pieces that Alfred and Jonathan had lovingly wrought from trees they had known and loved . . . the coffee-table that was heart-of-*totara*, the beechwood cabinet, carved and ornamented . . . She said to Mark, 'We'll go round to the window and peer in.'

They did, quietly, not to attract his attention. Charlotte was horrified . . . the big oak dining-table that had survived three months in a sailing-ship without a scratch was on its side, broken glass was everywhere from the vase that had stood on top, books were ripped out of bookcases, upholstery on the easy chairs torn. The boar was wrestling madly with some velvet curtains he'd torn from the far door, and the sound of his fury was spine-chilling. Oh, how long would the men take? . . . oh, if only she knew how to handle a gun, but then she'd never fancied killing anything . . . The pig turned, scored a deep gash along the wooden fender that was an antique piece, paused for a moment, then rushed at the dining-table. Charlotte got her eye on a rosewood writing-desk that Edmund had once told her Alfred's father had fashioned . . . it was exquisite, valuable, and in the light of family history quite irreplaceable. He might turn his attention to that next.

Charlotte knew she mustn't risk Mark's life or her own, by trying to open that door to let him out, but she must do something. She couldn't see years of tradition and history and craftsmanship destroyed. She said to Mark, 'Quick, I'll get one of the clothes-props,' and they flew to the kitchen lawn, grabbed one, came back to the little terrace below the drawing-room windows, and where there was a stone seat against them. Charlotte got up on the stone seat, pulled down the top of the sash window, and thrust the prop through like a lance; if she could distract that boar enough, it might give time for the men to arrive and despatch it.

'Mark, you're to go to the far gate, by the stables, where the men will ride in. You're to stay on the far side of it, with the gate shut. Even though I don't think there's a chance of him busting out. And direct the men round to this window, with a gun.'

Mark fled, obedient as children always were, in dire emergency.

Charlotte got the clothes-prop in, felt splinters running into her fingers, but no matter, and the boar turned, an animal at bay. How incredibly evil it looked! Charlotte lunged with the prop, not to strike it, but to tantalize it, to get its attention focused on something moving, to halt its trail of destruction. It worked. The prop was terribly heavy, and she had it at a very bad angle, but it worked! Charlotte hoped she wouldn't tire before the men got here. The damage in the room was awful, yet not nearly as bad as it might be. The boar didn't seem to be aware of her, only of this object that kept thrusting at him and withdrawing.

Charlotte felt as if her shoulder-blades were being torn apart . . . she must lever it round, balance it better . . . but it had stuck a little. She gave a terrific heave, the boar put all his weight on the next attack, then fell back, and to her horror Charlotte saw the end of the prop swing up, relieved of his weight, miss the chandelier by inches, and sweep the old black marble clock from the mantelpiece clean off it. It fell with a sickening thud . . . on to the boar's head. The next moment Charlotte was staring in disbelief as the boar collapsed, pitched forward, rolled over, then lay sideways, its neck bent back. She'd knocked it clean out!

With a clatter, as, unnerved, she relaxed her hold, the prop slid right into the room. Well, heaven only send that boar stayed out cold till the men arrived.

The next moment she knew they had. They were shouting, 'We're coming, we're coming!' and they were there, Mark in the lead.

Charlotte got down shakily, said, in the tone of one who didn't really believe it, 'I – I knocked him out – with the marble clock!'

The men stared. Rushed to the window, peered in, said, 'By gosh, she has,' and, 'Stone the crows, that's it!' Then they turned round and started to laugh.

Tod shook his head. 'I've never known anything like it. You look such a slip of a girl, Sharlie, but I don't reckon any woman has ever brought down a wild boar in unarmed combat before! But what presence of mind . . . to even think about it. Must have taken some levering off, and timing . . . you'd need just the right moment.'

Charlotte started to laugh too. 'Oh, I don't deserve that much credit. It was a sheer accident. I *knocked* it on to him. What do we do now? I mean what happens when he comes round?'

Tod took another look. He turned round. 'I don't think he will. I think you've broken his neck.'

Sharlie said, peering in, doubtfully, 'He's so huge he's hardly got a neck. Could I possibly have done that?'

Lance said, 'It was sheer luck, or providence or something. Anyway, we'll make sure of him. Well, I dunno. I've an idea that if we *had* been around, we'd have made a lot more mess despatching him. Gosh, the press will make something of this! You'll get headlines.'

Charlotte looked horrified. 'You mustn't! Owen would read it. He mustn't know I'm here. He would want to know why you have a housekeeper.'

The men looked cheated. They'd been looking forward to spreading a good story; they shrugged, laughed, said, 'Well, let's get cracking on the clearing up. Better get it under way before we ring Sandringhams' to tell Edmund. He'll never believe it, anyway.'

But the boar, dead as a dodo, was just being dragged through the door on to the back verandah when Edmund and Barbie arrived. They drove up to the yard gate, stared.

Edmund came striding across. 'What in thunder—?'

Tod said, 'You'll need a grain of salt. More than a grain. This chap chased Mark right down the hill from where he was building his hut ... Charlotte did the matador act, tried to divert him ... rushed Mark through the garden with the boar in hot pursuit. They dived into your room, the boar into the drawing-room, where he made a right mess of things. That made Charlotte flaming mad, so she shoved the clothes-prop through the window and attacked him, finally felling him with Alfred's marble clock ... she wasn't going to let him smash Margaretta's rosewood desk to pieces, not her. She certainly acts in the Leigh tradition, doesn't she? Wait till your father hears ... it even caps his story of falling on a boar!'

Tradition. But she was only a passing stranger to Edmund, someone he'd engaged in a moment of need and now despised. Someone she'd deceived, who'd be even more furious when he found out who she was ...

Edmund was looking bewildered ... or something. As if trying to take it in. As if he'd think it was a tall story if it wasn't for that carcase at their feet.

Then he looked at her and said, 'You tried to divert his attention from Mark to you? Why, you might have—' he stopped.

Mark was dancing with impatience ... it was *his* story. He'd been in it right from the start, he was trying to say. So Edmund didn't finish what he'd been going to say.

Mark rushed on, his account, through the eyes of a small boy not losing any of its drama, but also it didn't need embroidering. It was all there, every exciting moment.

Suddenly Charlotte sat down on the edge of the verandah and said shakily, 'Isn't it odd? My knees have gone all wobbly *now*.'

Lance said, 'We heard Mark's scream from where we were ... we had the glasses with us, and snatched them up and tried to focus them, but there was only a flashing movement – they moved so fast we couldn't follow them. At least *I* couldn't follow them. Tod tried to grab the glasses off me. We knew something was wrong, and were on the horses in a flash, and on our way ... then that frightful clangour broke out with the gong, so we knew someone was still above ground ... boy, did we fly over the fences? I reckon I could go in for show-jumping any time now.'

Tod came in – everyone interrupted, exclaimed, added bits here and there. Edmund said quietly to Charlotte, 'I'll thank you later, Charlotte, for saving my nephew.' It was the hardest thing she ever did, not to say she'd been saving her own cousin. She simply didn't answer him.

There was a lot to do, the damage to inspect, the damage that would have been so much greater without Charlotte's presence of mind. They restored the room as much as they could. Charlotte went to pick up the clock. 'My goodness, no wonder it broke his neck. I've never known such a heavy one. It must have been the swing and the leverage of the prop that sent it flying. But I don't suppose it will ever go again.'

It was the first time since the incident of the letter that Edmund had smiled like that. 'That clock hasn't gone since it left England more than a century ago, so don't blame yourself for that, you chump.'

That 'chump' after Edmund's politeness of the last few days sounded like an endearment to Charlotte, but she hardened her heart against it. They examined everything thoroughly. There would be scars, but nothing that couldn't be patched up in some way, in this household where their ancestor's skill with wood had been preserved to this generation. Charlotte had seen specimens of woodwork that Edmund and Owen and their father had fashioned. There would be hours of work ahead of them, but some day there would be only faint marks left to show what had happened in this day and age. But Charlotte would never see these things restored. Once Owen was home, all decisions would lie with him. She couldn't imagine any place for her here. Edmund despised her.

It was evening before he sought her out. He had an air of purpose about him, and she realized with a bump of her heart that the quiet conversation he'd had a few minutes or so ago with Tod and Lance had meant, in all probability, that he'd asked them to leave them alone.

Charlotte was sitting reading by the living-room fire, in a dress with russet stripes in its vivid green, a dress that brought out the auburn of her hair, the creamy ivory of her skin, the chestnut of her winged eyebrows, the green glints in the hazel eyes. She was quite unaware of the picture she made, there with only the firelight and the glow of the standard lamp upon her. She felt tired to death, with the excitement of the day, the sheer physical effort, her terror for Mark and herself, and underlying all, her unhappiness and anxiety.

She had shadowy hollows beneath her prominent cheekbones and her eyes, and a certain wistfulness that added charm. She didn't look up as Edmund drew near.

So she jumped as he spoke and at once recognized the purpose and the planning.

Edmund sat down on the couch beside her, possessed himself of one of her hands, smiled. 'We have some talking out to do, Charlotte. I've got to say how sorry I am I was so scathing about your hunting out that letter. I've been trying to fathom out my feelings when I saw you reading it. The disillusion I felt when you'd been so scathing about Avis doing just that. Tried to tell myself that all women must be the same ... deceivers. Like Phyl. But it's no good. I can't feel that way about you. And then today – that wild boar – the danger—'

He stopped, because she had risen, her listless hand withdrawing from his. Her tone was cold, none of the fine temper she'd been inclined to lash him with before, just complete indifference. She was proud of herself for achieving it.

She said, 'Don't bother, Edmund. I realize that having to be grateful to someone you despise must be very awkward for you. Think nothing of it. I was there – a child was in danger – I'd have done it for any child, *anybody* would have done it for any child. It's not bravery, or anything else, it just happens, and you act automatically. I can't stand gratitude. The fact that I saved your nephew from being gored by those tusks doesn't mean you have to overlook my sneakiness, my curiosity. After all, even criminals have heroic moments given the right time and right incident. And I couldn't care less. And right now I want to ring Ivan – my brother's partner, remember? He wrote asking me to ring. And after that I'm going to my room to write letters.'

She talked for quite a long time to Ivan, and very affectionately. She knew Edmund was sitting there in the living-room within earshot. As he hadn't tumbled to anything last time, he wouldn't now. Then she finished up by saying, 'Well, it's been a great relief that no one else on that plane seems to have contracted typhoid. Well, it ought not to be long now, Ivan, before we'll all be together again. Won't it be marvellous? Right back to Surrey days when there was always the four of us. When Edmund Leigh's brother comes out of hospital, he may know where his wife is. I'm sure he'll have some idea of where her fancy lay. And the responsibility for the children will be his, and I'll come down to you all.' And she said goodbye before the mystified Ivan could demand what she meant. Later he'd decide she had someone listening in to her end of the conversation, and had had to keep on pretending she was no relation.

Charlotte swept into the living-room, scooped up her book, didn't look at Edmund standing in front of the fire, said carelessly 'Goodnight, Edmund,' and climbed the stairs to her room.

CHAPTER EIGHT

THEY all grew a little tense as the end of the quarantine drew near. The hospital was reporting good progress now, though fortunately Owen had no access to a phone. Judy came over a lot, bringing her children to play with Mark and Barbie. She thought Charlotte was looking extremely thin . . . she added, 'So is Avis. Her mother actually asked me over for a chat the other day to relieve her boredom. I felt though that she really wanted to gossip over the situation here, but to my great surprise, Avis promptly shut her mother up. I felt slightly aggrieved at having to give her credit for that. And Avis looked terribly thin, and worried. Almost sort of hunted, but perhaps I'm being imaginative. When she went out to make afternoon tea Mrs. Weybourne said, "If only that unfaithful woman had never come here, Owen and Avis might have been married by now. My poor girl!" It's just plain ridiculous. Owen never looked her way.'

Charlotte kept her own counsel. Avis would be scared Judy would tell Tod and that Tod would see Avis's father about the mischief she'd tried to make. Judy went on, 'Avis did try to pump me later, though, when she came out to see me off. Asked had we heard from Phyl, said she was sure we would, sooner or later. Doesn't she come over here so much? Has Edmund had the sense to put her off?'

'Yes, I think you could say he was somewhat off-putting,' said Charlotte cautiously.

'Well, good for him. I had an awful feeling she might transfer her feelings for Owen to Edmund. Weybourne's boundary with Amberliegh's is near that little triangular paddock of ours, and Bill's been diverting the little stream there – it's been undermining a fence – and twice he caught sight of Avis, on horseback, watching Edmund through binoculars. Then she'd ride over to join him – as if she had just casually happened on him. Don't let her get her hooks in him, Sharlie.'

Charlotte boggled. 'What's it to do with me?'

Judy looked at her and smiled, 'Everything, I should think.'

Charlotte regarded her steadily. 'That's just not true.

Edmund and I clash a lot. Don't matchmake, Judy, it can be so embarrassing.'

Judy waved an airy hand. 'Oh, I never matchmake. I just let things take their natural course, but that girl will bear watching. That day Bill was over here borrowing Edmund's stapler, Edmund and Avis were in the stable. She was telling Edmund how she'd always adored Te-iti-rangi. Even Bill saw through it, and men are very obtuse about such things, usually, aren't they!'

All Charlotte said was, 'Then let's hope Edmund does too,' and changed the subject.

Two days before the end of their isolation, Judy came over and took the two children across to her place for the day. She said to Edmund in Charlotte's presence, 'You two have had a fearful lot of strain. Do you good to go for a long ride this afternoon, over the hills and far away. Have you ever taken Charlotte up Rainbow Gully? To the top ridge?' She turned to Charlotte. 'It's the most magnificent view, as far as the eye can see are range upon range of foothills, finally folding into the Alps. It might refresh you for what lies ahead. You both look strained.'

Charlotte said hastily, 'Nice of you to suggest that, Judy, but I'd be very grateful for the chance to stock up the larder without any interruptions from the children.'

Edmund backed this up. 'I can't spare the time either. I'm still busy on that boundary. But it will be good not to have to keep an eye on the children. That wild boar business has made us all a bit nervous.'

When they were gone and Edmund had ridden off and Charlotte had made gingernuts and peanut cookies, neither of which had turned out more than fair to average, she decided she wasn't in the mood for baking, and perhaps you needed a light heart for it, to say nothing of being able to concentrate on it, instead of milling about on this problem of Phyl. She pulled a polo-necked shirt on over her slacks, caught and saddled Floss and rode out into the hills.

The sunshiny golden peace of the day seeped into her, making all worries seem distant and hazy . . . discord and unfaithfulness and distrust didn't seem part of this scene. She followed one path after another, not caring where she went, but suddenly realized this one, along which Floss was picking her way so certainly, was leading to the ford below Te-iti-rangi. The poplars and the willows were so thickly leafed now that she was almost to the river before she could see the terraced garden.

She caught her breath in at its wild loveliness. Anemones ran in purples and reds in the long grass, their blooms smaller than the cultivated ones at Amberleigh, but reminding Charlotte of the wild flowers of the pastures she and Phyl had wandered over during a holiday in Switzerland, long ago. With Phyl. Oh, it was beyond bearing! Everything, even on a day of escape, always came back to Phyl and Phyl's defection.

Suddenly a glint of silver, moving, caught Charlotte's eye. What ... who ...? Then she focused. It was Avis, on her dapple-grey mare, a magnificent mount, riding swiftly away from the old homestead, on the overgrown drive that led up to the road gate. Charlotte reined in. What on earth was Avis doing here? Avis hadn't seen her, couldn't have. Charlotte watched till Avis was out of sight, then listened till she heard the sound of cantering hoofs on the metalled road above the house. She urged Floss on and splashed gently into the ford. Why on earth she felt this deep unease she knew not.

She'd come up out of the river and was halfway up the track to the house when she saw it, smelt it ... a thin spiral of smoke from the back of the house. She reined in, stood in her stirrups to see if it were rising from a chimney, then dug her heels into Floss's sides. There was no chimney just there ... and even if it were a bonfire behind the house, there was no doubt that the old beautiful homestead was in danger.

She turned Floss into the home paddock, flew up the terrace and into the house. She could hear a crackling ... it was along the passage ... then she saw the smoke belching out from the little downstairs guest-room. She grabbed the front door, pulled it shut ... any draught would fan the blaze ... looked helplessly around. It would take far too long to fill vessels for water, even if she could find any, and the taps might be so rusted up, there'd be no water anyway.

She saw the old velvet curtains in the hall, thick and smothering, gave a great tug at both of them. There was a terrific splintering sound as the old bamboo pole gave way and they fell down, enveloping Charlotte in choking dust. She scooped them up, dropped one against the door, flung it open and rushed in with the other. The old bed, wooden, with its flax mattress, was well alight, and the amount of smoke was terrible and terrifying. With a strength born of grim determination and the knowledge that she was the only one who could save Te-iti-rangi from total destruction, Charlotte thrashed frantically at the flames, thankful velvet was so solid, so little inflammable ... after the first onslaught she folded the curtain and bashed on, uttering little distressed cries and grunts as she did so. She snatched at some ancient cushions on the old basket chairs, crushed them down on other parts of the mattress, knew distress as she saw the floor starting to blacken from scattering fragments of the dry flax fibre.

At times she beat at the flames with her hands, so swiftly she wasn't aware of pain, and they extinguished so quickly like that. It seemed ages before the last flame died down. Charlotte drew in a deep breath to ease her tortured lungs. Then she heard it ... a really frightening roar from the dining-room. She caught up the singed curtains, thrust open the door. The whole fireplace was a sheet of flames and the chimney was obviously well away, roaring like an express train. A great mass of gorse, or the remains of it, was tumbling about on the hearth, crackling and spitting sparks everywhere and falling on to the wooden floor. Charlotte beat at them frantically ... the stone hearth could take care of the mass, if only she stopped these sparks from flying too far out into the room. The smoke billowed into her face, her eyes poured tears, she coughed, choked, spluttered. Great chunks of red-hot soot were falling down ... oh, if only she could summon help!

Like an answer to prayer she thought of the old gong by the door Edmund had pointed out. She flew out, seized the iron mallet and swung furiously and speedily at the gong till the whole valley seemed to reverberate with the sound, echoing back against mighty yellow cliffs and waking a hundred echoes further away against gorge walls and rocky peaks. It might be hopeless, because she thought Edmund was nowhere near, but there was always the chance that someone on Marsh's farm, the nearest, might hear it, if working on this side.

As she turned to fly in, hoping the flames had not roared right through the dining-room, she saw an old bronze flower-tub standing on the derelict verandah, full of slimy rain-water. She caught it up, staggered in, had to put it down to open the door she'd closed, went in to find the floor round the hearth ablaze and doused it with that precious rain-water.

The roar of the chimney was still scary, but she had an idea that if the chimney itself was sound enough, with no faulty creviccs to admit air and encourage flames, it might burn itself out. God send there were no exposed beams near, because the heat was blistering.

This was one of the things isolation brought you at a time like this ... prolonged danger. She did some more beating, finding the curtain starting to disintegrate, seized the flower-tub again, dipped it in an old water-butt, rushed back, and after using it to good effect, returned to find the flax mattress still smouldering. She got another lot of water, soaked it, then, when it was cool enough to handle, dragged it by the corners right out on to the stone terrace and tipped it over on to the lawn. The breeze fanned the fibres so that it burst into flame, but it could do no harm there.

Floss was charging madly round the paddock, whites of eyes showing, uttering horse-screams of alarm, shrill and wild, adding to the confusion. Flames were shooting out of the chimney and sparks flying up into the air and landing on the roof. Thank heaven it was corrugated iron! Charlotte hoped no spark landed in the birds' nests which were bound to be clustered under the eaves.

In with the tub again at the very moment that a huge mass of soot dislodged and, looking like an evil ball of fire from the heavens, fell into the hearth and burst, scattering sparks everywhere. Charlotte sloshed at the fragments nearest, the water sweeping them back into the hearth, seized the curtains again and with a tremendous gesture, shaking each one out, flung them over the glowing pieces on the tinder-dry floor, then flung herself on top, beating them flat.

She was only dimly aware of wild shouting, 'Charlotte, Charlotte, I'm coming!' then Edmund was in the room, and after one amazed and comprehensive glance was on the other curtain, beating as she was. In another couple of minutes it was all over save for the still roaring, though less flaming, chimney.

Edmund pulled her off her curtain on to her feet, let her go, went on stamping, picked the curtains up, shook them, trod on the remaining sparks and said roughly, 'You little idiot ... why didn't you just let it burn! You could have been burned to death, overcome by smoke ... of all the crazy things!'

Charlotte glared at him. 'How could I? I'm reading Dorothea's diaries now ... how she loved this place. That mantelshelf is the one Jonathan's Maori friend carved for them as a thank-offering when Dorothea saved their little boy from under the Falls. The whole house could have gone up. Dorothea loved every nook and cranny ... these are *her* bookcases, *her* china shelves ... and I've done it, haven't I? Saved Dorothea's Little Heaven?'

Her hair was singed at the ends, her face covered with soot so thickly her eyeballs glared whitely in it, tears were rolling down her cheeks, making grotesque rivulets down them, her shirt was indescribable, and her cream trews had one leg ripped from hem to knee and she was in a flaming temper.

Edmund caught her to him, soot and all and said, 'Oh, Charlotte, what does the past and Dorothea matter against a life ... *your* life ...? You ought to have let it all go up in smoke even if it was your fault.'

That did it! One moment Charlotte was leaning gratefully against him, the next she was struggling, beating at his chest. He was so astonished at the onslaught he let her go. She stepped back, stamped her foot, yelled: '*My* fault! Mine? What on earth do you mean? How *could* it be my fault? I was out for a ride on Floss, saw smoke curling up, just after I crossed the ford, and rushed in here to find the bed blazing – in the other room. Didn't you see that mattress blazing madly outside? I got it out, but it smouldered while I was trying to get this out ... I had the mattress almost under control when I heard this frightful roar from here.' She stamped her foot again, tears of rage spoiling over. 'What do you think I did? Came in here and tried to boil a billy or something? Oh, you're the most impossible man I've ever met! Honestly, if Owen's anything like you, I don't wonder Phyl ran away!'

The moment it was out, all anger left her. That was the most appalling thing to say. She clapped her hands over her mouth, then said in anguished tones, 'Now look what you've made me say! That was dreadful of me. Edmund, I apologize for it ...' then her sense of injury flooded over her again, 'but you are the most unjust man I've ever—'

She got no further. He seized her, clapped a hand over her mouth.

'Don't say any more, Charlotte. I deserve the lot and more, but don't say another word. Let me grovel first. And I didn't mean it as an accusation ... I did think you must've lit a fire in here ... this chimney would be full of birds'-nests, but I wasn't bawling you out for starting it, I was rounding on you for risking your life. Yes, I saw Floss ... and the mattress, so I knew *you* must be inside, since no one else rides Floss. I thought you must have tried to beat out the flames with the mattress. Charlotte, I was just terrified ... I thought I might find you overcome with smoke, badly burned ... now do you understand why I let fly?' And he bent his head and kissed her.

Charlotte tasted soot and the salt of her tears, all overlaid with Edmund's kiss. She felt him shake and knew he had been mad with terror for her. But perhaps you'd be like that for anyone in such danger? They drew apart slowly.

Edmund's face was streaked with soot too, some of his, some of hers. She felt laughter bubble up within her. Edmund's face broke up too, and they clung together laughing helplessly.

When they sobered up he said, 'I was only about half a mile away. I was clearing a culvert. I didn't go to the boundary, thank goodness, though, to be frank, you appear to have coped very well without me. I arrived only for the grand finale. I never heard anything like those echoes. I hand it to you, Charlotte, you've got a grand head on you in a crisis, from putting out fires to using marble clocks as missiles in time of need! I saw the smoke, knew where it came from, thought someone must have been along this road, saw the old place on fire and hand-banged the gong. I nearly went mad when I got over the ford and saw and heard old Floss.'

Charlotte said, 'Edmund, can we do anything about that chimney? It's not as bad as it was, but that roar is still terrifying.'

He shook his head. 'Much better to let it burn out. It should be clean in a few moments. If we got it out – which would be hard, away up in there – it might smoulder and break out again. In a house Alfred and Jonathan built, there'd be no beams too close to the chimney. But I'll not dare leave it till it's cold, and that'll be hours. How do you feel? You must be horribly shaken. Would you be up to riding old Floss along the top road, in a little while, to Jack Marsh's place and asking him to come along, and get him to see if he can get Tod or Lance on the phone? He might not get them, they might still be working away.'

Charlotte nodded. She did feel shaken, but it was only temporary, she thought, plus the physical effort of all that beating. She would not admit she was disturbed by his kiss and tenderness. 'I'll manage it. It's the first farm on the far side, isn't it? I won't go in, though, seeing our quarantine isn't quite over. I'll come back here. Or if he can't get the men, I'll ride on over.' She turned to go, but suddenly Edmund caught her, pulled her round again. He did it by her elbows. 'Charlotte, let me see your hands!'

Instinctively she put them behind her back. 'They're all right. They're very superficial burns, just singed really. I'll be able to hold the reins all right. It's not as if Floss could be described as a troublesome charger, hard to hold in.'

Edmund said, 'I want to see your hands. Instantly.'

Unwillingly she held them out. The backs were only filthy. He turned them palm upwards. Even through the soot he could see the angry red of the flesh. 'You can't ride like that, Sharlie.'

The tenderness of his tone almost brought on more tears. She blinked rapidly. Then she said, 'Well, leave me here to watch and you go over to Marsh's.'

'Never in your life! If that fire broke out again, there's no knowing what you'd do, Joan of Arc. We'll wait for a bit, then you can go to Marsh's on foot. When I'm quite sure you'll not keel over.'

She was indignant. 'I'm not the keeling over type!'

His lips twitched. 'I'm sure you're not. But we all have our limits. I'm not risking it. Now I'm going to bathe those hands of yours with whatever I can find here. It'll be painful, but I would like to get some of the dirt off the wounds.'

He found an old kettle, ran the tap till the water was clear of rust and sediment, went back into the dining-room and set it on the glowing remnants in the grate. 'I just want it lukewarm, I shan't be able to get the dirt off otherwise.'

He found some old pillow-slips in a cupboard, yellow with age, scoured out the wash-basin in the bathroom, tore up some more strips, and got Charlotte to immerse her hands to float off as much soot as possible. He was very gentle, but it was quite an ordeal, she'd lost so much skin, though they were all superficial wounds.

He rummaged till he found a jar of salt and soaked more strips in salt and water, then wound them round her fingers and palms fairly expertly. It stung, of course, but it would assist a little, till she could get them properly dressed, to ward off infection.

140

'Now I'll use the rest of the water to make you a bit of instant coffee. Tod and Lance brought some tins of stuff over when I sent them over to clear the guttering the other week. They had flasks of water with them, of course. They brought a tin of biscuits too, thank goodness. I thought we'd be coming here from time to time to do a bit of work on the old place, though it'll be long enough before we start to restore it, the situation being what it is at Amberleigh. I couldn't leave Owen on his own. But I don't want the property to deteriorate any more, so from time to time, we'll get in a bit of maintenance.'

He stopped, looked at her, added, 'Thanks to you, it's still standing. I think I know what must have happened, with both bed and chimney alight. Some old swagger – tramp to you – must have crept in here last night for shelter. I expect he was sozzled and had a cigarette in bed this morning and dropped it on to the mattress. It would smoulder for ages. And he would boil himself something on that open fire, though it's funny he didn't use the fuel range. But perhaps he was warming himself up too. Looks as if he brought in some dry gorse. That goes up like a rock, though, doesn't smoulder. Odd. Still, perhaps he left the heap there and it fell on to the hot ashes.'

Charlotte started to say something, then checked herself. No, she wouldn't say she had seen Avis riding away. She didn't want Avis brought into things yet. There was something very peculiar about this. That mattress fire hadn't come from a smouldering cigarette. It had been lit deliberately. Small twigs had been piled up in the middle of it and a charred bit of paper had fallen to the ground. Was it possible that Avis, as the woman scorned, was so eaten up with spite and malice that she'd deliberately started that fire? To injure the family she had hoped to marry into? The thought made Charlotte shiver. It was so unbalanced. But there were people like that, driven mad by their own possessiveness and jealousy, till nothing mattered but revenge. But it sounded so melodramatic. She didn't think she'd voice these suspicions to Edmund. He was aware that she disliked Avis. This gesture . . . Edmund's personal reaction when he had thought she might have suffered worse than a few skin burns . . . had been very satisfying. There had been nothing in it of the humiliating gratitude he'd offered her after the incident of the wild boar. She would do nothing to shatter this armistice. So she accepted the theory of the swagger.

At that moment they heard a car. They both rushed to the

terrace. What a welcome sight! Here was Jack Marsh coming down that overgrown drive from the road. He braked, leapt out, came charging up the steps to them. 'What's been on? I heard the gong, but I was right at the far end of the farm. I rode back, got the binoculars out, saw smoke, so I got the truck out. I've a fire extinguisher in the back, but it looks as if I'm too late. What happened? Did you light a fire and set the chimney going?'

Edmund shook his head, explained his theory, told back Marsh just what Charlotte had done. 'Would you take her back, Jack, and get Greta to fix up her hands? I'm frightened of infection. I'll get up on the roof with that extinguisher. I reckon all the old soot's gone now and it will be safer. Then if you run her to the homestead you could find the men and tell them to come over here to give me a hand.'

Charlotte set her chin. 'I'm not going if you're climbing up the roof. You might fall and break your leg.'

Edmund looked at her and grinned. Charlotte said hastily, 'It's just that things keep happening one after another. There are times like that, and I don't feel like coping with any more setbacks. As it is, I'm not going to be much use to you for a day or two.'

Edmund went on grinning in the most knowing and exasperating way. 'Of course, of course, it's not just solicitude for me, it's just that it would be such a darned nuisance.'

Jack Marsh grinned too, also knowingly. Charlotte turned away.

Jack said, 'We'll both get up on the roof if that suits you, Charlotte. Look, I know this is the first time we've met, owing to the typhoid scare, but I can't possibly call you Miss Smith when we've met like this. Besides, over the phone, Judy has been singing your praises non-stop to my wife.'

Charlotte thought indignantly, 'Yes, and probably hinting that Edmund and I – oh, bother these matchmakers. If only they knew!'

It was a very effective extinguisher. There wouldn't be much danger now. Nevertheless, Edmund decided he'd get Tod and Lance to sleep at the bungalow over here tonight in case of anything flaring up from a smouldering patch. They suggested again that if Jack would take Charlotte to his place, she could have her wounds dressed properly by his wife, then—

'No,' said Charlotte very firmly. 'We aren't quite out of the safety margin, and dressing my hands would mean close contact. Jack, would you go over to Amberleigh, get hold of Tod and Lance and send them over here? They could come in the car. The horses would be here for them tomorrow – even if they both despise poor slow old Floss – and Edmund can drive me back. No sense in making more contact than we need.'

Jack looked at her admiringly. 'She's not only brave, but she's got a head on her shoulders too!'

The children were vociferously sorry they'd missed all the 'fun!' Barbie added mournfully, 'And I missed that pig chasing Mark and Sharlie too!'

There was a sweetness in having Edmund helping with the dinner, asking her advice on what to do, and he bathed the children, insisting, and rightly, that she must keep her hands dry now. Charlotte had refused to let him call the doctor or take her into his surgery. 'I honestly can't face the thought of the long drive, Edmund, and as for calling him, in a remote area like this, it just isn't fair. Someone else might take seriously ill and need him. I've had tetanus immunization, so there's no danger of that.'

They had a very up-to-date first-aid kit at Amberleigh, a necessary thing on so remote a farm, and Edmund proved adept at bandaging when he had proper supplies. He wrapped her fingers firmly and with confidence and the dressings he used were cool and soothing.

Nevertheless, they were oddly ill at ease with each other once the children had been put to bed. Perhaps it was because Edmund had so much to do for her. He had insisted on washing her face and brushing her hair, carefully separating the singed strands and snipping them off. He seemed to take an inordinately long time about it. Charlotte found herself growing tense. She was glad ... or was she? ... when he finished. Then he prowled round like a restless lion in a cage. Was he resenting having to be grateful to someone he really despised? Was his tenderness towards her over at Te-iti-rangi just a reflex action born of the attraction she had once held for him? Something he had later vowed was in the past tense. Finally Charlotte said, 'Do put the television on. I would like to see that film.'

That effectively put a stop to conversation. Charlotte pretended to be completely absorbed in it and when it ended, rather late, Edmund said, a little stiffly, not to say gruffly, 'I really think you ought to have been in bed sooner than this. I'll make us a pot of tea and you'd better turn in. I've switched your blanket on and turned the bedspread back. What would you like? A custard square?'

He insisted she took aspirin. 'Your hands might throb a bit and keep you awake.'

She rarely took any form of sedative, so fell into billows of sleep and sheer exhaustion almost immediately.

At three she woke, conscious she had been dreaming about Phyl, about Phyl's letter. Only it wasn't the same letter, because as she held it, reading it over, trying to reconcile what it had said with what she knew of her cousin, the words disappeared and other words came to take their place. But because it was a nightmare, she couldn't read them . . . they kept wavering and dissolving in front of her eyes. But she knew Phyl was trying to tell her something, was asking her for help, for understanding.

Charlotte found her pillow was wet; she'd been crying in her nightmare. Then it began to recede, though the depression on her spirits remained. Yet her mind had a clarity and freshness she had not known for some time.

And sitting up there in the dark, she knew beyond a shadow of doubt that Avis had deliberately lit that fire. That Avis would do anything. Her mind swung back to that dreadful moment of discovery when Edmund and Avis had surprised her with the letter. How Avis had enjoyed that! The look on Avis's face rose up before her . . . the triumph of it. Then that look had been superseded by another, a sort of tremor of fear. It had been glimpsed for a moment and gone, as if it had been written in water. Could it have been that she had feared Charlotte might read something between the lines, something revealing, or extenuating? But why? There'd been nothing ambiguous, only a sort of vagueness, an incoherency that didn't really explain anything. The only thing that could explain that was that Owen must know who the 'he' was, so she'd not needed to explain much.

But why had Avis looked like that? All Charlotte had been doing was peeling back that fragment of a page that had adhered to the top of the second page of Phyl's note. Something clicked in Charlotte's mind. Avis had stared, almost fascinated, at that piece of paper as Charlotte had dropped it on the desk. Again, why? Later Charlotte had swept it impatiently into the waste-paper basket.

She sat up in bed, put her light on. She drew her knees up, rested her elbows on them, and put her bandaged hands to her brow. Was she being over-imaginative? Could it be possible Phyl had written a *three*-page letter? Those pages hadn't been numbered. Phyl had been in too big a hurry for that, she supposed. That letter had been blowing round the room when Avis had found it. Was it possible a middle page, a more explanatory page, had been blown away, gone missing?

But ... but the letter had run on very smoothly. There wasn't any gap. There were no missing words. At least, she didn't think so. She thought one paragaph had ended on the first page and a new one had begun on the second, so perhaps a complete paragraph could have been blown away. The thoughts swirled in Charlotte's mind, confusing her. She wished she had looked more closely at that fragment, instead of just absent-mindedly peeling it off.

... But that basket hadn't been emptied. She was sure of that. Because Edmund used the office one far more, and they'd always had fires at night, and most scrap paper had been fired into the flames. That scrap would still be there. Charlotte thrust the bedclothes back, wincing at her vigour, picked up the torch she used for peeping at the children, and crept downstairs. Edmund's bedroom was well away from the living-room and there were no creaking boards in this house. She gained the room, closed the door stealthily and switched on the standard lamp near the desk. It cast a pool of light round her, enough for her purpose. She knelt on the carpet and tipped out the contents. Her hands clumsily spread them out. A small piece of paper would be easily distinguished from the rest. Ah, here it was. Oh, what a pity it was so tiny. It might only have been a damaged sheet of paper Phyl had thrown away. She peered at it closely, then her heart thumped. It *had* been used for writing on. The lower torn edge had one or two loops on it.

The first from the left could have been the top of a capital 'O'. That might have been Owen. Then something that could have been the upright of a 't' and the loop of an 'h' next to it. So it might have read, 'Owen, the ...' But what of it? Perhaps Phyl *had* gone on to that page, decided she wasn't expressing herself well, or saying too much, or something, and ripped it out. She could have crumpled it up, flung it into the basket, and it would have been thrown out, probably, between the time of

145

Phyl's flight and Charlotte's arrival.

A wild surmise shot into Charlotte's mind. She knew it was a wild one and shook her head for even thinking of it. She mustn't become obsessed with the idea that the blame for it all could be laid at Avis's door. If there *had* been a middle page, and Avis *had* destroyed it, nothing could reverse the fact that Phyl *had* run away – and had a divorce in her mind. Besides, it was hardly likely that Avis, who would have read straight through the letter, would have leapt to the fact that a page concealed could make matters worse. Oh, no, it was too tortuous, and she was being stupid. She'd better go to bed and try to sleep again. If Edmund caught her on the prowl again, he'd go up like Vesuvius. She was getting over-fanciful, the result of weeks of strain, the terror of their chase by the wild boar, the excitement of the fire, the quarrel with Edmund. She was probably not even right about Avis having set fire to Te-iti-rangi out of spite. Civilized people didn't do such things. Impossible to associate criminal tactics with a spot as lovely as Tapuwharua.

Besides, Judy had said Avis had been making up to Edmund, had been telling him she thought Te-iti-rangi was charming. That didn't tie in with trying to burn it down. Dawn was streaking the sky when she fell asleep again and she didn't waken till the children, bursting with virtue, were in her room, carefully carrying a tray of toast and a cup and saucer and a pot of tea. Edmund was behind them, but just looked in to say, 'Good . . . the aspirin gave you a good long night. We've all had our breakfast. Glad you didn't waken. How are the hands?'

'Not nearly as sore, thanks. I see the toast is already buttered. Mark can put some marmalade on and Barbie can pour the tea, thanks very much.'

'You deserve it. I'll get back as quickly as I can to give you a hand, but I'm just riding over to the other homestead to see how the chaps got on. It will be safe enough now, if there were no more outbreaks, but I'd like to inspect the damage myself. So long.'

The men were agreeably surprised when they got in just before lunch to find it ready for them. Charlotte had donned rubber gloves over the bandages, some very large ones she'd unearthed, and the children had managed the things she found most awkward.

'It's a real pest just the same,' she said. 'I'd promised myself

146

that I'd get those flowerbeds under the living-room windows weeded this week. You can hardly tell the violas from the chickweed.'

'Oh, plenty of time for that, Charlotte,' said Edmund. 'I'll get the boys on to it next week before Owen comes home.'

Barbie's face lit up. 'Oh, Uncle Edmund, will Daddy really be coming home as soon as that? And what about Mummy? I was just thinking: if we're going back to school tomorrow, I suppose she'll be able to come home now the quarantine's over and Daddy's out of danger.'

Edmund said hastily, 'Well, we've managed so well without her, I expect she'll want to stay in to keep Daddy company till he gets home, but we'll see. We'll leave it to her. Right, chaps, let's go out. No, sorry you can't come today, kids. I think you'd better stay round to help Charlotte. There'll be the vegetables to peel for dinner and so on.' Charlotte guessed he didn't want the children to keep asking him questions. The time was nearly on them for confession, both to Owen and to the children. What a really hideous situation!

That night, early, Edmund got a ring from the doctor in charge of Owen's case. They all fell silent, unashamedly listening to Edmund's answers and piecing the situation together, glad the children were in bed and asleep.

'Yes,' said Edmund, and his voice was heavy, 'I do realize that now the quarantine's over, we can't put off the evil day any longer. Oh, did he? Yes, I thought that would happen. Once he knows he's going to be walking, he'll plan on ringing Phyl. Well, it gave us a respite. You'll be there? What time, exactly? I'll make it very punctually. You're a busy man and we do appreciate all you've done in a problem situation. We've hoped against hope that we might have heard from her, but time has beaten us. No hope now. Well, only if it were a last-minute reprieve, but that's too much to expect. May I meet you for a few moments before we go into Owen's room? You could brief me a bit on how to answer the sort of questions he's bound to ask. Thanks very much. Then I'll meet you at two-thirty. Thanks once again, and goodbye till then.'

He came back to the table and buried his head in his hands. They all sat in silence. They'd been over this eventuality so often there was nothing left to say.

Edmund lifted his head. 'He wants me to take that damned

letter with me. If Owen doesn't see it, he'll torture himself with his imagination. The doctor's going to break it himself, though. But he feels my presence there will bring it home to Owen he still has someone of his own. But what's a brother against the loss of a wife? He thinks also that I ought to let Mother and Dad know soon, and bring them home. He thinks Mother should be here when Owen gets home. If this doesn't set him back too much, he could be out at the end of next week. I'll ring my parents at my sister's place in British Columbia when I see how Owen's taken it. They'll want to know. They're back from Alaska, so it won't take them long to fly home.'

He pushed back his chair, grabbed his pipe, went outside. Tod said, 'Let him go alone. He'll feel blue-devilled. He'll want to think out what to say to Owen, once Owen's taken in what the doctor's going to tell him.'

Young Lance said savagely. 'If only we could *do* something. But Phyl's vanished into thin air. I feel I want to pluck her out of nowhere. And there's still a part of me that won't credit that she – above all people – has done this.' But they had to, they all knew that.

It was late when Edmund returned, deep lines graven each side of his face, his shoulders sagging for once. Edmund was a beaten man. Charlotte said quietly, 'Let's have some tea, Edmund, and get to bed. There's nothing any of us can do now, and if you torment yourself by milling over it all night, you'll be in no fit state to help Owen tomorrow.'

He nodded. 'Yes, I've got to accept the inevitable now. And Owen may have had his suspicions. I mean, she referred to "he" as if he would understand.'

Charlotte nodded. She brewed the tea. They had it, eating and drinking in silence. Charlotte felt she didn't dare try to cheer him by saying miracles do sometimes still happen ... there's still time for Phyl to ring ... it would be too cruel at this juncture to even breathe of hope.

She was halfway up the stairs when the phone rang. How extremely late for anyone local to call them! She hesitated, as Edmund, also on his way to bed, took it in the hall. Could it be a last-minute reprieve? Or, frustatingly, a wrong number?

Edmund's voice was very ordinary, then it quickened with surprise and excitement. 'Where from? Oh ... right, put them on, I'll hang on.'

He covered the receiver with his hand, said urgently,

'Sharlie, this is *it*! It's Phyl . . . get on the other phone, quick, and copy down everything she says if you can, so I don't get it distorted —I'll have to repeat it to the doctor, and Owen. I must have it word-perfect.'

Sharlie was at the other phone almost before he took his hand from the mouthpiece. Despite the bandages she had the pencil at the ready in a trice and pressed the earpiece of that phone so hard against her ear, it hurt. Oh, Phyl, Phyl, let this interview go as it should. Oh, please God, don't let Edmund lose his temper so that he can persuade her to come home. . . .

Then she heard some words that knocked the props from under her: 'Amberleigh? Fiji is coming on now. . . hold the line.'

Fiji! Oh, no, it couldn't be. . .Edmund had said it was Phyl. She mustn't panic, perhaps Phyl *was* in Fiji . . . it was an island paradise . . . oh, dear God, don't let it be from *my* people, not with Edmund listening in.

But it was . . . it was her stepfather's voice. 'Is that you, Owen? It's Hugh Ward here. Look, I believe Sharlie's with you. Oh, well, I expect that, like Phyl, you call her Lacey. We're a bit anxious about her. We met some New Zealanders at a party tonight who asked hadn't my stepdaughter been on that plane that had a typhoid case on board. We thought she must be with you by now. We wondered — what did you say? Sorry, I can't hear you very well. Can you hear me all right?'

Charlotte knew why he couldn't hear very well, it was because Edmund had muttered something incoherent, as he very well might. She heard Edmund clear his throat, say, 'Oh, sorry, is that better? Well, it isn't Owen, it's his brother. But *Lacey* is right here. Just one moment. *Lacey*, take this call, will you?'

His voice was silky with rage. Charlotte gave a great gulp, waited to hear Edmund's receiver put down, didn't hear it, and knew that, justifiably, he wasn't going to put it down. He was going to listen in, so that at last he could get at the full truth about her.

How Charlotte managed to reply and sound as ordinary as she did, she didn't know. She said, 'Oh, Dad, I'm sorry. We didn't let you and Mother know because we thought you'd only worry. Yes, we all had to go into quarantine, plus all our contacts here, and Di, John and Ivan, at the Hundalee. I've kept in touch with them by phone and they've been fine too. I don't suppose this chap was anywhere near us, but they have to be most careful, don't they? I haven't heard about anyone else contracting it, so

149

that's pretty good. I think the authorities acted commendably swiftly.

'Oh, yes, Dad, I'm having a wonderful time. Amberleigh is the most beautiful estate. Yes, the children are just sweet. You'd hardly know them, the way they've grown. Barbie's very like Phyl, and Mark's like Aunt Susan. No, Phyl's well, but she's not in, or she'd speak to you, too. She'll be sorry to have missed you. Yes, it was a good idea to ring as late as this, you're sure of getting me, then. Yes, do put Mother on, though I hope it's not costing you too much. You can tell her all I've told you, anyway, and I'll try to keep it short. Oh, glad you're enjoying Fiji so much, it sounds fabulous . . .'

Her mother came on, asked a few more questions, was fobbed off in the same manner. And then – and then came the moment when saying good-bye and putting up the receiver was upon her and she must turn and brace herself to face Edmund's wrath. Not till she hung up did she hear the click of the hall instrument as he replaced it. She swung round from the living-room phone, with her back to the telephone table, put her hands on it, behind her, for the support she so badly needed. She felt the pressure of it against her burns, but physical pain didn't matter in that moment of exposure and accusation.

Edmund, for a ruddy man, was white round the nostrils. His lips, for once, were a thin line, and she'd never heard his voice so cold. She'd far rather have had fury than this sneering tone.

'Let me congratulate you, Miss Charlotte *Lacey* Smith, on your ability to lie and lie and lie. Of course it was easy to deceive a simple rustic like myself, from Down Under. We don't look for such guile in *our* women! I suppose you thought this no end of a joke . . . sniggered over it every time you rang your relations when I was safely out of the way. I can just imagine it!

'What in the world you wanted to come here for, when your precious cousin had just brought our world tumbling about our ears, I don't know—' He held up his hand. 'No, Miss Smith, don't attempt an explanation. Hearing your fluency at lying to your parents, I wouldn't believe a word you have to say. Not a word, do you hear? I've *had* it. I can't do anything about this till after I've seen Owen tomorrow and seen his reaction. I can't take any more tonight myself. I won't add distress to distress to Owen by telling him how you wormed your way in here. I'll simply tell him I got a competent woman—' his lips curled with sardonic humour – 'in to look after the children, and before he gets home I shall have engaged someone else. I'll tell him you could stay only a few weeks. Now go to bed. Don't bother to cook my breakfast tomorrow. I couldn't bear to sit at the same table with you – it would choke me. Keep out of my way. I'll get the children to take you up a tray – those hands will make a good excuse. And I'll finalize things with you – and about you – tomorrow night,' and he strode off to his room.

CHAPTER NINE

CHARLOTTE was heavy-eyed and bone-weary when she woke next morning. It seemed incredible she'd slept at all. Tod came in in the wake of the children, bearing the teapot, sure they'd trip up the stairs with it, he said.

He looked at her. 'Glad you didn't wake too soon. You look all in. Aftermath of your fire-fighting, I suppose. It catches up with one sooner or later. I think you'd better have the morning in bed. Edmund cut the children's lunches himself. I think he's worried about you.'

Charlotte would have liked to have cackled derisively.

Tod added: 'And as to what the poor beggar's got to face today, I wouldn't be in his shoes for anything. I'm sure there was no need for him to set off for Christchurch as early as this; I know he's got some business in town with the stock and station agent, but he was off and out as if his life depended upon it, soon as he cut the lunches. I'm taking the kids to the bus. He tells me he's arranged for Judy to pick them up today. She's having them for the night too. I expect he wants to talk things over with you, without the kids there.'

Tod frowned at the look on her face – she'd looked startled – and said, 'Well, it's only natural, isn't it? He'll want to tell you how Owen took it.'

Charlotte said faintly, 'Yes, of course. He'll want to discuss it with us all.'

But she knew that wasn't the only reason he wanted the children out of the way. Because he was going to send her packing. He might not even deign to tell her how Owen had taken it. He would be classing her with Phyl – untruthful, deceiving.

He was going to stand over her till she packed her things; he would carry them down to Diana's car, and see her off the premises. She knew it. And she couldn't blame him. She'd had to come, to see the situation for herself, to find out if the children were being properly cared for, not neglected or resented, but she ought to have declared herself, defied his command to her not to come, in that letter he'd written to someone he'd thought was called Lacey Ward, and it might just have been, for Edmund was a fair man – given a fair deal, that was – that he might have conceded her the right to stay to look after them. At least it would then have been done in a proper fashion. Now he was antagonized beyond hope of reconciliation.

She washed herself sketchily with the tips of her fingers, came downstairs and, despite protests from the men, managed the chores.

They came in at ten-thirty for coffee. Tod stayed on, smoking his pipe. On an impulse Charlotte said to him, 'Tod, you know that awful morning when Edmund discovered me with Phyl's letter and you butted in and saved me from the full extent of his anger?'

'Yes, Sharlie?'

'And you told Edmund that Owen had ordered Avis to keep away from Amberleigh . . . did Edmund ever refer to it again to you?'

'He sure did. After he'd gone after Avis and told her that what went for Owen went for him too. That he strongly suspected she'd put undue pressure upon Owen's marriage, and that might account for Phyl's behaviour – that she could have cracked under the strain and turned for comfort to someone else. Then he came back and told me what he'd done. He wouldn't tell you, of course, because at the time he was mad clean through with you. But why?'

Charlotte's eyes were very bright, and shrewd. 'Then that accounts for it. It was sheer badness – spite.'

'What was? Come on, Sharlie, no more mysteries. This one about Phyl's just about got me down.'

Charlotte said slowly, 'I think she deliberately fired Te-iti-rangi. Just before it went up in smoke, I saw her riding away from there. I don't like thinking those things about anyone – I felt horrible for even giving credence to it, and didn't dare risk Edmund thinking I was being catty about her. I thought he'd say I wanted to believe those things of her. So, in case I'd not thought it through properly, when he said it must have been an old swagger, smoking on the bed, I let him think it. But swaggers don't pile up bits of bark and wood and paper in the middle of a mattress and set it alight. Or bring in great clumps of dead gorse by the roots and thrust it up the chimney. It wasn't just piled on the hearth, you see, as a swagger would do. It kept falling down. If a swagger had done it early in the morning, that gorse up the chimney would have been alight long since. And there was no smoke from the chimney when I first saw the smoke coming out of the bedroom window – she'd left that open for a draught, I'd think. But she must have lit that chimney fire last, and ridden away.'

Tod got up, thumped the table. 'That's finished it! You've got to be right. I'm going over there to tear her liver out!'

His fury steadied Charlotte. She didn't feel hot, she felt cold. She caught him by the arm. 'No, Tod, not today. It could bring Avis over here like an avenging fury, an accusation like that, and Edmund's got enough on his plate today. He's going to be like a chewed rag when he gets in tonight.'

Tod saw the force of this and stumped off, muttering to himself.

Then Charlotte set about doing what she must do. It was a long chance, but it might just come off. She'd use the almost-certain knowledge of Avis's arson in a desperate attempt to clear up a mystery. She'd nothing to go on, apart from intuition, except a scrap of paper, but Avis's sense of guilt over the fire might just make her betray herself.

She rang Longbanks and luck was with her, for Avis answered.

Charlotte's tone was crisp. 'I want to see you. It's important. It's about Owen.'

There was an appreciable pause. 'What about Owen?'

'I can't tell you on the phone. I have my reasons.' She made her voice sound mysterious. 'I don't think you'd better come here, though. Tod knows about this too and he's in a terrible rage – I had to stop him coming over to your place and confronting you. I don't think you'll want me there, either. Meet me at the corner where your road joins this road. By those old stone gates. Right away.'

Avis, more than a hint of uneasiness in her tone, consented.

Charlotte found her knees were shaking, but she got the Mini out and drove along. She hadn't long to wait before she saw Avis's Mini come along the road.

Avis got out, came across to Charlotte, then said, as if glad to be able to find some small talk. 'What have you done to your hands?'

Charlotte looked down at them off-handedly, said, 'Oh, that . . . I got that putting the fire out the other day.'

'What fire?' But Avis's voice had wobbled, sounded scared.

154

'As if you didn't know!' snapped Charlotte, holding Avis's eyes. 'I mean the one you lit at Te-iti-rangi, of course.'

Avis visibly blanched. But she said, feebly, 'I don't know what you're talking about.'

Charlotte's voice was contemptuous. 'Oh, don't give me that. You were never meant to embark on a life of crime, Avis. You scattered clues like confetti, believe me! Besides, I was on the other side of the river, watching you. Tod's got the evidence in safe custody. I had to forcibly stop him not only from coming across to tackle you about it, but from going to the police in Oxford. Arson's a pretty nasty crime. There'll be a terrific scandal if he does, of course. You're going to cut a pretty fine figure!'

Avis was as white as a sheet. She licked her dry lips. 'I don't believe you *have* got proof. I think you're just trying to blacken my character. I think you like Edmund and—'

Charlotte was amazed at the menace in her own tone. 'I don't care what you think. We can prove it was you. But I've held Tod back for one reason and one only. It's over to you. You can save yourself from prosecution if you wish.'

She shut her lips tightly together, stared ahead of her, as if she knew she was in command of the situation. As if she was tough.

Avis crumpled. She looked this way and that, as if seeking an escape. Charlotte pressed the point home. 'You'd better hurry. Tod was livid. He won't wait too long. Do you want to save yourself or don't you?'

Avis was completely puzzled. 'But how do I do that?'

Here it came ... the long chance ... Charlotte drew in a deep breath, then let her have it: 'By telling me what you did with the middle page of the letter Phyl left for Owen!'

Avis gave a gasp. If possible she turned even whiter than before and croaked out: 'You know about that, too? But how – how—?'

Charlotte said, 'You saw me peel off a bit of paper from the final sheet. It came back to me ... coupled with that odd look on your face when you saw me do it. The wastepaper basket had never been emptied – there was part of a sentence on it – incidentally, I'm Phyl's cousin. Edmund Leigh didn't know that when I first came. I applied for the post of housekeeper because, quite frankly, I just didn't believe Phyl *would* run out on her husband and children. How dare you conceal that page!

Where is it, and what did it say? If you don't tell me and tell me true, supposing you can't produce it now, I'll put Tod on to you and he'll *wring* the truth out of you. And we'll let Edmund take over tonight. *Did* that page give any clue as to Phyl's whereabouts? Come on – where is she, and who's she with?'

She braced herself, but the answer almost knocked the stuffing out of her.

Avis said sullenly, 'She's in Australia with her first husband.'

Charlotte stared at her, quite unable, for a time, to form words. Then she managed: 'Have you gone completely and utterly crazy? Phyl's first husband is dead, has been dead for years. He was lost overboard from a freighter.'

Avis said, 'Then presumably his body was never found, because in that page Phyllis said that he'd been in touch with her . . . had been trying to get money out of her to keep quiet about himself. And then he'd rung her on the very day Edmund was coming home. He was in Sydney between ships. So Phyl was flying there to see him before he could join the ship and get away. So . . .' the malice and spite showed up in Avis's close-set blue eyes, 'so it's still a hell of a mess, isn't it? You haven't solved a thing. *That* will still be a terrible scandal, much more than my setting fire to that old derelict house. Owen Leigh living for a year with a woman who's someone else's wife!'

Charlotte could have throttled her, but she didn't allow her fury and dismay to show. She said with scorn, 'Who's going to make a scandal out of something even the authorities assumed was correct? Oh, poor Phyl . . . the agony of mind she must have endured. But why, why did you conceal that page? I mean—'

Avis didn't answer. Charlotte said: 'You're going to tell me why, or the whole district is going to hear about you . . . the trick you played with the letter, the arson you committed. Come on, tell!'

Avis said slowly, 'Well, the pages were blowing about. You know that. I only saw two to start with, and naturally assumed Phyl had run off with someone else. And I was glad – glad, do you hear? It served Owen right. I was glad he was going to suffer. Then I saw the other page, under a chair, fished it out and read it. And I realized that he'd suffer even more if he believed the first – oh, I knew he'd only believe it for a little while, because on that page Phyl had said she'd ring him from Sydney, but she never has. I wonder—'

It hit Charlotte with a sickening awareness ... then Phyl had disappeared. She'd been gone for weeks, without ringing, without writing. Where could she be? Phyl was vindicated, she wasn't an unfaithful wife; she hadn't callously deserted her children ... but she was gone, without trace. Remembrance of all Ranulf's cruelty rose up and hit Charlotte with a physical blow ... had he used violence towards Phyl? had he – oh, horrors – forced her to accompany him somewhere? This was ghastly!

Charlotte couldn't have told afterwards how long she'd stood there, her thoughts a whirlpool. Sheer terror of what they didn't know swept over her with a physical impact and she came up out of her immobility.

She took a step to Avis, seized her by her shoulders and, despite her burns, shook her fiercely. 'Come on, you, speak! Tell me exactly what was in that page, what Phyl meant to do, if she said she'd get in touch ... where exactly in Sydney was she going? Oh, when I think you destroyed that page I could – I could murder you!'

She was horrified at the sound of her own voice, but nothing mattered save Phyl's safety ... the thought of all that Phyl might have endured during these passive weeks when they had done exactly nothing to find her!

Avis was terrified, and no wonder, but her answer was so unexpected:

'I didn't destroy it. And it did give an address ... if it can still be read.'

'Still be read ... why? What—?'

'I crumpled it up a bit and pushed it behind a bush outside the window.'

'What on earth for?'

'Well, I knew that in a day or two Phyl would ring. She'd said she would. I only meant Owen to squirm for a day or two ... to pay him out for all I've suffered over him. I've been nearly out of my mind wondering what's happened. I thought that when she rang, and they talked at cross-purposes for a bit, and then she spoke about her first husband, they'd remember the pages were blowing about and look for it and no one would dream I'd been the one to throw it out in the garden.'

Charlotte digested this. If only she'd done that wretched

weeding, she'd have found it ... or would she? Because she might have just thrust it into the bucket with the weeds.

She said, 'Right ... you're coming back to Amberleigh with me. You're going to show me *exactly* where you put it, and I can only say heaven help you as far as Tod is concerned if the address is all washed off. Can you remember it at all?'

Avis shook her head. 'Only that it was a suburb of Sydney.'

'Well, while we're driving over you can start thinking, start trying to remember. No, you aren't going in your own car – you might give me the slip. I'd put nothing past you. You're unspeakably vile!'

They got in. Charlotte's heart was racing so much, she had to use all her will-power to steady her hands and to discipline her nerves so she wasn't a danger on the road. Not that it was far, thank God.

As they reached the stock-grid by the drive entrance, Avis said in a dry, cracked tone, 'If the page is gone, or the writing all washed off, what are you going to do?'

Charlotte was surprised at how ordinary her voice sounded. 'Tod and I will drive into Christchurch with you, get hold of Edmund before he leaves the yards – he's at a sale – and go straight round to the police station. Phyl's got to be traced, so you'd better start trying to remember something of that letter. It will be over to Edmund, of course, but if that page is gone, or illegible, only the police can do anything.'

Avis was struck dumb by the enormity of what she had done and her terror of the consequences.

Tod and Lance came out on to the verandah as Charlotte stopped the Mini and said to a reluctant Avis in a tone they'd never heard Charlotte use before, 'Get out!'

Charlotte turned to the men, said slowly and distinctly, aware that it was going to be hard for them to take it in, 'Phyl *hasn't* run away with anyone! She'd had contact with her first husband. It seems he wasn't drowned. He's very much alive. All of this was in a missing middle page of that letter Phyl wrote that this ... that this ... that this beastly woman here concealed! It would have been bad enough, that news, that Ranulf is alive, for Owen to read, but Avis picked up the first and last pages first, surmised what we all surmised, then saw the other page. So she decided she'd twist the thumbscrew on Owen just a little bit more. ...'

Avis took a hasty step backwards as Tod uttered an indescribable sound and took a menacing step towards her. Then he checked, breathing hard, and said, 'Go on . . . quickly, Charlotte.'

'She didn't destroy it . . . quite. She dropped it out of the window so that when Phyl rang after she'd seen Ranulf, and Owen got the true story, everyone would assume it was just an unfortunate accident. We've had rain and dew and wind . . . it may be quite illegible now, or even gone. But she's here to show us where she put it. Then we must find Edmund before he sees Owen. And if we can't find the page, or read it, then it's the Christchurch police for us. They'll contact the Australian police. It's like a nightmare. Because what's happened to Phyl between then – and now – with a husband who's cruel and vicious as well as weak?'

It was young Lance who grabbed Avis's elbow as if he'd like to twist her arm off and said, 'March, you!'

Tod said, 'Thanks, Lance, because frankly I just can't trust myself to touch her!'

Round the corner of the house they moved at speed, into the rectangle formed by the east and west wings, to the weedy flower-bed beside the living-room window. In silence they watched as Avis bent down beside a lilac in full bloom against the wall, parted the grass that was still heavy with dew because the sun hadn't got round there yet, and saw her scrabble madly. Then she straightened up with a piece of sodden paper, her face expressionless.

Tod said quickly, 'Handle it carefully, don't open it out quickly . . . here, let me do it.'

He took a corner carefully, eased it back a fraction at a time, then he had it spread out, damp, crumpled, but . . . he gave a shout of triumph. 'It's okay . . . it's okay! It's all here, smudged but readable . . . and I can see the address!' Then, quickly, 'Lance, watch her . . . catch her!'

He'd seen the blood leave Charlotte's face as he looked up from the page and her knees begin to buckle beneath her. Lance caught her, pushed her head down, bent her over. The blood came back to her head, she recovered immediately.

Tod said, 'Let's get her inside and on a chair.' Charlotte shook her head. She wanted to look at what Phyl had written right now. But they were adamant.

She did feel better sitting down. They spread it on the

159

kitchen table, Tod smoothing it out with calloused fingers that were gentle as a baby's. The three of them leaned over it. Oh, poor Phyl! The agony of mind she had been enduring! It had been as Charlotte had thought, from that scrap of paper: it had indeed started 'Owen, the most horrible thing has happened to us....' and went on to say she'd had several letters from Ranulf, disguised in innocent-looking envelopes, demanding money from her for keeping silence about his survival. He'd heard she'd married well. It had been a strange tale, because he'd been lost so far out at sea, no one had dreamed he could survive. The first had come when Owen had been working late and early, lambing. She hadn't wanted to worry him, and although Ranulf had always written his letters on a portable typewriter, she'd doubted it could be him. She'd wondered if it might have been some rascally shipmate, able to at least copy his signature.

So she had written saying she must have positive proof. The proof he had supplied was to ring her ... and it had been unmistakably Ran's voice. He had said she'd have one more chance, only one. She would hear from him at Rio de Janeiro next. He was joining a ship in two days' time, bound for there. She was to airmail him some money immediately. If not, he'd sell his story to one of the sensational papers. Phyl had written, 'I tried to ring you, Owen, to say I must fly to this address immediately to see him, to plead with him not to do this. To allow me to approach the courts and see if there was any way out of it. I know if once he gets on a boat for South America and jumps it at one of the ports, it could be months before we trace him. And we'd go through hell during that time. We'd have to part till a divorce could be arranged, if one can get a divorce for that. I don't even know if you'll still want me.

'I rang Harewood, and I must get this next plane. I can't wait for you to arrive. Owen, forgive me, but I never doubted I was a widow. But here's the address he gave. I'll ring you as soon as I can. Just keep it quiet. I'll leave the car at that garage and take a taxi from there.'

Tod, Lance and Charlotte all finished reading together. They gazed at each other and their hearts were like lead. What had happened to her?

Avis said, 'Perhaps she's gone with him. Perhaps seeing him revived old feelings,' and then shrank back at the look on Tod's face. He said, 'Stay out of this. It's nothing to do with you. But

160

you'd better pray we *are* able to contact her at this address, or *you'll* be the one to assist the police with their inquiries. If Phyl has met with any harm because of you, I'd hate to be you. Now we're going to Christchurch to get hold of Edmund. I'm going to make Charlotte some strong coffee first. Lance, pull that kettle forward on to the heat. And you, Avis Jezebel, are going to walk back to where your car is and go home. Your people will have to know about this, seeing they think Phyl ran away with another man. I'm sorry for your father. Grant is a decent bloke – I don't know how he landed a daughter like you. And I'm recommending one thing. If I were you, if you want to make a fresh start, get right away from here. Take that overseas trip you're always talking of . . . that is, if we find Phyl and you don't find yourself charged with concealing evidence and arson and goodness knows what. Now march!'

Avis marched. Charlotte was surprised at the trend of her own thoughts. Normally she always felt sorry for anyone found out in bad behaviour – but not for Avis. Phyl was missing, Owen was recovering from a serious head injury and all their lives had been torn with fear and discord.

Tod said, 'We've plenty of time. Don't rush that coffee, Sharlie. Ed will be at the yards some time yet. Then he'll have lunch there before going to the hospital. He'll be like us, know a terrific relief he's not to tell Owen his wife has eloped with someone, but will be aghast at her disappearance. I can't even begin to imagine what's happened. That's better, your colour is coming back. Well, it will be over to the doctor what or what not to tell Owen. Lance, when we've gone, will you ring Judy to put her and Bill in the picture?'

Charlotte was so glad of Tod's presence. It was a road she'd never been on before, the road to Christchurch; she would have been completely lost in a strange city and Tod would know his way round the sale-yards and would find Edmund easily. Or so she thought.

The beauty of the surrounding countryside was lost upon her, rolling south, with purple foothills and jagged mountains on her right, beyond the gentle curves of the fertile North Canterbury countryside; occasionally they got glimpses of the sand dunes that edged the Pacific coast, on their left; they swung over bridges spanning swirling rivers, ran in between pine plantations and avenues of poplars that were rippling green waves of leafiness up above them. They passed through Belfast, Styx, and turned into Cranford Street to take them quickly to the city, by-passing Papanui.

This was a city of the plains ... Tod was spreading himself partly because this was his birthplace and he loved it, but mostly, she guessed, to take her mind off the fearsome implications of Phyl's disappearance.

Colombo Street, going directly north to south through Cathedral Square, led right to the Cashmere Hills that surrounded the harbour of Lyttleton that served the city as a port. The hospital lay against those hills, a few miles out, but the saleyards were nearer.

'I think,' said Charlotte, breaking into Tod's descriptions quite without knowing she was interrupting him, 'that the doctor will advise Edmund not to visit his brother today. He'll concoct something to excuse his non-appearance. Edmund will have to have time for inquiries. Not that Owen can be fobbed off much longer. Gosh, what a convalescence he's had, scarcely any visitors!'

Tod agreed. 'That quarantine business was a godsend in disguise. Otherwise he'd have been fretting for weeks, convinced by the portion of letter we had that she'd run away with someone. No wonder none of us could credit it. My word, Edmund's going to be eternally grateful to you, Sharlie. You were the one who bludgeoned the truth out of Avis. I say, what's the matter? You're crying ... been too much for you, has it?'

Charlotte hastily dived into her suede bag for a handkerchief. 'I haven't told you all, Tod. I've been the most terrible liar ... and Edmund found me out last night. That's why he left the house so early this morning. He can't bear the sight of me. I've – I've deceived him all along. I'm – I'm—'

'You're Phyl's cousin,' said Tod calmly, and laughed.

Charlotte gulped, stuttered, finally managed, 'How—? Oh, he told you. You see, he—'

'Hang on. Ed didn't tell me. I'm afraid it amused me. I've known for a long time and thought good on you. I knew Edmund had written to this cousin of Phyl's saying not to come. I can't quite fathom why Edmund didn't know what Phyl's cousin's name was, but I guess it was something to do with you being called Lacey by some people. It was the night of the broadcast, though the truth didn't hit me till later when I was in bed. It came in a flash. I'd once posted a letter to you from Phyl, and could suddenly see her writing before me:

162

"Miss C. de L. Smith." Somewhere in Wales. I wondered what on earth you'd been up to, but worked it out, and I got a good deal of amusement out of it. You brick! I knew old Edmund had dashed off a reply to you telling you not to come here, within minutes of receiving your letter to Phyl, and he was in one hell of a temper, but how on earth—'

'I'd signed it Lacey and had just scribbled c/o H. Ward on the back of it, and our Wellington address, so he addressed me as Miss Lacey Ward. I applied for the position as Charlotte Smith. I'd no idea how many lies it would involve me in, nor—' she let that go. She'd almost said, 'Nor how much heartache.' She continued: 'At the time all I wanted to do was get down here to look after my cousin's children.'

'Then what in thunder is Edmund so steamed up about?'

'I suppose it was the *way* he found out. My stepfather rang last night from Fiji. Edmund thought it was Phyl and motioned me to the other phone with pad and pencil to take it down. It was ghastly. As soon as they said Fiji I knew what I was in for.'

Tod gave an expressive whistle. 'What a conversation that must have been!'

Charlotte dabbed furiously at her eyes. 'Yes . . . but the one that followed was even worse. And Tod, if *you* can understand, why can't he?'

Tod said slowly, 'It's a bit different. Edmund's feelings are – are more involved than mine.'

'You – you mean because Owen's his brother, and he thinks Phyl has been unfaithful to him, and classes me with her, seeing we're cousins?'

'I didn't mean that at all. I've never seen Edmund look at a any girl as he's looked at you, Sharlie, and I've known him since we were nippers. Our ancestors came out on the same ship. He's very idealistic. First he caught you opening his desk and going through private papers. Then last night you got caught out, rather flagrantly, in another deception. It won't last, with Edmund. He'll get round to admiring you for it just as I have. I've known longer, and anyway, it wasn't me you were deceiving. I do admire you. It's nice to see loyalty between women instead of cattiness. And your faith in Phyl has been completely justified, Sharlie. When Edmund finds out how you forced the truth out of that white sepulchre of an Avis, he'll feel nothing but gratitude and admiration for you.'

Charlotte said, between her teeth, 'I don't want gratitude. I — I want — well, never mind. I'm sure *he* won't admire my tactics. It amounted to blackmail, Tod. I really brought pressure to bear. He'll think me quite unscrupulous, a liar and a blackmailer. As soon as we find Phyl, because that's all that really matters, I'll go up the Hundalee to my brother's. I'll never come back to Amberleigh again. Phyl can come to Huntress Hill to see me if she wants to. I hate Edmund Leigh, I just hate him!'

'Methinks the lady protests too much ... leave it to time, Sharlie. Edmund simply felt a fool, being taken in by you. He'd probably think you were laughing up your sleeve at him, thinking him a simpleton. As a sex we men are pretty vain. Ah, Moorhouse Avenue. Nothing now. You just wait, Edmund will fall on your neck.'

But they couldn't run Edmund to earth. Yes, he'd been there for part of the sale. Yes, he'd bought some stuff in. But that had been very early on. Then he'd cleared off. Tod wasn't perturbed. There were plenty of places he could be — their stock and station agent's for instance. But he hadn't been there. Tod rang their bank, and some friends. No luck.

'Not to worry,' he assured Sharlie. 'I'll give the hospital a ring, say that Edmund has an appointment with Owen's doctor, at two-thirty, and that we'll have to see them then, and that on no account are they to let either doctor or Edmund see Owen for discussion, till we see them first. We'll get there in plenty of time, anyway. I'll get you some lunch first, Sharlie. I don't think I'll ring before about ten past two. If I do it earlier, they'll change shifts at two and the message might not be passed on.'

It sounded fine. They had lunch, began to feel better, because of the food, about the ordeal ahead, then decided to phone. Every slot telephone they came to was either occupied or out of order. 'I'll stop along Colombo Street South,' said Tod. 'There are plenty of phone-boxes along there. And a couple of post-offices.'

It happened before they found one. A child flashed across the road without warning, in front of the car ahead of them. The driver braked, slewed round, skidded, missed the child, ran into the edge of the kerb and bounced back, striking their bumper bar. Tod made a magnificent effort, managed to bring their car to a halt, then felt the car behind take them sideways.

So there they were, three cars locked together, sideways in the road, traffic coming to a halt and a crowd gathering. No one was hurt, apart from Tod's elbow receiving a terrific jolt, but it took some sorting out, and none of them could leave till the traffic department officers arrived.

At first Tod said, 'It's all right. We've still plenty of time. We can get a taxi if only some garage can come along with a breakdown truck and separate these cars.' But it became evident that this was going to take longer than expected. Tod would have to stand by. He finally said, 'Sharlie, I see a telephone box about four lamp-posts down. Would you go and ring the hospital? It would be unthinkable for Owen to have one shock on top of another. I mean, if anything else delays us and we get there too late to stop the doctor giving him the first version, then he'd just have to hear the second, which, while less disillusioning, will send him frantic with fear. He'd be like a caged lion, tied to a hospital bed while the police were trying to trace his wife. The poor beggar would go mad.'

Sharlie took to her heels and ran. She asked for the Sister. It seemed ages before the Sister came to the phone. She'd just been posted to this ward, and quite evidently knew Owen's medical and surgical history, but not much more.

So Charlotte didn't dare embark on long and detailed explanations. It was too involved, too dramatic. Besides, Sisters were busy people. She simply said that Mr. Owen Leigh's brother, in company with his doctor, were about to see him, to tell him of some family trouble. This problem had just been resolved, and could the Sister make sure that neither the doctor nor Mr. Edmund Leigh saw Owen Leigh till she, Miss Charlotte Smith, had arrived at the hospital. Then she rang a taxi, instructed it to come to the scene of the accident and made back to it. Edmund and the doctor would think an eleventh-hour message from Phyl had come in.

The breakdown gang had just taken over Tod's car when the taxi arrived and they rushed into it in such a hurry the driver asked them if it was a maternity case, which at least gave them a laugh. Traffic was slow, part of the road was up and they had to take a diversion channel, and by the time they got to the hospital time was almost running out and they were both convinced there was a hoodoo on them. They were almost running the length of the corridor, sure that the message would have got garbled and that even now the harm might have been done. It was a wonderful moment when they actually arrived at the ante-room to the ward and walked in to find Edmund and the doctor there, looking apprehensive, as indeed they might.

They must have been wondering, frantic, imagining having to concoct another delaying excuse for hospital visits, if, as they would naturally suppose, Phyl had at last rung.

Sharlie said breathlessly, 'You'd better tell them, Tod, you'll be more coherent than I feel at this moment. I feel – oh, go on, Tod!'

Tod did. He told it concisely, with no distortion of the basic facts, neither sparing Avis, nor dramatizing their own part in it. Then he handed them the missing page. Edmund and the doctor read simultaneously, each holding a corner.

Then they lifted their heads. Edmund made a sort of hopeless gesture. 'Where now?' he asked them.

Tod said, 'We've had a bit more time than you to adjust ourselves, Ed. We can't rush anything – with regard to Owen, of course – so – oh, sorry, Doctor, that's over to you, naturally. But I should think we'll have to go to the police immediately. We can only work through them. They've got all the magnificent organization necessary to trace people. They can contact their opposite numbers in Sydney, who'll go to this address ... they'll find out which ship was leaving for Rio about that time. He probably won't be under his own name – maybe he was so in debt, he found it best not to reclaim his identity when he was rescued. Oh, hell, what a mess!'

They talked it out at length. The doctor said, 'I think your course is clear, Leigh. Just about exactly as this chap suggests. It gives you a breathing-space. We weren't too specific to your brother about the end of the quarantine. He doesn't know you're coming today, does he?'

'No. He'll know it won't be long before he sees his family, though.'

'Right, I'll drop by shortly, and during the course of a bit of chit-chat, I'll say that in a few days he'll be having family visitors for sure. That's indefinite enough to give the Sydney police a bit of a chance, though—'

They all knew what he'd bitten back. Though there was precious little to go on, really. Edmund said crisply, having now accepted the situation and feeling the need for action, 'I'll go to Sydney immediately. If that fellow has done my sister-in-law any harm, I'll—'

The doctor rose, patted his shoulder, said, 'Don't do anything too quickly, at least as far as going over there is concerned. Get into action right away with the police at our end. I must go, unfortunately. I've another appointment here at three. But I'll see your brother on the way and just mention what I said about seeing you all soon. When you've seen the police would you come back and let me know what's transpiring. Just use this room then if you want to discuss anything. Or now.' He went out.

Edmund looked across at Charlotte, said, 'Charlotte, I want to apologize for my behaviour last night. I owe you—'

He got no further. She held up a protesting hand. 'You don't owe me any gratitude, Edmund. I couldn't stand it. Even if I *was* the one who wormed the truth out of Avis, I still did it by the most unethical means. I'm still a liar and a cheat, and now a blackmailer. I don't want your gratitude. And I don't care if I am all those things. I'd do it all again.'

Edmund's blue eyes were calm, not resentful because she'd flouted and spurned his overture. He put out a hand to her across the little table, and was smiling. Actually smiling! She could have throttled him.

She kept her own hands tightly clasped in front of her. Her red hair was in disordered tresses on her shoulders, her back very stiff.

Then, unbelievably and maddeningly, Edmund was laughing helplessly. 'I wasn't going to say I owe you a debt of gratitude. After all, you didn't do it for me. You did it for your cousin. You'd rather have wrung my neck, wouldn't you?'

'Yes,' said Charlotte, 'I certainly would.'

'And I'd have deserved it. I was mad last night, mad clean through. I thought you'd made a fool of me, that you'd been laughing about the way you'd duped me, behind my back. I could imagine you giggling like mad about it every time you rang this Ivan up. I don't suppose you can understand my feelings because you aren't a man, but no man could relish being made such a fool of, especially by the woman he loves.'

'I *didn't* make a fool of you,' said Charlotte furiously. 'I never even thought of that. I'd never met you in my life before. You simply didn't count. I was desperate. I *had* to find out what was happening to Phyl – especially when I knew she just wasn't the type to do a thing like that. *You* were only a signature at the foot of a letter . . . the obstruction that was forbidding me to come to the valley! I knew from the tone of that letter that I'd never get you to consent to my coming to look after my little cousins, so I *had* to resort to subterfuge. There was no thought or intention of making a fool of you, you were just an impersonal object in the way.' She stopped, looked thunderstruck, as the recollection of his last words registered. 'Oh, Edmund, what did you say? What *did* you say?'

The old battling light was back in the blue eyes, replacing the hopeless look of a few moments ago, when the baffling problem of Phyl had been the only thought in his mind. 'I said I loved you, Sharlie. I said it loud and clear and you practically ignored it. And I'm damned sure, for all the way I've treated you, that *you* love *me*, you incredibly brave and clever girl!'

Charlotte's feelings rose up and swamped her, all the misery, doubt, delight, torment, frustration of the past few weeks. She didn't hear the door had opened behind her just as Edmund was half-way through his declaration. She swept back the red hair from her shoulders as if clearing the decks for action, stamped her foot and said, 'Ah, bah! You make me furious! Just because I've solved the mystery, you've now decided this stupid attraction I seem to have for you must be love! Let me just tell you that when I go looking for a husband, I won't be wanting a moody, unreasonable man like you, blowing hot and blowing cold . . . just because I've been vindicated you can now approve of my deception. If I'd lost, if I'd proved nothing, if my cousin *had* been an unfaithful wife, you'd still treat me the way you treated me last night. Believe me, Edmund Leigh, once we find Phyl, I'm off to Fiji to join my parents!' Tears of real fury were standing in her eyes. But she had paused for breath out of sheer necessity before sweeping on, and into that small silence, a cough sounded. The sort of cough made to attract attention. They'd been too engrossed to notice that door opening. They swung round.

It was the Sister. She had stopped dead in her tracks, as well she might, her eyebrows arched, lips parted, the very personification of bewilderment. Tod laughed out loud, irrepressibly.

Sister got control of herself. 'I thought,' she said with some asperity, 'that you were discussing a police matter . . . tracing a patient's wife. Or so Doctor Bellaby has just informed me. Not—'

Tod still had a trace of delighted laughter in his tone. He came to her rescue. 'Not witnessing a proposal of marriage . . . I take it, Ed, it *is* a proposal of marriage?'

'It sure is,' said his boss wickedly, grinning broadly. Charlotte could have struck them both.

She said icily, regaining her temper, 'She's witnessing not only a proposal of marriage, but also a refusal! I wouldn't marry you if you were—'

Edmund interrupted her, eyes dancing, 'I know . . . if I were hung from top to toe with diamonds. You've said that before and it makes no difference to the final issue. We got our wires crossed, that's all, and no wonder.'

The Sister's mouth fell open again. She was very bonny and she seemed ridiculously young to be a Sister. She had black shining hair and the bluest of eyes and the most betraying dimples. They weren't under very good control at the moment, even though she was trying.

Tod said to her with audacity, 'Look, sugar, this is no place for either you or me at this moment. These two have been at either cross-purposes or loggerheads ever since they met, and no wonder, as my boss just said. The circumstances haven't been anything like ideal for courting. Any chance of leaving them alone here for a few moments? I'd back Edmund to make his wicket good if only he could get a few moments alone with her. Honestly, the last week or two I've felt like a frantic mother with two squabbling children! Can you lock this door, sweetie, so for once they can have it out without people barging in?'

Edmund gave a great shout of approving laughter that was cut short and turned into a groan as a very hasty and peremptory sort of knock sounded on the door. Whoever had knocked didn't wait to be told to enter but burst in. Edmund looked straight over Charlotte's head to the intruder, a double crease between his bleached, craggy eyebrows. Now who in hell could this be?

He saw a tall girl with nut-brown hair caught back behind her head and with slanting brown eyes that reminded him of someone. She had a brown skin, yet it was fairly pale as if . . . yes, as if she'd been ill. From her left cheekbone to the centre of her cheek was a recently-healed scar and she had great shadowy hollows beneath her eyes. What a moment for another patient to come bursting in!

Tod and Charlotte had swung round, and they were both, had anyone been watching them, caught into camera-stillness for one surprised moment, then, in perfect duet, they cried: 'Phyl!' and surged forward. Only then did Edmund became aware that behind this girl were two more people, still in the passage ... and he knew these two ... Lance and Judy were standing there grinning like conjurors. Just look what *they'd* produced out of the hat!

Tears were tumbling down Charlotte's face as she caught her cousin to her, but Phyl was dry-eyed, beyond tears, even of joy.

Charlotte was saying, 'Phyl, Phyl, Phyl! Oh, where have you been?'

It didn't seem to register with Phyl. She said simply but quietly and with terrible urgency in her tone, 'How is Owen ... does he know I've been missing? Has he been told?'

Tod said, 'No, Phyl. Oh, no, Phyl. Don't look like that. We got here in time to stop it.' Then he stopped, banged at his forehead with his fist in utter bewilderment. 'But how do *we* know what *you* mean? And how did you arrive so pat? Why have we not heard from you all this time?'

At that moment the Sister's trained eye told her something, and she seized a chair and slid it under Phyl. 'Easy,' she said. 'There's no hurry now. You've been ill, haven't you? You've had an accident.'

Phyl subsided into the chair and gave her a grateful look. 'Yes,' her hand came up to her scarred cheek. 'But I'm almost right again. This cut wasn't much more than superficial, but I had some head injury and suffered from amnesia ... lost my memory! I can only tell you by hearsay what happened to me. I've been in a Sydney hospital and when I was convalescent they gave me a room so they could keep an eye on me. They couldn't have been more kind. It was in the nurses' home. Of course Australians are like that.

'They tell me I worked as a sort of nurse-aide. They thought some sort of occupation would help me – as it must have done. I can't remember any of that. But this morning, evidently one of the nurses, coming off night duty and wanting to give a message to the girl in the room next to mine, barged in and woke me up. It must have sort of jolted me, because she says she apologized, explained, and said, "I'm Barbie Newcombe. I've not been here long," and I remembered my Barbie. Remembered everything up to my accident. Nothing more.'

She laughed faintly at the look on their faces, the way they all said: 'Just this morning?' She nodded. 'Seems incredible, even to me.' Her eyes suddenly fastened on Edmund. 'Oh, you *are* like Owen . . . you must be Edmund. Oh, how sorry I am that I messed up your homecoming like that!'

He made a gesture meant to say it was less than nothing, came to her side, put an arm round her shoulders and said, 'Nice to have another sister, Phyl, but go on, darling.'

'I can only remember missing my step and crashing down these stone stairs. It wasn't a very nice area – down by the docks. And it was getting dark and – my mind was in a turmoil.'

At the word docks Edmund and Charlotte and Tod grew rigid. Lance and Judy, behind Phyl, didn't seem affected. But it was Phyl's story, and she'd been through a terrible ordeal, and they must just let her tell it her own way. If they put her off, who knew? Her memory might relapse. They didn't know enough about this sort of thing.

But had Phyl crashed before she saw Ranulf, or after? Was all that ahead of her still – tracing him, facing the publicity of a spectacular divorce?

They would spare her all the pressure they could. She was alive and reasonably well, and God be praised for that!

So Edmund said, very gently, 'Phyl, didn't you have anything in your bag to give the police your address?'

'It must have been stolen from me as I lay there. There was nothing to even remotely connect me with New Zealand, to spread the inquiries, and of course when I came to, after being unconscious some time, I had an English accent, so they assumed I was an immigrant or something. It was sheer ill-chance that everything I had on had a "Made in Australia" label.'

Edmund said, 'And how did you know to come here to the hospital? I mean, why are Lance and Judy here?'

Phyl smiled. 'I got such a shock when they told me the date and I realized I'd been missing for weeks, and I couldn't understand why Owen hadn't had inquiries made about me in Sydney. It was so completely beyond me – seeing I'd even left him an address – I absolutely insisted I get the first plane over. That is, I insisted on that, after I'd rung Amberleigh and got no answer. I couldn't understand why no one would answer so early in the morning, then they reminded me that it would be a bit later in New Zealand because of the time difference. I nearly went mad, thinking the family could be out all day — thought Owen must be on the hunt for me somewhere. Oh, it was just too frustrating!

'I rang Judy — no answer. I didn't want to give away too much to the local exchange, because knowing the reason I'd gone to Australia, I thought none of you would have let that out. I was at my wits' end — time was so short if I wanted to catch the plane, so I sent a cable — one that didn't give too much away — to Owen at Amberleigh and to Judy, thinking that if Owen was away, she might be round. I worked out that if Owen was prosecuting a search, the children would be with Judy. I simply said: "Will explain all when I get home stop arriving from Sydney this afternoon" and gave my flight number and arrival. I couldn't know, of course, if anyone at either place would be home to receive the cable and meet me, especially in the short time it takes by jet, but I thought once I got here I'd probably make contact by phone, or get a taxi no matter what it cost. That is, as long as it could be paid for at the other end!' Her voice wobbled. 'But it was marvellous. I came through Customs, which was easy because I've only got what the hospital gave me, to see Judy and Lance waiting. They'd made it with just minutes to spare. The hospital provided me with money, got my tickets — a great blessing you don't need passports between Australia and New Zealand — and they sent a member of the nursing staff with me. She's sitting out in the car right now. All I wanted to do was get to Owen as soon as possible, and when I heard — what had happened to him, from Lance and Judy, I—' She broke off, struggling with tears.

Judy took on for her, standing behind Phyl's chair and stroking her shoulder. 'Lance and I thought we'd never make it to the airport in time. We'd no idea, of course, where Phyl had been or what had happened to her. We just dared not take the time to phone the hospital here. Lance was marvellous. He took no risks, but every possible short cut. Lance, fortunately, had rung me as instructed, all about Avis and the missing page and that you were going to stop Edmund telling Owen anything yet, so we knew our best plan was to meet Phyl and get her here. So at least we could tell Phyl why no one had been trying to trace her. We've not filled it in much — it's such a short distance from the airport to here.'

Edmund said, 'We'd better fill in anything she doesn't know.' He pulled a chair forward, possessed himself of Phyl's hand, as if to transmit reassurance and comfort. He made a gesture to Charlotte. She took Phyl's other hand.

Judy said, 'Basically, she's got the lot. About what we all assumed, even though we couldn't – at times – credit it. Phyl thought we were mad at first, as she'd no idea a page had gone astray, of course; well, that a page had been concealed with malicious intent is more correct. Nor could she believe, right away, that two pages could make one story, and three quite a different one!'

Phyl said, the colour coming back into her cheeks now, 'Who could think, Lacey, that so small an omission as being in too big a hurry to number pages could have caused all this? But for that, inquiries would have been instigated by you folk weeks ago, and I'd have been identified.' A small crease appeared between her brows. 'Lacey, Judy didn't seem to realize you were my cousin. I haven't had time to work that one out. When she kept saying that Charlotte Smith, this girl who's been looking after the children, was just marvellous – she absolutely forced the truth out of Avis, I said, "Of course . . . if anybody would, Lacey would. She's got a genius for leaping to the right conclusion, streets ahead of anyone else, because she goes by instinct more than reason," she didn't know who or what I was talking about. But by that time we'd got here and were rushing into the hospital, so I've not fathomed it yet.'

Edmund squeezed the fingers he held. 'My dear sister-in-law, it's a long tale. Lacey – Charlotte to me – wrote you a letter on the plane, posted it on landing, signed it Lacey and put care of H. Ward on the back of the envelope. So I wrote to a Miss Lacey Ward, at that Wellington address, forbidding her to as much as come near us.'

Phyl looked amazed. 'Forbidding her – why, Lacey would be the ideal person to look after two children on a farm. She's a trained nanny and—'

Edmund said, 'It was that letter. Please forgive me, Phyl. You see, I'd never met you. Everyone else went round unable to believe you had left Owen for another man. I'd made up my mind you must be the sort of woman so utterly charming you'd bewitched everyone into thinking you incapable of unfaithfulness and deceit. So I decided this cousin of yours might be the same. My letter was forwarded on to Sharlie at the

Hundalee. Her brother and family had seen my advert and—' he started to chuckle, 'what do you think she did?' Coolly applied for the job of housekeeper as Miss Charlotte Smith!'

Phyl gazed at her cousin and her face broke up. 'Oh, Lacey, Lacey ... you're just the same as ever. How absolutely marvellous!' She began to giggle and looked years younger.

Charlotte's tone was dry. 'Edmund didn't think it so funny when he found out, believe me, Phyl.'

'That's all in the long ago past,' said Edmund outrageously. 'I was only cross temporarily, and it doesn't matter now, anyway, because Charlotte and I are now engaged to be married.'

A cry of protest was wrung from Charlotte: *'Edmund!'*

Edmund's smile was in his eyes as well as on his lips. His face was so close to Charlotte's, and there was a meaning in it she could not fail to understand, though in any case he made sure of it by saying, 'It's okay, my love. I know you don't want me to over-excite Phyl.' He turned back to Phyl. 'She's afraid it may be too much for you.'

Charlotte was struck dumb. This was no time for a resumption of hostilities. Phyl needed tranquillity, reassurance. She'd have to play it Edmund's way for a bit. Inwardly she was consumed by rage, outwardly she managed what she hoped might be taken for a happy smile. But just wait till she got Edmund to herself!

He positively smirked! Lance uttered a sound of delight, 'Boss! Gosh, you're not half lucky!'

The Sister remained rooted to the spot. She only just hoped she wasn't called out for something in the ward. To have to leave now would be maddening. What crazy people! Though there was something about them. . . .

Tod was doubled up. Edmund said, 'What a peculiar effect this announcement seems to have upon him.'

Judy had stars in her eyes. 'Oh, I wish Bill was here! I told him it was bound to happen. I could see it coming a mile off.'

Phyl looked puzzled and delighted all at once. 'But – but do you mean it's *just* happened?'

Edmund nodded. 'But it's been a dead cert for some time. Charlotte has fallen for Te-iti-rangi. I think she's a reincarnation of Dorothea or something. So it was foreordained. It's her idea of a little heaven too. We're doing it up. I reckon we could get part of it habitable by Christmas.'

Charlotte breathed heavily. If it wasn't for Phyl— Her cousin leaned forward and kissed her, eyes shining. 'Oh, Lacey, how wonderful! You'll be my sister-in-law as well as my cousin. I can't think of anything more wonderful than having you on the same estate. Oh, how I wish Owen's mother and father were back home! They'll just love you. And if you're half as happy as Owen and I are, you'll be happy indeed.'

Mention of Owen froze Charlotte and Edmund and Tod. Judy and Lance didn't appear to be affected. Charlotte's anger with Edmund was swamped by another feeling – anguish. It stabbed her with a physical pain, even as it stabbed Edmund and Tod. As happy as Owen and Phyl were! *As they had been,* she meant. Because they weren't even married. There was a ghastly obstacle in the way of the resumption of that happiness. Ranulf. Ranulf, who had come back from the dead.

Phyl continued, unknowing, 'But now I must see Owen. Doesn't it seem strange, he doesn't know anything of this! What a blessing Laccy and Tod got here in the nick of time. I mean how terrible if he'd been told either of the stories, that I'd presumably run away with another man, or that I was missing. I – I think we'll just have to go and see him as if none of it had happened. As if at first I was down with a chesty cold, and then that we were in quarantine because of Lacey being on that plane.

'Judy seems to think he'll be home in a week or so. We'll let him get settled in at home, then tell him. He'll hardly be able to credit that so much has happened. Isn't it odd? *He'll* have a gap in his consciousness, and so will I. But at the moment all that matters to me is that he's alive and well, and in blissful ignorance of events that could have given him such a shock it might have affected him badly both physically and mentally. All I can think of is that in a matter of a week or so he'll be back at Amberleigh with us and all will be well.'

Charlotte heard Edmund swallow and clear his throat. Pity for him rose in her and nullified every other feeling. Poor Edmund, he'd had to face up to so many distasteful things these horrible weeks ... now he was faced with the necessity for asking Phyl *her* plans.

She was surprised to hear his voice so steady, so matter-of-fact. It said, 'You mean you won't tell him Ranulf is alive till he's quite recovered? We'll have to tell his doctor, of course. And I'll get legal advice right away. You must be free.'

Tod and Charlotte and Edmund were completely unprepared for the radiance that broke through the gravity of Phyl's face. 'Oh, my dears, do forgive me . . . having told Judy and Lance on the way in, and having all this excitement and relief since, I'm completely addled. I was only concentrating on explaining my loss of memory. Ranulf *isn't* alive. It was his twin brother – a bad egg like his twin. I'd never met him. He had run away from their home in England long before I met Ran. He was a crew member on that ship that took Owen's mother and father to Canada, and through various things dropped, worked out who they were, and to whom I was married. He thought they were very much wealthier than they are. He's not only an identical twin, but he's like Ranulf – always in debt, always gambling, living it up one moment, living from hand to mouth the next. But Ranulf had a very noticeable scar on his forehead. Eric didn't. Ran always typed his letters and his signature was fairly easy to copy, though I did have a very faint doubt – more a hope than a doubt. It was all flourish. But when he rang, I felt sick at heart. Their voices, on the phone anyway, couldn't be distinguished. That can happen, I know.

'When he rang and said he'd be leaving for Rio so soon and I couldn't get hold of Owen, I knew there was only one thing to do, go and see him myself. It was like a nightmare. I'd no intention of parting out with any money. If the report of his death was false, then I'd get a divorce, somehow. I knew the courts would see justice was done. But it would be far more likely for Ranulf to disappear, hoping I might send some money, but not staying in one place. I thought he'd start to try to wear me down. But if I could get to him and pin him down, convince him I was only going to set legal proceedings going, he just might co-operate, but once he got on a boat for Rio, if he were under an assumed name, it would be hopeless.

'I put the letters he'd sent me into the bottom of my jewel-case – the one Owen's mother gave me – it has a false lining. I thought they could be used against him in court, as evidence of trying to extort money. But it was like some hideous nightmare.' She closed her eyes against the impact of the memory for a moment. 'He wasn't in when I reached that seedy rooming-house, but the woman who owned it said he was coming back that night. I only asked for Mr. Seymour, not Ranulf. It was only a long shot, using his correct name. But as he had put it on the letter, it was all I could do. I couldn't understand why he'd put it – because I was sure he'd be using an alias. So I didn't ask for Mr. Ranulf Seymour. What a blessing I decided to wait for him, because if I hadn't, and his landlady had told him my name, he'd have cleared out.

'I'll never forget the moment when I heard his footsteps coming along that passage. The door was pushed open and he came in and just boggled at me, because of course, I was a perfect stranger to him. I stared at him in amazement, because I noticed in a split second the absence of that scar, and at that very moment his landlady called out: "Is that you, Eric? I've put a lady in your room."

'Till then my mind had felt half paralysed, but it came crystal clear instantly. I didn't give away the fact that over the phone I'd been persuaded it was my husband's voice. I stood up and said, "Well, well, at last I meet my notorious brother-in-law! Did you honestly suppose I wouldn't know my first husband's voice? Ranulf wasn't much of a man, Eric, but you're a lot worse! And you're right in trouble."

'At the look on his face I felt a little bit afraid, yet the relief was so magnificent, it sort of strengthened me. I said quickly, "I've got it in the hands of the police. They know I'm here. They only wanted me to identify you." The speed with which he acted was quite incredible. There'd been a duffle-bag half packed on his bed. He yanked open a top drawer, scooped some stuff out, crammed it in, and ran.

'I walked out without seeing his landlady again. I didn't want to discuss it. I felt as if I was walking on air. The awful weight that had lain on my heart for weeks was gone. I just wanted to go and get a room for the night and ring Owen. I was half running – it was a horrible area. I took a wrong turning, saw some steps that would save me a long walk back, I thought, to get me going in the right direction, and I slipped. The rest you know. So, when Owen comes out of hospital, he can come back to me. It's like a miracle. It is a miracle! I thought that never again might I know peace of mind. I—' Her voice cracked.

Edmund kissed her. 'You brick! You utterly wonderful girl. You kept it all to yourself because it was lambing, and Owen would be tired to death, especially with that late snowstorm.' His eyes sought Charlotte's. 'I like the women of your family, Phyl. They've got guts!'

He swung round on the Sister, still absorbed in this real-life drama. 'Sister, will we have to wait to tell the doctor, or can we just go in to see Owen, as if nothing has happened except that we've been confined to the estate because of the quarantine?'

She said, 'You can go in. The doctor might not be free for some time. I'd like you to see him then, though. I'll send him a message that he must come to see me, before he goes to see Mr. Leigh again. But there's one thing you've forgotten. You've got to think up an excuse for that scar on Mrs. Leigh's face.' She peered at it closely. 'If I were you I'd say you slipped in the cowshed . . . I presume you do have a cowshed? Oh, splendid. That you struck your face on the rim of a bucket. It looks exactly like that – slightly curved. And you didn't want him to know in case he imagined it was worse than it is. By the way, they've made a very neat job of it. In a few weeks' time you'll hardly see it.'

Tod said admiringly, 'Got a head on her shoulders, hasn't she? And a fertile imagination too. She'd suit the Amberleigh set-up immensely. We can all lie our heads off at the drop of a hat. I tell you, sweetie, you're exactly the sort of nursing Sister to get involved in an affair like this. We must see more of you. How about coming out to our valley some time?'

Her lips quivered, one dimple flashed, but only for a moment. She cleared her throat and tried to look severe. 'Well now, I'll take you along to Mr Leigh's room. Then I'll get that Australian nurse out of your car – what kind of car is it and where did you park it? – I'll get her myself, because we don't want any gossip about this. Not a single nurse on this ward is going to know a thing about it.' She disappeared through the door in a would-be aura of white starch and efficiency.

Phyl said, 'I want you all to come. Otherwise I'll make a baby of myself when I see him. It will be easier to be ordinary with all of you there – a sort of grand reunion after the quarantine period. Come on.'

They trooped along the corridor in pairs, Edmund and Phyl, Charlotte and Tod, Judy and Lance. They pushed Owen's door further open, and there he lay, propped against a mound of pillows, a capelline bandage round his head, evidence of bruising down one side of his face, but otherwise looking reasonably recovered.

His eyes widened as he saw them, then he said, 'Stone the crows! That doctor just told me the quarantine wouldn't be over for a day or two yet. It's been an eternity . . . Oh, Phyl, Phyl, come here!'

As he clasped her to him, Edmund said hastily, 'Well, they made a mistake in the time. It was shorter than they thought.'

Owen just accepted that and they breathed again. In all the excitement of the last half-hour, they'd forgotten that detail.

Owen was questioning that no further. He said, 'Darling, darling, what on earth did you want to get a chest cold then for . . . it's been awful lying here without you. Just imagine, the only time you were at my bedside, I was unconscious!' Then suddenly he pushed her away from him, scrutinized her closely. 'What on earth have you—'

Phyl achieved a laugh that did her credit. 'You're not the only one to have accidents, but mine wasn't as dramatic. I had an argument with a bucket – fell on it in the cowshed. I can tell you, Owen, the doctor has just about had me – a chest cold, then quarantine, and a cheek to stitch. He said anybody'd think I didn't want to go into hospital to see my husband. You and I make a pretty pair, don't we?'

Charlotte saw admiration flickering in Edmund's eyes for her cousin. He's admiring *her* acting . . . yet he was furious with me for mine. Called me a fluent liar, said I was full of guile, that I'd probably sniggered about it to my relations. I detest him . . . condoning in Phyl what he loathed in me. I detest inconsistent men!

Owen said, 'To be quite candid, none of you look exactly blooming. Edmund's lost a lot of weight. Look at his face. He looks five years older than when he left for Canada. Judy's got a wild and dishevelled look . . .' he laughed as Judy, dismayed, put her hand up to her hair. She'd not even looked at it when she got the cable, just tore off her apron and rushed over to Lance. Owen went on laughing. 'Lance and Tod have still got farm-boots on and haven't even scraped the mud off . . . I expected V.I.P. treatment, not this, after lying at death's door . . . which I suppose is fairly correct? And from the photos I've seen, this must be Lacey, whom no one's bothered to introduce, and her hands are covered in bandages! What *has* been going on, anyway? Hi, Lacey!' His eyes narrowed. 'You've all got a guilty look . . . come on, give. What's been happening?'

There was a horrible silence. Everyone's inventiveness was exhausted, seemingly. Owen Leigh was even more astute than

Edmund. He sighed. 'You aren't going to tell me, I can see that. Okay. I daresay Doctor Bellaby has said no excitement. Gosh, and I'm bored to tears. I could use a bit of excitement right now. But if you won't, you won't. Phyl, you might introduce your cousin properly for a start.'

Edmund came to himself. 'Let me do the introducing. The relationship isn't quite that . . . and is going to be even more involved soon. She's not just Phyl's cousin . . . she's your future sister-in-law and my fiancée!'

It was a splendid red herring. Owen put out a hand to Charlotte, said, 'How magnificent!' He started to laugh. 'I bet Phyl had a hand in this. She said, when she first knew you were coming out, Lacey, "Wouldn't it be marvellous if she and Edmund fell for each other?" A real matchmaker, my wife. I can just see her, taking advantage of every moment of that quarantine to throw you together. Was that how it happened so quickly?'

Tod came in, 'Yep. I reckon you could say it was due to Phyl that they were left alone together in the house on so many occasions.'

Phyl started to giggle. 'I couldn't have put it better myself.'

Suddenly Owen looked puzzled. 'Surely the doctor didn't think a bit of happy news like that would excite me too much? How daft!'

Edmund said, 'Well, you see, Owen, it's just happened, come to a head. Good job you're on the mend. If Mother and Dad are home for New Year, we'll make it a January wedding. Then we can honeymoon in high summer, and get back for harvest.'

Owen was nothing if not persistent. 'But this still doesn't explain the farm-boots, Judy's ruffled and excited air . . . the bandages.'

Judy realized he'd have to know a little bit more. 'Well, so much happened in so short a time. Let's just tell him.' As she heard them gasp she rushed on . . . 'About the fire. They very nearly lost Te-iti-rangi.' She picked up one of Charlotte's hands. 'But thanks to Charlotte — we call her that, not Lacey — who saw Avis ride away, the old homestead was saved.'

Owen said, 'Saw Avis ride away . . . what? This is as clear as mud.'

Edmund said, quietly, 'She committed arson, out of spite.'

He grinned. 'She transferred her unholy passion for you to me, saw I was falling for Charlotte, knew we both loved Dorothea's homestead and out of sheer malice set alight to it. Charlotte rode across the river, tore down the hall curtains, checked it a bit, realized another fire was going – Avis had lit two – and Charlotte beat that old gong as it's not been beaten since the day Dorothea saw the landslip coming down on the barn; I heard it, and got there just in time to help her beat out the last of the flames. Charlotte got rather singed, and lost a lot of skin off her hands, so Judy was over at Amberleigh giving us a hand, because of course Phyl's just recovered from that fall, and suddenly they let us know the quarantine was over. We knew visiting hours would soon be over, so we just piled in and thought you wouldn't care.'

'I don't,' said Owen. 'I was only suspicious – thought you'd all been up to something.'

Judy added hastily, 'We hadn't time to bring the kids in – they were at my place. Bill's looking after them.'

Owen said, 'I gather you would tear strips off Avis later. She's a—'

'Pain in the neck,' said Edmund. 'Charlotte wasn't quite sure she'd done it, didn't want to accuse her if she was innocent, but trapped her into an admission. So in response to a suggestion . . . if you can call it that . . . by Tod here, the charming Avis is taking a trip to Europe.'

Owen's face lit up. 'Good! She was giving Phyl hell for a bit, but Phyl was too sensible to let her make any real mischief. I forbade her the place, in fact. But I never realized spite would carry her that far. Was the old place damaged much?'

'Not really. Only superficially. We're having the chimney rebuilt. The carved mantel is intact, just blistered. I'll restore that. We're going to do the surround and hearth in the amber-coloured stone from the falls. Charlotte and I are going to have an enormous lot of fun doing it up, aren't we, Charlotte?'

She didn't want to have to meet those audacious eyes, to play it along with him, but must, seemingly, for Owen's sake, for Phyl's. So she found herself, slightly to her surprise, saying: 'Yes. But apart from the fireplace, which was crumbling, I'd like it left as much as possible as Dorothea and Jonathan had it. Everything's thick with dust, but things like that old rocker, and the spinning-wheel and the spool beds up in the dormers, could all be restored.'

Edmund added, 'And when that portrait comes back from that picture-dealer's in Christchurch, it will be hung over the drawing-room piano again. Mother and Dad had to take it to him, to have the glass replaced. It's been at Amberleigh for many years, of course, when Te-iti-rangi was sold out of the family in the hard times. You haven't seen it, Sharlie. A famous painter of the old days came out to New Zealand. The girl Dorothea had worked for wanted her portrait painted by him, and her father could well afford it too. This chap, the painter, was wealthy in his own right and could afford to be choosey. He refused. It so happened he was taken out to Amberleigh by a geologist, to see the Waipungapunga rocks, had a meal at the homestead and asked Jonathan if he might paint Dorothea. He said she was patrician in every inch. So she was. It shows in the photograph. So even if she was a London waif, I expect her father was a gentleman. Anyway, it was poetic justice. It gained publicity, and I believe Olivia, who must have been of the same breed as Avis, was livid.'

Owen, sounding puzzled, said, 'Why is it you didn't call her Lacey from the start? I've never heard Phyl call her anything else.'

Charlotte saw Edmund was at a loss and found herself coming to his rescue. 'Oh, Phyl was at your bedside when I arrived, Owen, so it happened I arrived at the homestead unannounced and said I was Charlotte Smith. That meant nothing to your brother. He thought Phyl's cousin's name was Lacey Ward — because of my stepfather.' She fixed Edmund with a limpid innocent gaze. 'But we soon sorted that one out, didn't we, Edmund, my love?'

Owen said, 'How strange it all seems. I haven't even the haziest recollection of you sitting at my side, Phyl. When I first came round Edmund was here. You'd gone for a breath of fresh air. I must have lapsed again. And you developed that cold, so I expect they packed you off home. Gosh, I felt funny the first time I asked the date. It's so strange to have a whole chunk of your life disappear. I don't suppose any of you can imagine what a very peculiar sensation it is, to have weeks of your life blotted out. Makes me realize what a terrible thing it must be to lose your memory.'

A silence fell on them all, to be broken by everyone talking at once. After that the seeming ordinariness of their conversation seemed unreal, to belong to another world. They all felt relief when their time was up. They walked out to give Phyl a few moments alone with her husband. When she joined them her eyes were very bright.

The Sister appeared as at a signal. 'Doctor Bellaby is here. He was almost stunned, poor man, but much relieved, and I've got a cup of tea ready for you all. What an ordeal that must have been!'

Nevertheless, they had the idea that she'd found this a pleasant change in a sphere where they saw so many stories with less happy endings.

Lynne MacIntyre, the Australian nurse, was there and was coming out to Amberleigh with them. She'd given up some home leave to come. She was starry-eyed at the prospect. 'I love riding, and I've been able to do so little while I've been training.'

Lance said, very quickly, 'You can ride my Hiawatha. He doesn't get as much exercise as he should.' Charlotte saw Edmund look quickly at Lance and his lips twitch.

Sister Rossiter laughed. 'I'll be sorry to say good-bye to you all. It's been such a tangle, but it's all unravelled now.'

Tod scratched his chin, looked sly. 'I expect, like lesser nursing mortals, probationers and what-have-you, you have days off, Sister? Why not come out to Amberleigh? We've got scads of room, haven't we, Phyl? We could drive in and pick you up if you haven't a car of your own.'

The dimple quivered, was repressed. 'Well, it's most kind of you. But at the moment I'm rather busy and—'

'Utter nonsense!' said Doctor Bellaby. 'You know quite well you're hoping they'll press the invitation. She'll come.' He grinned at Tod, who, much relieved, stretched out his legs, caught sight of his mud-caked farm-boots and endeavoured to tuck them out of sight under his chair again.

Edmund seconded the invitation and said calmly, 'And when Owen is quite up to it, we'll throw a belated engagement party and seeing you've all been in on it, what about all of you coming? Bring your wife too, of course, sir. We've had a helluva time with anxiety and deception and cross-purposes and even downright villainy ... I reckon we deserve a really good celebration!'

Suddenly Charlotte could have screamed. She'd fix Edmund Leigh later tonight!

Tod and Lance drove Judy and the Australian nurse. Charlotte found herself with Phyl and Edmund. By now he was in an irrepressible mood, making outrageous plans, telling Phyl of all their clashes, misunderstandings, setbacks. When he got to the phone call from Fiji, Phyl was laughing helplessly.

Charlotte brought them down to earth by asking, 'How are you going to explain to the children? Oh, I know they think you stayed in Christchurch to be near Owen, Phyl, but when they do see him, they're bound to let it slip that you weren't at home. And how on earth are you going to tell them I'm your cousin Lacey?'

Before they reached the leafiness of the Forbidden Valley, Phyl had made up her mind. 'I'm going to tell them the truth. It's the only way. Owen made me promise to take them in on Saturday. They'll give the show away otherwise. And while he looks fit, I don't think anyone with a head injury as severe as this one has been ought to be burdened with such a tale. He'll just lie in bed thinking about it. Children are credulous creatures. They'll probably assimilate it more than we could ourselves. I'll do it myself, when I tuck them up tonight.' She looked at them, twinkling. 'That should give you two a bit of time together on your own.'

Yes, thought Charlotte vindictively, and I'll use it to full extent. How dared Edmund Leigh take advantage of a situation like that one at the hospital today!

But Edmund didn't second Phyl's suggestion. Just when Phyl was taking the youngsters up to bed, having told them she was going to tell them a long and exciting story of how she cut her face, Edmund looked in and said, 'I'm off out. Don't wait up for me. It will be a long session. I'm going over to Longbanks. I'm going to brace myself to do some very straight talking to Avis in front of her parents. I want her out of the district for some time to come. See you tomorrow, Charlotte.' It wasn't fair. She had to go to bed with it all unsaid.

CHAPTER TEN

CHARLOTTE woke to the warmth of a November morning, with the sun spilling goldenly through her windows. The last month of spring here. December would be the first month of summer in this gloriously crazy topsy-turvy world. Just imagine ... this time yesterday morning none of this had happened ... they'd been bowed down by an intolerable load of anxiety, hadn't known where Phyl was, knowing this was the day Owen must be put in possession of what they had thought were facts.

But Phyl was home, and asleep in this very house, her small son and daughter blissfully happy to have their mother home and their small world secure. . . . Owen was well on the mend. And they all thought that Charlotte's and Edmund's differences were resolved too. But they weren't. No man should have acted like that. Like Edmund had yesterday. It had been overbearing, outrageous, unforgivable, to push her into a position like that. She didn't know how to meet him this morning, how he would behave.

She just couldn't lie here thinking about it. The sun rose so early these mornings. What time was it? She looked at her bedside clock, dismayed. It was only four-thirty. Two and a half hours before she could get up. And there would be breakfast to get through, trying to be ordinary. Oh, if only Edmund had stayed home last night and she could have – could have what? Well, she didn't know. But she still couldn't lie here, waiting, thinking. She'd slip out, saddle Floss, and go over the hills and far away.

She didn't disturb anyone. She washed sketchily, slipped into some russet-coloured stretch trews, pulled a cream silk shirt over them, and a chunky-knit loose yellow sweater, because the morning air would be dew-fresh and cool. She tied a yellow and russet scarf triangular-wise round her throat, brushed her hair back from her ears, to lie in tresses on her shoulders, curling up at the ends.

She stole downstairs, had a glass of cold milk, went outside and saddled Floss, trying to hush her eager whinnyings. Then she was into the saddle and away. Oh, how glorious to have an hour to oneself.

Was there ever a fairer morning? The poplar leaves, aquiver, looked as if they'd been dipped into green enamel, the willows bent down with caressing green fingers to stroke the surface of the river . . . yes, she'd come, as she had known she would, as if compelled, to the ford below Te-iti-rangi. Floss lingered in the water, drinking. Then they began to climb up the other side.

Buttercups dotted the grass with shiny gold circles, the over-grown geraniums and daisies were scarlet and white against the old, mellow grey house, the scent of lilac, fresh as any English lilac, drifted across the garden to her. Had Dorothea ever come out here in the early morning to think things out? She must have had her problems, as she applied herself diligently to ac-quiring a culture to match her husband's. But that had been a love-match from the start. He had championed her, and in championing, had fallen in love with her. There had been a chivalrous impulse behind it all, protective, cherishing. Whereas she, Charlotte Smith, had been brazen, deceptive, had menaced Avis, had used any method on Phyl's behalf. No, the atmosphere hadn't been a romantic one.

She turned Floss into the paddock. The last time she'd been here had been the day of the fire. She would go up into the house, see if she could sense, as she had before, the kindly presence of Dorothea's spirit. As she climbed up the last of the terraces she saw that the old house was plumy now as she had imagined it would be, with the purple of wistaria, drooping pendulously from huge gnarled branches, and an archway was almost bowed down with starry pink clematis blooms. The old burnt-out mattress still lay forlorn on the grass. Here was a house waiting to be stirred to life, like a sleeping princess.

She went through and into the still-elegant drawing-room with its small-paned set of French windows. As she did so, she stopped. What was that? It was Floss whinnying . . . the sort of whinny she gave when she greeted another horse. Charlotte went back down the hall, out on to the terrace. Edmund was coming out of the paddock gate. His Cavalier was turned in with Floss. The sunlight shone glintingly on his bare fair head. He looked up and waved to her and advanced, tall, bulky, and confident.

Charlotte turned and fled back into the drawing-room, and stood there, her hands nervously clasped together, waiting.

His step, on the bare parquet, sounded purposeful, measured.

He stopped in the doorway and looked at her, one eyebrow raised.

'Well?' he said.

It seemed as if she had to answer that. He was impelling her to by the very force of his personality.

But she muffed her line. She ought to have run to him then, her hands outstretched. There'd have been no need for any other answer.

She knew her voice sounded petty, on the defensive. 'I wanted to be alone.'

He shook his head. 'You didn't, not really. Don't pretend any more, Charlotte. Let's be honest with each other.'

She didn't answer.

He said, 'I'm going to be just as proud of my bride as Jonathan was ... perhaps more proud. After all, he didn't have a wife who could wring truth out of a Jezebel of a woman ... or put out fires single-handed ...' he started to laugh, 'or knock out wild boars with heirloom marble clocks!'

She said resentfully, 'Does that add up to love? Or is it just admiration and gratitude? I thought love was something that came without rhyme or reason.'

His voice was quite calm. 'It's that, too.'

She sounded unconvinced. 'I've seen no evidence of that. You only feel like this towards me when I've – I've helped the family.'

He smiled. 'Rot. Utter rot. Charlotte, I loved you first when you saw Te-iti-rangi for the very first time. You had no idea of its Maori meaning, and you called it a miniature paradise. And I *knew*. You looked at me the next moment, and I had to wipe the expression off my face, because it had hit me for six. And then there was the night we heard that announcement on the TV. I was terrified you might contract typhoid. And when you said it would have been better for us if you'd never come here, I was suddenly appalled at the thought that I might never have known you.'

When she didn't answer, he said roughly, 'You've got to believe me. Have you any more questions, because believe me, Sharlie, I'm not going to wait much longer.'

Oh, she believed him ... you couldn't get away from that look on his face, but for some reason she wanted to prolong this moment. She said, wistfully, 'But proposing like that ... in front of everyone ... you absolutely browbeat me into

187

accepting you. You acted like the lord of creation. I wasn't even *asked*. Why?'

His laugh held pure merriment. 'And I'm not going to ask you now. Why? . . . because what a position I've been in . . . talk about romance! It's usually up to the man to rescue the woman he loves from some terrible situation or other. Like Jonathan, for instance. He found Dorothea's mistress beating her and rode off with her on his saddle-bow. Well, in his buggy, anyway. But what happens to me? *You* do the dragon-slaying . . . well, the wild boar! *You* save my house from destruction! *You* tear the truth from the serpent in Eden . . . oh, Charlotte, Charlotte, I couldn't beg you to marry me. I had to bludgeon you into accepting me. . . . that's how I love you, girl . . . in real caveman style. Now, wench, come to me!'

She came, was folded into his huge embrace, knew in the strength of his kiss how much he had hungered for her. . . .

It was a long time before they drew apart. Charlotte said shakily, 'I haven't any breath left!'

Edmund laughed. 'What do you want breath for? Going to do more talking? It's an awful waste of time.'

She laughed, pushed her bright hair back, looked at him in the way he'd hoped for so long she might look at him. 'Edmund, despite all I said just now, I think I knew when I climbed the terraces this morning that I would surrender. I felt as if this place was like the garden of the palace of the Sleeping Beauty, awaiting the touch of our hands to make it live again. I felt as if Dorothea and Jonathan were here, welcoming me. Only I was alone.'

'You thought you were alone,' he corrected her. 'I went to your room to waken you, to tell you to come out, to saddle up, to come over here. And at that moment I heard Floss whinny to you. I knew you would come to Te-iti-rangi. I just followed.' His eyes swept round the room, dusty, cobwebby. Hers followed his. They both saw it as it would be again . . with a grand piano in the corner, brought back from Amberleigh. With Dorothea's portrait hanging above it, her china in the little glass-doored closets in the alcoves. . . .

'We'll have a Dorothea and a Jonathan, won't we?' asked Edmund. 'For some reason those names have never been used again in the family. But we'll use them.'

A little thrill ran over Charlotte. Edmund knew it because her hand was in his. He kissed her again, then turned her to the end set of windows. They began to walk towards them.

Edmund said, 'This garden will be your domain, your refuge, just as it was Dorothea's. She gathered lavender here for her lavender-bags, rose-petals and cinnamon pinks for her pot-pourri. Oh, look,' he had unsnecked the door, 'the rose tree has thrown out a new tendril right across it.' He took hold of it, gently detached it from the far side, held it back, and she passed through.

Charlotte thought Dorothea had already been there, preparing for them. She said so. 'Look, Edmund, the roses on the far wall are bursting their buds ... see, apricot and crimson. ...'.

They walked to the little fountain. Edmund said, 'Let's make that the first restoration of all. Jonathan built that for her and it played for the first time the night they came here after their wedding.'

Far above them, an infinitesimal speck in a blue, blue sky, a lark was singing as sweetly as it had ever sung above Edmund's ancestors and Charlotte's ancestors in the Surrey woods of long ago.

A little zephyr sprang up, ruffled the curling tendrils of auburn hair at Charlotte's temples, blew coolly against Edmund's face. It decided that this garden had been left to dreams of yesteryear for far too long. It ruffled along the edge of the fountain basin, and with sudden caprice, swooped on the dry rose-petals of long ago, and scooped them up into the air, to fall on the ground below.

'Then let's get on with our bit of tradition-building,' said Edmund. 'We've got a lot of work before us if we want a New Year wedding.'

The little zephyr went on its way, over fields of growing green wheat, over grazing flocks, and the hills where native evergreens and English deciduous trees grew in perfect harmony, till down in the forbidden valley, it decided to sweep up to the little pit-sawn timbers of the Church of St Francis of Assisi, and around the mossy gravestones that clustered it.

It lingered longest near one that bore two names ... Dorothea and Jonathan, bent down, whispered, and was gone.

Why the smile?

... because she has just received her **Free Harlequin Romance Catalogue!**

... and now she has a complete listing of the many, many Harlequin Romances still available.

... and now she can pick out titles by her favorite authors or fill in missing numbers for her library.

You too may have - a **Free Harlequin Romance Catalogue** (and a smile!), simply by mailing in the coupon below.

Golden Harlequin Library

A Treasury of Harlequin Romances!

Many of the all time favorite Harlequin Romance Novels have not been available, until now, since the original printing. But on this special introductory offer, they are yours in an exquisitely bound, rich gold hardcover with royal blue imprint. Three complete unabridged novels in each volume. And the cost is so very low you'll be amazed!

Handsome, Hardcover Library Editions at Paperback Prices! ONLY $1.95 each volume.

This very special collection of classic Harlequin Romances would be a distinctive addition to your library. And imagine what a delightful gift they'd make for any Harlequin reader!

Start your collection now. See reverse of this page for **SPECIAL INTRODUCTORY OFFER!**